RECLAIMING THE L-WORD

SAPPHO'S DAUGHTERS OUT IN AFRICA

RECLAIMING THE L-WORD

SAPPHO'S DAUGHTERS OUT IN AFRICA

EDITED BY ALLEYN DIESEL

Publication © Modjaji Books 2011
Copyright © 2011 is held by the author of each story

First published in 2011 by Modjaji Books PTY Ltd
P O Box 385, Athlone, 7760, South Africa
modjaji.books@gmail.com
http://modjaji.book.co.za
www.modjajibooks.co.za

ISBN 978-1-920397-28-9

Edited by Alleyn Diesel
Copy editor: Gill Gimberg
Cover and book design: Natascha Mostert
Cover photograph: Zanele Muholi
Author photographs: Courtesy the authors

Printed and bound by Mega Digital, Cape Town
Set in Minion Pro

CONTENTS

FOREWORD

As I write this we are celebrating the 20th anniversary of the unbanning of the ANC in 1990 and the subsequent release of Nelson Mandela. What a truly remarkable journey we have made from our dim past! We celebrate, among many things, a Constitution that has been rightly lauded as one of the most progressive in the world. We have, indeed, come a long way. And we should never forget that.

But we still have to travel further on the road to a full democracy. The long walk to freedom is indeed long.

While formal rights are guaranteed in the Constitution, there is much that still needs to be achieved. Rights must be translated off the paper on which they are written. They must become part of the ground on which we walk. They have to be clearly understood, and easily accessed.

As a feminist, I have always been prodded to push the boundaries of awareness and critique, to recognise the lurking oppressions that continue to be relegated to the margins. As a woman of faith, I am continually compelled to ask in new and daring ways, "Who is my neighbour?" *Reclaiming the L-Word: Sappho's Daughters Out in Africa* assists me in this ongoing journey, expanding my understandings of "community" and "sisterhood". It makes me appreciate that there are many permutations of "the woman-identified woman".

In a time of increasing fundamentalism in every sphere, and of narrowing definitions of the Other, we are constrained to address again our common humanity and our connectedness. The struggle for human dignity, equality and justice is neither divisible nor partial. It is certainly not selective.

We have to acknowledge that our Constitution does not automatically guarantee a change in public culture and the mindset of individuals and communities. This is why feminist activism must be ongoing, and feminist intellectual work that intersects with womanism and lesbianism is vitally important. While women's groups have fought for socio-political rights and gender justice, we have to continue to ensure that hearts and minds are changed, especially on matters of sexual orientation.

It is fundamentally necessary to link women's concerns with lesbian concerns. Apart from structural and economic discrimination encountered by lesbians, we must also address the social and cultural stigma that is experienced and endured. Such stigma is not only debilitating; it can also, in some instances, be life threatening.

This collection is therefore invaluable as it draws attention to the lived realities and experiences of lesbians. It reveals disquieting truths of the hostility and violence against lesbians. The stories remind us again and again that the feminist dictum that personal is political is indeed true.

We need efforts such as this to raise consciousness and on-going activism at all levels, so that homophobia, among other prejudices, is addressed. Moving lesbianism away from spectacle and the exotic, the collection emerges from the wellsprings of lived experience. It tells flesh and blood stories – stories of the values, loves, struggles and challenges of living in a society that continues to perpetuate many myths, mythologies and misconceptions about lesbians. Moving in their honesty, and brave in re-imagining the world, they tell of highly-wrought decisions to live with integrity and with grace. They remind us of the great diversity among women of our continent and region, and the need for sensitivity and openheartedness to the many faces of lesbian and transgender experiences in our time and place.

The following poem by Lebogang Mashile, in her collection, *In a Ribbon of Rhythm*, evokes the compelling and redemptive power of telling stories, of bearing witness:

> After they've fed off of your memories
> Erased dreams from your eyes
> Broken the seams of sanity
> And glued what's left together with lies,
> After the choices and voices have left you alone
> And silence grows solid
> Adhering like flesh to your bones

They've always known your spirit's home
Lay in your gentle sway
To light and substance
But jaded mirrors and false prophets have a way
Of removing you from yourself
You who lives with seven names
You who walks with seven faces
None can eliminate your pain

Tell your story
Let it nourish you,
Sustain you
And claim you
Tell your story
Let it feed you,
Heal you
And release you.
Tell your story
Let it twist and remix your shattered heart
Tell your story
Until your past stops tearing your present apart.

Reclaiming the L-Word: Sappho's Daughters Out in Africa is a "triumph of courage" at reclaiming the voices of those who have long endured being "sister outsiders".

Dr Devarakshanam (Betty) Govinden
Senior Research Associate in the Faculty of Education,
University of KwaZulu-Natal, Durban, South Africa

INTRODUCTION

*"You can see that there is no easy walk to freedom
anywhere, and many of us will have to pass through the
valley of the shadow of death again and again before
we reach the mountain tops of our desires."* [1]

Although lesbians have existed in Western societies throughout
the centuries of written history, at least from the time of Sappho,
the woman-identified poet of the island of Lesbos in ancient Greece
(7th century BCE), their lives have remained largely invisible,
unknown to, or ignored by, historians. Indeed, even after the rise
of the second wave of feminism in the 1960s and the emphasis on
recovering the history of women, separate from that of men, most
feminist historians tended to overlook the existence of lesbians in
their midst.

Just as the patriarchal suppression of the position and
achievements of women throughout most of Western history
has been disempowering by keeping them hidden, so, too, has
the deprivation of knowledge about lesbianism resulted in
their separation from one another, and their contribution to
society as women with an alternative view of the world has gone
unacknowledged, thus effectively prohibiting many from forming
any positive self-image. Ignorance of one's past inhibits an ability
to grasp or learn from experience, and so to be enabled to make
informed decisions about the future. This tends to suppress the
knowledge and motivation needed to change a pernicious and
damaging situation to allow for a full flourishing of one's humanity.
Enforced isolation fosters ignorance, withholding the support of

---

1   Quoted by Bernedette Muthien from Nelson Mandela's "The Struggle is
     My Life" (1986:42) in *Performing Queer: Shaping Sexualities 1994-2004*.
     Vol. One.

others that is necessary for emancipation. "Women together are strong!" – but, as South Africans learnt through years of apartheid, separation is truly disempowering.

Too often, stories involving lesbians have been written, or re-written, so as to conceal their real interests and motivations, in order to make them appear more acceptable to mainstream views and values, and less threatening to the status quo. How shocking for some young woman to find that her adored role model was in fact deviant! This has meant that, as well as traditional (usually male) historians expunging certain details from the stories of women suspected of being lesbian, the women themselves have usually imposed a self-censorship, hoping to pass themselves off as "normal" heterosexual women. Which all means that until very recently stories of lesbian women, whether biographical or autobiographical, have tended to conceal the nature of their sexuality. Few honest, explicit writings exist which allow us a clear insight into the fears, agonies, secrecy and joys of lesbian lives, providing the kind of understanding which brings an empathetic appreciation of alternative relationships, and their ability to provide enrichment and fulfilment for both partners.

In general, until fairly recently, the only knowledge available of lesbian lives in the modern West has been of those famous/notorious women such as Virginia Woolf, Vita Sackville-West, Mary Renault, Nancy Spain, Ethel Smyth, Natalie Barney, Bessie Smith, Billie Holiday and Josephine Baker, or of those relatively few women brave enough to write honestly about themselves, for example, Gertrude Stein and Alice B. Toklas, Colette, Radclyffe Hall, Audre Lorde, Pat Parker, Mary Daly, Rita Mae Brown, Martina Navratilova and Ellen Degeneres, the highly visible talk show entertainer. But, of course, none of these exciting and stimulating figures was South African, leaving a great gap in possible role models for contemporary local lesbians. Apart from women such as the pop diva Brenda Fassie, Eudy Simelane, captain of the South African women's football team, Ruth Morgan, lesbian activist and author, and many unnamed women school teachers, South African lesbians have been bereft of iconic female figures to encourage them in their lonely search for identity.

The genesis of human sexuality is complicated. Essentialists believe that sexual orientation is fixed by biology (hormones, genes, etc.), whereas constructionists hold that sexuality is shaped by psychological and social factors that interact in complex ways. Some eclectically embrace both perspectives. Neither group endorses the belief that sexuality or sexual orientation is a matter of choice, as one cannot choose one's genes or the psycho-dynamics of one's family. However, for the constructionists, choice or agency is involved in matters of identity and the process of identification. One may be homosexual, but choose not to identify oneself as a lesbian, as this may involve political, social and familial decisions which are too painful, and in some communities in South Africa too dangerous, to handle. Even though there is no convincing evidence yet that sexuality is biologically determined, what is important for the daily lives of lesbians is the way in which this (mis)information has been exploited by patriarchal societies to create various myths about lesbian women.

The idea that homosexuality is congenital – that people are born homosexual – and therefore cannot help who they are, so that no attempt at a cure is possible, is widely discussed. The typical argument is, "Who on earth would choose to be this way? It's something that one cannot help and therefore just has to learn to live with." This also provides the justification that if one cannot be held responsible for who one is, then this is not a sinful state, as "God" created one this way.

This appears to be an argument more popular with male homosexuals than with lesbians, with many feminists strongly objecting to this view. Based largely on the existentialist view that each person must assume responsibility for who they are, that every aspect of life involves choices, and that we can never hide behind the claim that we are mere victims of circumstance, this feminist argument tends to insist that one's sexual preference is a matter of personal choice. Whatever circumstances in life might be seen as contributing towards the way we develop into adulthood, ultimately, as responsible individuals, we have to accept who we are and choose to live with this in as full a manner as possible.

Many feminists would also view the overwhelming emphasis on heterosexuality as the norm of human behaviour as a patriarchal construct aimed at maintaining the subordination of women. Women, some would argue, are born with the ability to respond sexually to other women as well as to men, but are deliberately conditioned to seek out emotional and sexual relationships exclusively with men. Every aspect of their upbringing urges them to view men as the objects of their sexual interest, and they are inundated with role models who promote their "femininity", and sexual attractiveness, to men. Thus, women who flout these social and sexual expectations, refusing to define their lives by their relationship to men, are perceived as being a political, as well as a sexual, threat to the patriarchal status quo and are labelled as deviant, even at times, in many societies, being criminalised. Another aspect of the lesbian threat is that these women are perceived as aspiring to usurp the power of the male by wanting to be men.

The enforcement of heterosexuality, viewed as the "proper" control and "protection" of women, is sometimes seen as the only way to defend (patriarchal) society from being undermined by deviant and perverted women who refuse to conform to their traditional role in society. So persecution, legislation, being locked up as suffering from mental illness, and in some places stoning, burning at the stake, and, more recently in South Africa "corrective rape", are all viewed as justifiable methods of containing and suppressing such dangerous, sinful and subversive behaviour.

Despite great strides being made recently in society's attitude towards lesbianism, much misinformation persists, consciously or unconsciously, and continues to contribute to a generally negative attitude towards such women.

I think the stories in this collection largely dispel these misconceptions about lesbians.

The need for successful, responsible, well-adjusted, professional, happy, attractive and vulnerable lesbian role models is essential to break down damaging stereotypes and demonstrate that this is an appropriate and acceptable choice open to women. Coming to terms with the many implications of a lesbian lifestyle often involves the invariably painful defining and constructing of a new identity: one that flies in the face of all the heterosexist clichés and expectations with which young girls are indoctrinated in heterosexual societies.

The new, much lauded, progressive and liberal South African Constitution of 1996 decriminalised homosexuality with an equality clause that forbids either the state or any individual from discriminating against anyone on grounds of race, gender, sex, pregnancy, marital status, ethnic or social origin, colour, sexual orientation, age, disability, religion, conscience, belief, culture, language and birth. This has allowed same-sex couples to receive pension and medical benefits, and to adopt children. These rights were further extended in 2006 with the passing of the Civil Union Act that permits same-sex couples to have their relationship legally recognised in either a civil union or a marriage, which has helped enormously to normalise life for most lesbians and gays. It is also significant that this legislation accords South Africa the status of being the only African country to sanction same-sex unions, as well as placing it in the company of the few countries which similarly recognise the rights of lesbian/gay/bisexual/transgender and intersex (LGBTI) couples, for example the Netherlands, Belgium, Spain, Canada and some American States. In 2009 the Delhi High Court abolished the law declaring homosexuality illegal.

The African continent does not have a reputation for tolerance towards homosexuality in general, with the recent denunciation of homosexuals by Zimbabwe's Robert Mugabe providing a vehement example. Even more recently, reports from Uganda and Malawi have provided frightening evidence of severe penalties, up to life imprisonment, imposed on homosexuals, with Uganda considering the death sentence for homosexual acts. A Ugandan government spokesperson has stated: "[Homosexuality] is not allowed in African culture. We have to protect the children in schools who are being recruited into homosexual activities" (*The Mercury*, Durban: 8 January 2008). However, despite such threats and intimidation, as well as acts of violence, the sense of solidarity and determination to survive among homosexuals living in Africa appears to have grown. The desperate claim by various denouncers that homosexuality is "un-African" appears to be entirely without foundation.

However, in spite of the South African Constitution's progressive view of sexual orientation that has, rightly, been the cause of much rejoicing in the LGBTI community, there is still a long way to go before same-sex couples can feel completely accepted and safe in their day-to-day activities. There is, of course, much less overt homophobia, which has provided the space for many to live their lives more openly.

But the legal situation must not allow us to be lulled into complacency that all is well and that the battle for equal rights is won. South Africa remains a profoundly conservative society where the attitudes of generations will not be altered in a few short years. The recent rise in fundamentalist religion and the seemingly unabated scourge of AIDS, with all the shame and secrecy still surrounding those who are HIV positive, are salutary reminders that discrimination and intolerance of difference still flourish in numerous areas.

Paradoxically, more visibility for lesbians has also resulted in an increase in hate crimes, with many being terrorised, attacked and subjected to "corrective rape" to "punish" and "cure" them of their "deviant" sexual orientation. Recently it has become clear that in townships like Soweto and Khayelitsha women risk their lives by coming out as lesbian. During the last few years rape, particularly of women who challenge gender stereotypes – even by wearing trousers and other items of what are considered to be "male" clothing – and who are therefore not considered to conform sufficiently to traditional notions of "femininity", has become a national epidemic. The Triangle Project, a gay rights organisation, claims that up to ten cases of "corrective rape", particularly of "butch-looking" women are reported every week. Further evidence from women suggests that the police show little enthusiasm for pursuing and prosecuting male perpetrators, possibly in some instances actually sharing some sympathy with the perpetrators' attitudes and actions. Numbers of black lesbians have been killed by vigilante groups of men for daring to walk the streets in the company of their female lovers. Eudy Simelane, the footballer and high-profile political activist, is one of these: gang-raped, beaten and stabbed to death for her perceived flouting of conservative/ traditional gender stereotypes.

Yet more cause for concern are recent ominous rumblings in even the highest political and religious circles which bear witness to the fact that public denigration of alternative sexualities is very much alive and well. In fact, very recently, one of our writers, the internationally acclaimed photographer and human rights activist, Zanele Muholi, had her work featuring lesbian women together in loving poses denounced by the Minister of Arts and Culture as being "immoral, offensive and going against nation building". To have a liberal constitution is only a beginning to the eliminating of prejudice and unfair treatment, and promoting tolerance and respect for the humanity of all people. Government leaders and the police are in urgent need of more enlightened attitudes and more political muscle if women are to be allowed to live in safety in all areas of this country. All South Africans must recognise that one of the essential responsibilities of a democracy is to protect the rights of all citizens by denouncing discrimination on grounds of race, gender and sexual orientation (as well as all the other possibilities spelled out in the Constitution); that this is a matter of guarding fundamental human rights, not merely protecting the wellbeing of certain (minority) groups.

The stories in this collection are told by women who come from a wide variety of communities, with great differences in ethnic, social, educational, economic and religious or secular backgrounds, that offer very diverse opportunities for advancement and success in life. But their accounts of growing up as lesbian in South Africa all reflect in some way the difficulties, uncertainties, fears, sometimes rejection and discrimination that have accompanied their attempts to achieve recognition in society.

A number of women represented in this anthology have happily availed themselves of the enlightened post-apartheid Constitution to legalise their relationships, which frequently proves crucial for their rights of inheritance and in child custody issues. And a significant number of stories tell of the decision by lesbian couples to adopt children, or have children by in vitro fertilisation. But two women share courageous accounts of abuse and rape that depict the dark side of lesbian life in this so-called enlightened country. And the fact that three of the contributors have opted to use pseudonyms, and others were reluctant to have their photos included, is indicative of the lack of security and acceptance they still perceive in South African society.

It seems appropriate, in the present climate of the general decriminalising of homosexuality in most Western countries and the new higher profile that this has allowed to many whose lives were previously largely marginalised and invisible, that the stories of these women (not famous in any usually recognised way) should now be shared with a wider audience. This is not, in any way, to try to attract spurious interest in unconventional lifestyles, but to present those who, unfortunately, are unable to claim, "Some of my best friends are gay!" with some insight into the lives of women who love other women, in the hope that some understanding of their fears, achievements and happiness will create a more empathetic appreciation of ways of life and relationships which are alternative to the majority.

If something as simple as a story can help to create understanding and build a bridge, then this country, and in fact the world, could become a better place for all.

Alleyn Diesel
Pietermaritzburg, 2010

ACKNOWLEDGEMENTS

To all the women who have bravely and enthusiastically agreed to contribute to this collection, my heartfelt thanks. I know that some have found it quite alarmingly demanding, and at times, like myself, experienced a failure of nerve. For me, it has been exciting to meet some new and very stimulating women, and to be alerted to aspects of lesbian life of which I was previously only vaguely aware. I hope that all participants will be pleased with the finished product and finally convinced that it was all worthwhile.

I am most grateful to Betty Govinden for her encouragement, and for writing a thought-provoking foreword. Her endorsement of the project is much valued.

To Michael Lambert of the Classics Department at UKZN, many thanks for all the discussion and suggestions on dealing with the subject of homosexuality.

My appreciation to Michel Friedman and partner Louise Minna of Cape Town who gave valuable help in suggesting and contacting possible contributors.

Thank you to Colleen Lowe Morna and Deborah Walter of Gender Links for their very willing help.

Thank you to *Agenda* for permission to reproduce the article "Thinking Through Lesbian Rape" by Zanele Muholi, and to Michael Stevenson Gallery in Cape Town for permission to include Zanele Muholi's photographs.

Many thanks to Colleen Higgs of Modjaji Books for her faith in the value of this collection, and publishing it, so enabling these stories to get the audience they deserve; and to editor Gill Gimberg for her meticulous and sensitive editing.

Finally, much gratitude to Mary Kleinenberg, my partner of 26 years, for all her loving support, encouragement and critical comments throughout the project.

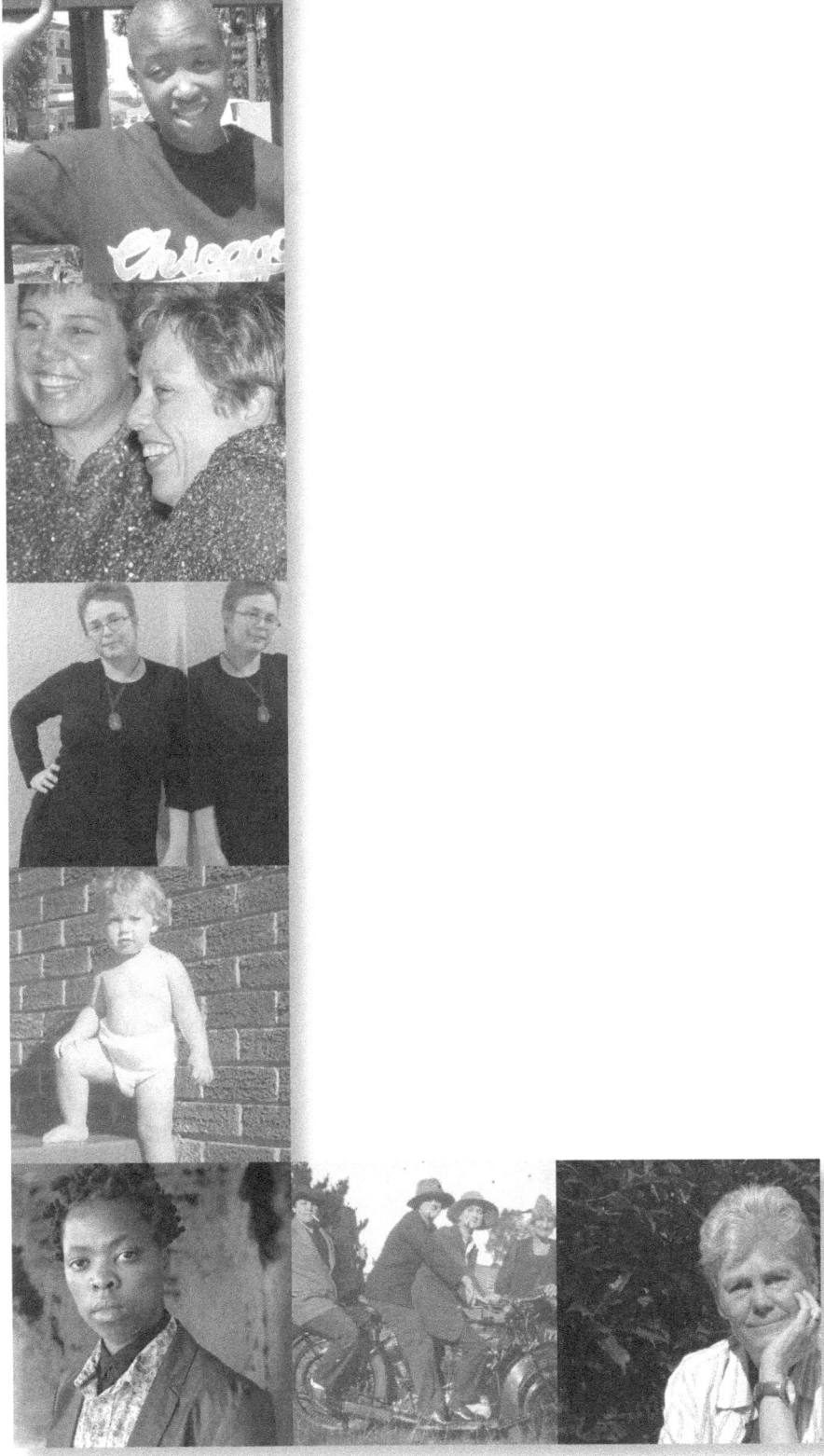

HEIDI VAN ROOYEN (PhD) works for the Human Sciences Research Council. She is the Head of Office at the HSRC's Sweetwaters office in rural KwaZulu-Natal and oversees the operations and implementation of three large, multi-year, internationally funded social and behavioural trials. All the studies evaluate various types of interventions that address the wider context of vulnerable children, as well as families and communities at-risk, infected and affected by HIV/Aids.

Heidi lives with her partner Monique Salomon in Pietermaritzburg with their two mixed-breed dogs – or coloureds – Kylie and Odie.

PULLED OUT OF THE CLOSET INTO MY FAMILY'S EMBRACE

HEIDI VAN ROOYEN

I thought deeply about the invitation to be part of an anthology of South African lesbian writing. I liked the fact that the book would attempt to provide a set of stories about positive, strong and successful women. I could live with that! What pulled me up short was that this was not just a story of successful South African women, but of successful South African *lesbian* women. My discomfort was not because I am uncomfortable with my sexuality, or that I am in "the closet" in either my personal or professional life – far from it. What gave me pause was the singling out of one aspect of my identity – of seemingly placing my sexual orientation – in neon lights. I struggle with being overly defined by any concept, label or circumstance. I feel that I serve these issues better (for example my race, my gender and my sexual orientation) by authentically living and being these things – by simply being myself.

It also seemed that the very act of singling out one aspect of me – my lesbianism – would do so at the expense of other parts of me that could claim equal rights in shaping who I am. And, perhaps, my discomfort also pointed to some last traces of internal homophobia. I hardly ever refer to myself as a lesbian – preferring the safer, neutral and easier-on-the-palate term "gay" to describe my sexual orientation. Also, no matter how out you are, committing your story to paper exposes you to a much larger (unknown) audience and outs you even further. I finally decided to take up the challenge offered by this anthology to claim the lesbian-in-me, and explore how this one aspect of me interacts with the many others – my race, my working class background and my conservative and traditional Catholic upbringing – that define and shape who I am.

I was married – to a man – almost twenty years ago. Ironically, the period of time of my marriage marks the beginning of the process of coming to terms with the possibility that I was gay. So much of our lives are clearer in retrospect. It would certainly help, and it would save us all a lot of pain and trauma if we had some of these hindsight-insights smack bang in the middle of a difficult period. But, it doesn't quite work like that, does it? The clarity of hindsight can seem so cold and calculating when stripped of the emotions, turmoil and struggle of the time.

Here are a few of my moments of clarity about this significant period of my life. Firstly, I got married too young. At 24, I had no business getting married. It was a time in my life when so much was in flux and key aspects of my identity were being formed and shaped. I was trying to figure out who I was in relation to the world and my place in it, particularly with respect to issues relating to gender roles, sex and intimacy, and how I should be in relation to another person, let alone a wife to a husband.

Here's another: we got married too soon. We met and were married within about six months. And, being the good Catholic girl that I was, I certainly wasn't pregnant. In retrospect, I think that I got married with such haste as a way out – as a way to escape home, and a mother who was dying of cancer. Given my background, leaving home to either live on my own or with my boyfriend was simply not an option available to me. I got married so that my mother did not have to worry about me – it was my way of saying that she could go: I was in good hands and I would be OK without her. She heard me. She attended the church ceremony in a wheelchair, and died about eight weeks after the wedding. This was a difficult time for me. I struggled with her death and it was hard to talk about.

I was also in the middle of my clinical psychology internship year. An internship period is an intense practical period when, after all the years of clinical training and preparation, you finally get to work with real cases. Like most interns, I went through a period of profound and significant personal change during that year. It's almost inevitable that this happens. In working that closely and intimately with others, I came into close contact with my own issues and personal struggles that I had either pushed aside or not fully dealt with in the past. One of the issues I confronted in the relationship was that of gender and, particularly, the roles that society assigns to men and women based on the physical characteristics of their sex. For example, even though we both worked full-time, there were certain things that I *had to do* simply because I was the wife – such as cooking. I actually love cooking, but it became such a heated source of conflict. I chafed under the seemingly immovable set of expectations that I had to cook, irrespective of the circumstances of my or his day.

It was a lot for a new relationship to deal with: coping with all these significant and stressful events, and also trying to figure out how to do this relationship, how to do this thing called marriage. We struggled. Throw into the mix a growing awareness that I might be gay. At the time, I did not know this so clearly, nor could I state this so unequivocally. The realisation was on a much more physical, non-verbal level. You can all relate to this – a moment in your life when a truth, an aspect about yourself, a knowing of something about yourself clicks into place. It's as though your internal mechanics all shift a gear and settle into a comfortable groove that was meant to be.

Throughout my life, from primary school up until this particular point, there was always an older woman – a teacher, a guidance counsellor, a lecturer, a supervisor – to whom I had an emotional connection and attachment. These women gave comfort, support and a safe space, and it was to them that I took all that mattered to me. In my relationships with men I took on a different role. I was the one they came to and talked to, and brought their problems to. The big shift at this time was that, in addition to the emotional connection with the older female supervisor, there was a knock-me-down, physical desire for another woman. This floored me. Completely! For the first time I was consciously aware that I was both emotionally and sexually attracted to someone of the same sex. I was terrified, but this awareness moved me at some deeper level that overrode some of my anxieties.

It was becoming clearer to me that the marriage happened too soon and perhaps for not all the right reasons. This was difficult to admit to myself and to others, and especially to my family. Being from good Catholic stock, a divorce was not an easy topic to raise. In fact, it's a topic that should not be raised at all. There were many examples of couples in my community who stayed together under extremely taxing and heartbreaking circumstances. My unhappiness and desire for something more seemed so insignificant compared to these marriages that surrounded me. There was a strong sense from my family that I should try to make the relationship work. Leaving the marriage meant that, probably for the first time in my life, I would be going against family expectations. In doing so, I risked losing the understanding and support of those closest to me. It was a very lonely time for me. But, it was also an important time in learning that I was ultimately responsible for my own happiness. As I have gotten older, at other life-altering decision-making times, when all around me is in chaos, I have learned to listen to this part of me that quietly speaks its truth, and demands to be heard.

Did I leave the marriage because I knew that I was gay?

This is one of the hardest questions that I have ever been asked. It's hard because there isn't a simple "yes" or "no" answer. It's hard because something as big as this – love, relationship, sexuality, sexual identity and sexual orientation – is never this straightforward.

The short version is that, on its own, the marriage was not working. If anything, the marriage, in what it couldn't give me, gave me a clear sense of what I wanted and needed. I wanted a relationship that was more equal, that was more about give and take, that was based on individual strengths, abilities, and inclinations rather than being tightly defined by gender and gender roles. And, with the growing realisation that I was sexually and emotionally attracted to women, some of the blanks were being filled in – that this future relationship I desired and wanted could be with another woman. Perhaps, knowing that I did have other options, as yet unexplored, gave me the strength and the courage to leave.

But leaving the marriage and coming to terms with being gay wasn't easy. I was taking a leap into the unknown. There were no examples of other gay people where I came from. Together with many other coloured families we were relocated as a result of the Group Areas Act to an area called Wentworth on the outskirts of Durban, mindlessly close to a major oil refinery. The place we called home was an old army barracks that was now a makeshift "community" for many displaced families. Wentworth soon became synonymous with drugs, alcoholism and gangsterism – signs of a disparate group of people, with competing value systems and beliefs, thrown together against their will and trying to find a way of co-existing together.

I come from a large family of eleven – nine girls (including me) and two boys – a case of yours, mine and ours. My father had three children from a previous relationship, my mother had three of her own and together they had five of us. My father moved in with the children from his previous marriage and we grew up together; we have always felt like a large family of eleven children. We were poor. My father worked too little, and too inconsistently for it to be of any consequence. And he drank far too much! My mother kept the family going by working three jobs: she worked by day in a factory as a seamstress and by night did dressmaking for private clients. On weekends and month ends she sold food and cakes to bring in extra income. It was tough. My parents struggled with each other's different understandings, responses and capacities for marriage, parenthood and responsibility.

While growing up, I always felt different from the others in my family. There were several reasons for this. As is typical with many coloured families, the children were all different shades of brown. I was one of the lighter-skinned ones in the family. I stood out and took some flack for this from my siblings. It didn't help matters that I also wore the good girl mantle. I felt that, in the chaos and difficulty that characterised my parents' relationship, and the struggles of our home life, I had to be the good girl. I had to be the one good thing that would make everyone proud. So, I did well at school. At home I played the clown and tried to get my mom to laugh, and tried to live up to all the expectations. I believed for the longest time as a child that I was accidentally left at my family's doorstep by the proverbial stork. I felt different in so many ways. I wanted more. I was determined to get beyond the unemployment, drugs, alcohol and violence that characterised many lives in Wentworth. Of the brood, I was the first to "use my brains" as my one sister said, to help me "get out" and make the most of my life. I was the first to pass Matric, get a degree, and more recently, the first with a PhD. Perhaps this feeling that I was different also came from the fact that I was gay. I don't know. I certainly didn't know it at the time.

I wear my race and the relative disadvantage of my upbringing lightly. Somewhere along the line I felt that if I allowed these things – the hardship, the squares of newspaper used as toilet paper, the salt for toothpaste, the ill-fitting clothes, the hand-me-downs – if I allowed these things to define me too closely, I would become defined by the deficits, by what I didn't have. Going this route meant that there would be little space to acknowledge all that I did have. We are a family rich in the right things: love, an ability to laugh at ourselves and our situation, a closeness and support for and of each other that is remarkable.

When I left the marriage, I didn't come out to my family. I needed time to internalise the fact that I might be gay and to become more comfortable with it. I had my first relationship with a woman several years after my marriage had ended. It didn't last too long, but it helped confirm what I was beginning to grapple with. I was gay. My first time with a woman was a moving and incredible experience. It sounds clichéd, but it felt like I had come home. The entire struggle and the confusion of the past few years just seemed to disappear. While on a personal level this was making more and more sense, this knowledge did not transfer to more public spaces outside my relationships with women and the gay social circles that gave me a home.

Comprehending and accepting that you are gay in a world that is so predominantly and overbearingly heterosexual needs to be worked through on so many levels. There's the personal acknowledgement and acceptance that is required – many of us struggle with this – as your newly found sexual orientation has to compete with the norms, values, culture and religious beliefs of your upbringing and of society at large. This is tough. Even if one works through this with a reasonable level of success, you have to also deal with others' views, fears and prejudice about your sexual orientation.

As I wasn't quite ready at this time to deal with my family's views and reactions to being gay, I started to live a split existence. I had my relationships and gay friends on the one hand and my family on the other. I offered my family very few glimpses into my new life and "friendships" with women, some of whom they did get to meet. Like many other gay people, I was afraid to come out to my family. I feared that they just wouldn't understand it. Loving someone of the same sex would be a foreign concept to them and I had no way of knowing how they would respond to this. My greatest fear was that my family would keep the children from me. I have a large clutch of nephews and nieces who I am close to and have been very involved in their upbringing and their lives. If I came out, I worried that they would prevent me from seeing the children.

In the end, I was unceremoniously pulled out of the closet by one of my sisters. I am thankful to this sister for many things. She brings much to my life. But none more so than this single act, and the asking of the all-important question: "Are you gay?"

So much for me thinking that I had my family fooled with my various girl "friends"! They had been wondering about the nature of these relationships for a while. Our families and those close to us know us intimately and know us well, and are able to see us in our entirety even when aspects of ourselves are hidden or obscured from our view. I also believe they ask the all-important questions when they are ready to hear the answers. I responded to her question in the affirmative. It was a wonderful conversation and we discussed how we thought the other siblings might react to the news. I left feeling lighter than I had in years. I was slowly working on a plan that would probably have taken me about ten years to come out to my remaining siblings.

My sister phoned in excitement on the Monday after our conversation. "You won't believe it," she said. "Things are not as bad you thought!"

"I know," I replied, "I've been feeling so much better since we spoke."

"No, no," she said, "I'm not talking about that. After you left, I phoned everyone and told them that you are gay!"

I couldn't believe it! After our chat, she had promptly phoned all my siblings to tell them that I was gay and needed their support. She had also set up a family meeting for the next day. Given that the agenda for the meeting was to discuss the fact that I was gay, she thought that it was a good idea for me to attend. For added emotional effect – just in case any more was required – the meeting was to take place on the anniversary of my mother's death. Most of my friends gasp at the audacity of my sister when I tell this coming out story. They feel outraged on my behalf that she took into her own hands what should essentially be my story to tell, at my own pace and in my own time. I was initially shocked at her behaviour, but mostly I was relieved, and grateful for her intervention.

I had reworked and replayed coming out to my family so thoroughly over the years that it was starting to silently choke me rather than build my confidence to enable me to eventually voice my story. By "outing" me, my sister did me the greatest favour. She forced me out of myself and my fears, into my family's love and embrace, and acceptance of who I really was. I was lucky in more ways than one, not only for the infamous sister-act, but also for my family's lovely response. There were the usual questions: "How come I am gay? What made me gay? How did I know that I was gay?" I envy straight people, who never have to answer such awkward and profoundly difficult questions. It's like trying to find simple answers to what is complex and complicated, and defies such simplicity. I fumbled my way unsatisfactorily through their questions. Eventually, my older sister, who is often teased for not being clever enough, smartly rescued me. In response to the questions about what made me gay, and after several shaky attempts from my end, she piped up and said: "You know what – it's just the way you are." Why didn't I think of that?

But mostly, in that family outing, there was a reminder that they loved me no matter what and that I should not have doubted it for a second. I was humbled by their response, and a little ashamed that I was so afraid that they would reject me when they found out. I should have known. I should have known that this family, which the world would harshly dismiss as having so little, always had a good dose of the things that mattered, and unwavering love and support of each other, no matter what the circumstances. Sadly, the reality is that far too many gay people are not so fortunate. I remain thankful for my family's generous response and love at a time when most gay people anticipate, and very often get, the opposite. I don't have too many regrets about how long it took for my story to emerge. I believe that, like most important things, it happened at the right time – for me, and for my family.

That out-of-the-closet experience happened about thirteen years ago and it marked the start of an important period in my life – one of greater acceptance for who I am. A family's love and acceptance for who one really is can do that. Their acceptance of my sexual orientation expressed that day has not wavered. They have warmly embraced Monique, my partner of ten years as one of the family.

At our wedding two years ago, I told another story of family acceptance. It took place at the beginning of our relationship, and Monique was still trying to figure out who everyone was, and how to negotiate her way through these events. Family gatherings are often large, noisy affairs with loads of food and drink. My brother-in-law, who was slightly drunk, spent the afternoon trying to get a moment with her; she spent the afternoon trying to avoid him, unsure of what he was up to. He eventually followed us out to the car as we were leaving. All he wanted to say was: "I don't care about your *praaitjie* (I don't care that you are gay), I love you both. But Monique, if you mess around with Heidi, we'll fuck you up!"

We laughed all the way home, cheered by those colourful, beautiful words of acceptance for our relationship – Wentworth Mafia style.

ZANELE MUHOLI   Born in Umlazi, Durban, in 1972, Zanele Muholi currently lives and works in Cape Town and beyond. As a gender activist, photographer and proudly South African lesbian, Zanele captures images of black lesbians in order to highlight their existence, and to challenge stereotypes of lesbianism. She explains that, "In each township there are lesbians living openly regardless of the stigma and homophobia attached to their lesbian identity, both butch and femme. Most of the time being lesbian is seen as negative, as destroying the nuclear heterosexual family; for many black lesbians, the stigma of queer identity arises from the fact that homosexuality is seen as un-African. Expectations are that African women must have children and procreate with a male partner, the head of the family." So she attempts to depict the wide range of lesbian roles that women play within the black lesbian community: actress, soccer player, scholar, lawyer, dancer, gender activist, and so on. Her many thought-provoking photographic exhibitions have brought her much-deserved recognition as one of the most innovative and creative South African photographers.

I HAVE TRULY LOST A WOMAN I LOVED
ZANELE MUHOLI

I take photographs to remember those who cannot speak freely and to be remembered. I believe photography to be my first language, a calling that I received from my ancestors so that I could voice my issues and concerns. Whatever I have captured and still capture is for the world to see that we exist as black lesbians, women, trans men, intersexed, bisexuals, trans women – as queer Africans.

© Zanele Muholi. Courtesy of
Michael Stevenson, Cape Town.

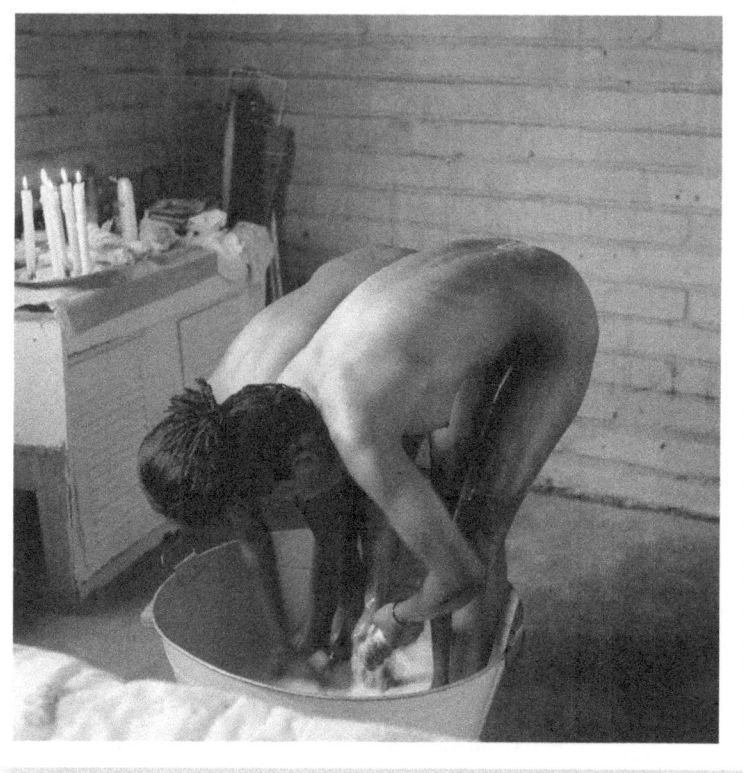

© Zanele Muholi. Courtesy of Michael Stevenson, Cape Town.

© Zanele Muholi. Courtesy of Michael Stevenson, Cape Town.

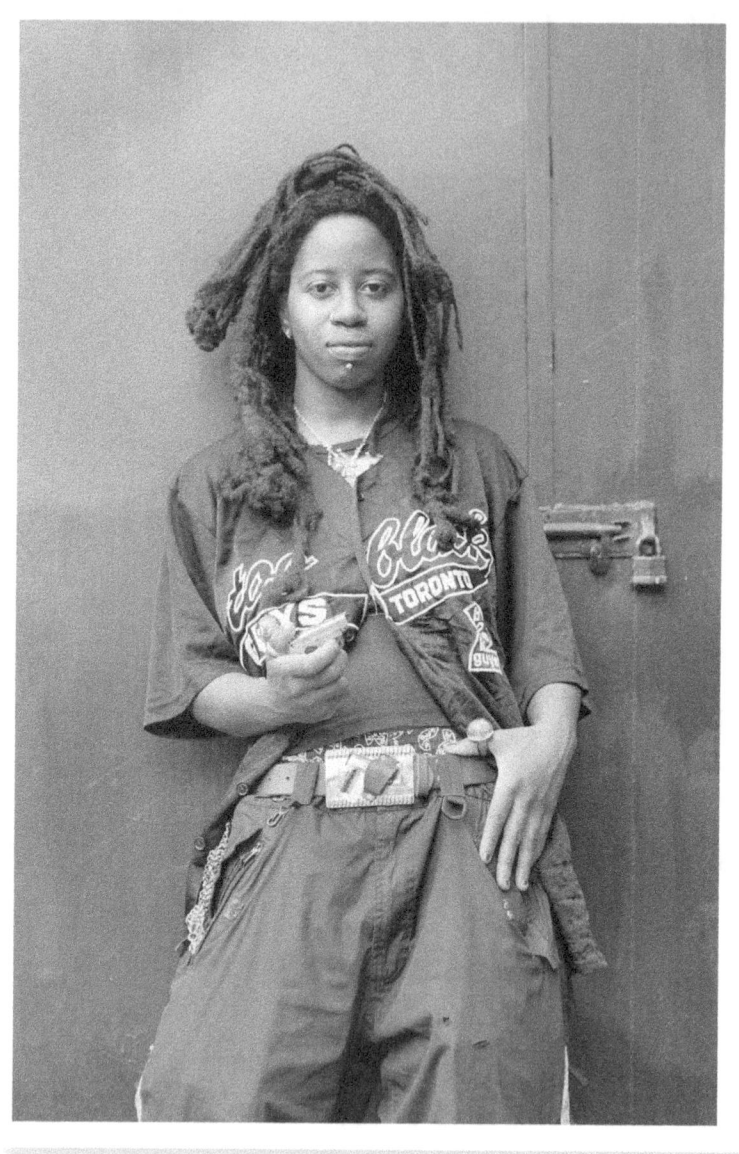

© Zanele Muholi. Courtesy of Michael Stevenson, Cape Town.

© Zanele Muholi. Courtesy of Michael Stevenson, Cape Town.

© Zanele Muholi. Courtesy of Michael Stevenson, Cape Town.

© Zanele Muholi. Courtesy of Michael Stevenson, Cape Town.

© Zanele Muholi. Courtesy of Michael Stevenson, Cape Town.

I identify as a visual activist, though many say I am an artist now. I continue to document the many layers of my community, and I aim to create positive images for our future generations. For almost a decade now, I have captured black South African queers ranging in sexualities and genders from black lesbians to effeminate gays, lesbian men, drag queens and trans men. They represent my alternative, extended family. Yet I have been feeling a longing in the past two years for something else. I realised some time ago that none of my pictures – at least none known to the world – are of my bio family. I have travelled and related experiences of my adopted family and community in so many places, but I feel an emptiness, a kind of guilt, about the lack of time I have spent on my own bio family, and this haunts me, because it is my family that defines so much of who I am today.

As an insider in the black queer community – being an African lesbian myself, I have shied away from capturing my personal life and my background. I have rarely invested the time to explore the intimacies I shared with my beloved family, including details of my mother's life and my childhood with my siblings, their children, and the many other relatives who shared space with us. Few people know I come from KwaZulu-Natal, and fewer still know I was born and raised by a single mother in Umlazi township, Durban.

Today, I am ready to share more because I am in mourning.

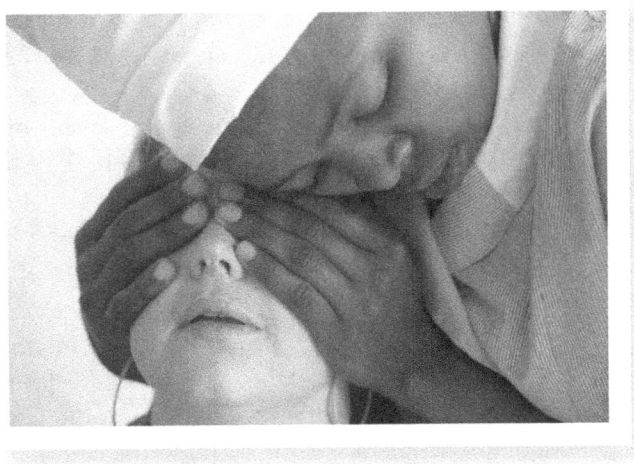

Massa & Mina(h) 2008. Photo by Neo Ntsoma © Zanele Muholi

There is a photo project I never had a chance to complete, because my beloved mother Bester Ziqubu Muholi passed away from us on 27 September 2009. The project is called *Massa & Mina(h)*, and it is conceived as a tribute to my mother who worked as a domestic worker for forty-two years.

Her last stable job was with the Harding family. It was only sickness that forced her retirement in 2002. The last time I saw Mrs Harding was more than a decade ago, though she was part of my mother's life long after she stopped working for the Harding family. It was always curious to me that two women could share parts of their personal lives and struggles despite the years of apartheid that kept one woman in the perpetual role of servant and the other in the life-long role of Madam. I remember in 2006 when my mother was very sick and in severe pain, yet she insisted on calling Mrs Harding while in the hospital. In 2007, Mrs Harding came to my mother's house in the township to help her bury Goodman, my brother. I recalled that my mother nursed Mrs Harding's two sons when they were babies. I remembered so many things as I saw her again at my mother's funeral.

I was not even in South Africa when the cloud of death enveloped us. I received the sad news while in Amsterdam. I received a call from my lover Liesl. "Please call your sister Ntomb'zane at home – it is about your mother." When I insisted on knowing "what about my mother?" she told me my mother had passed away at five-thirty that morning.

I tried to calm down, but my mind did not indulge. The last time I had called Mama was about two weeks before. I had promised to phone her that Wednesday, but I never did due to my hectic production schedule. I went upstairs to the bedroom I had occupied for more than two months. Tears did not come. Thoughts of procrastination and making empty promises haunted me. Even when she died I was busy with photography – projects, deadlines and being worried about other personal assignments. I had always wanted to avoid thinking about what might happen to her when I was far away from home. The last time I had seen my mother was in July when I was home for a few days before I departed for Amsterdam.

The night before her death, I had an exhibition at the studio at which I was an artist in residence. At the end of the evening, I shared some photos of my mother with six friends. The morning after, when I heard the news about Mama, a sharp pain hit my chest. I took a glass of rosé instead of a painkiller. I sat down next to the "beamer" that had projected the photos of Mama the night before and continued talking about my mother's struggle of raising eight children on a domestic worker's income. What was on screen was the last newspapers clipping titled "Work as usual for Bester Muholi".

It is an article that was published in one of the community newspaper in the area where she worked. It spoke about her dedication to her work in order to fend for her children. My father's name is mentioned, too, though I never met him. He died a few months after my birth. Unlike my other siblings I am the only one of his children who never knew him. He was a foreigner in South Africa. He came from Malawi to seek employment as a tradesman in the 1950s. I always wanted to know more about him from my mother, but it is too late now. What is left behind for me now is the

photo of him, a memory for us and our children. All I know is that my mother loved him.

Liesl last visited my home in May, and I requested that she take photos of my mother for me. She did. At least we have that record. You know, for me photographs are evidence of existence. They are part of the process of how I am able to understand life. Taking photographs and looking at their likeness is healing.

I remember one evening in 2006, when I visited home, my mother was not well and her feet were swollen as a result of the diabetes she suffered from. Sabine was my partner at the time and she offered to rub Mama's feet. Mama brought one foot up to her. Her soft foot, though burning, was embraced by *white* hands, and I could see from her eyes that she enjoyed that sense of touch. I recall thinking, *Gone are the days when white people recoiled from black skin, and they were not allowed to spend time at black people's homes.* That very night, my white lover and I shared a bed with my beloved mother, who was in pain. The four-room house is sparse in furniture, but we never minded sharing. Sabine is my former lover, and though we have parted, she is still a close friend. You know, it is crazy, but we never bother to think about how sometimes the women we love remain in our mothers' lives forever. My mother never stopped asking me about Sabine, or about her mother, whom Mama welcomed into her home in 2005.

Mama saw all my past lovers as part of her family. I write this keenly aware that some of my friends have difficulties with their same-sex lovers being accepted in their homes. But I never had such challenges. My ex-lovers are still welcomed at home even though my mother is gone, because she taught my family to accept and respect the intimacy and love between me and them. She accepted each one, not as a friend or as my sister, but as my lover. I never had to officially "come out" to Mama either. In 1995 I moved in with a woman who was quite abusive and, when I called my mother for help she simply came to Johannesburg and spoke to us both, just like she would with any of her other children who happen to be heterosexual.

At Mama's funeral I know many relatives I have not seen in years were mistaking my white lover for Mama's former Madam. But to this day, my sexuality has never been up for too much discussion among my relatives because my mother always responded positively and with respect on my behalf. I remember one day when my aunt asked me about when they would meet *umkhwenyana* – the husband. My mother just said, "Zanele is not interested in men." I knew from that day that even though my Mama had never had the opportunity for higher learning, she understood love. Love for her children, and especially for me, her "special" child. I had supported my mother financially and emotionally as much as I could and therefore she had no expectations of *ilobolo* – the traditional bride price. I know it is not the same for many of us. My mother treated me like all her other children when it came to love and spouses.

My mother came home to us for one last night on Friday 2 October 2009. She slept at home though her movement and voice were silenced by death. According to our Zulu tradition, if a person has died from natural causes, the family may bring the deceased home one last time. Her presence was felt by all of us. Catholic Church women in royal blue uniforms carried her coffin into the house at four-thirty in the afternoon, singing songs in celebration of Mama's life. This proved that she was indeed a staunch member of the church. We held a vigil that night, and in disbelief I looked at the people, my family and especially the young ones, and I bled. I felt as though I had never said enough to Mama for her to understand how much she meant to me. She was my child, my next of kin.

I have truly lost a woman I loved.

My mother had her children, and then I had her till the last day I spent with her in July.

I regret not hearing her last words. I hate the thought of not being called the day she was taken to hospital. I wonder if she thought of me that night when she was passing. Did my Mama ask for me when she got to hospital?

I still want to hear her story. I want to hear how apartheid affected her, impacted on her. I want to hear about her domestic work and the challenges that came with it, both for her family and her relationship with Mrs Harding. I want to know how she managed to support us with her meager salary and still pay for our Bantu education. I still need to know so much more about her. You know, for so many years I thought that my mother was not a dying type. She survived so many storms, lost so many close people in her life – all her family, her mother, three sons, and even grandchildren.

My sister Ntombi told me that I must not worry – "Mama suffered from so much pains Zanele, do not worry. Uphumlilemanje!"

October 3, 2009, was the day of Mama's funeral. I had only three hours of sleep and I spent these in the one other bedroom in the house. I see it clearly now. Two white plastic chairs covered with some blue upholstery material became my bed for those moments. On the actual bed two female relatives slept head to toe. The space was limited as the room was also full of groceries. Silver pots adorned the top of the imbuia wardrobe. There was cow bile in the corner. Fresh air came in from the window parallel to the bed. In the kitchen and outside women were peeling vegetables. Samp and beans was boiling in the three-legged pot. My nephew Xolani cooked beef. Everybody was occupied and every room in my mother's house was full of people on that day.

The funeral itself was held at St Alphonse Roman Catholic Church which is situated only a few metres away from our home in Umlazi. It is the landmark that we use when we give directions to people who want to come to visit home.

I took a bath before the funeral, though I did not bother looking for any fresh clothes to wear. I had no change to spare on clothing for my mother's funeral. When I heard the news of her passing I had no funeral policy, no big bucks in the bank. I had just finished school abroad and I was still in debt. At the art residence in Amsterdam I only received a stipend; I had nothing to spare. When I received the news, friends who heard my muted screams gave me some financial support. So, I dressed up in my black cargo pants, black striped shirt and the black jacket that I had bought at a second hand shop in Toronto. It happened to be one of my favourite items. I put on my crazy, not so clean, Nike sneakers and jumped in the car that my lover had hired for that weekend. For sure, those who had heard from my mother that I was overseas expected wonders in terms of dress code. Unfortunately for them, I was so plain. There is no glamour in mourning the passing of my beloved. Some strangers were probably astonished by me wearing pants in church, let alone at a funeral: in my culture, good African women are supposed to wear skirts. But I reminded myself that my Mama would not have minded about what I was wearing.

Because of my mother's funeral, I rediscovered church. Seated in the front row was my family. Usually when functions like this happen family members get special attention and better seats.

I decided not to sit with them as I needed to take photos of this journey. My mother's coffin was placed on the front podium, with just one wreath of flowers, a blanket, and a framed photo of her that I had taken in 2003. She had just turned 67 and I wanted to capture her as she transitioned through different stages of her life. She had on a purple *doek*, her glasses, and an orange and white two-piece skirt and shirt. She looked so healthy then.

The last time we had spoken Mama had complained about painful feet and a swollen stomach. The doctors had drained water from her stomach and were still conducting further tests to check what caused all the complications. She had known that she had diabetes and heart problems that caused difficulties for the blood to circulate. Then the doctors had discovered that she had cancer of the liver.

As the songs were sung, and minimal speeches were delivered in church, I moved around trying to capture the best shots, but all in vain as I could not concentrate. In Zulu they call this *uzodlula* which means that one becomes an extremist during bereavement in the family. I guess that's what happened to me as I continued to document Mama's passing journey. Luckily Thora Matekane agreed to document the major part of the funeral for me pro bono, and Bongi Louw had a second camera. Inside the church the man who managed the service, our pastor's deputy, requested the men to take off their hats in church. He walked close to Bongi and me and said to me, "Men are not allowed to wear hats inside church." Then, after looking at Bongi, who is more masculine than me, he said "For you women, it is fine." I was stunned. I did not know that I was so obvious … my blackness/lesbian identity/sexuality was pronounced.

The beat goes on! – a personal journey to be continued.

YULINDA NOORTMAN and her partner Karen share their home in Hilton, in the KwaZulu-Natal Midlands with their numerous canine "children", clivias, birds and their many friends.

THE DOG, THE CAT, THE PARROT AND THE PIG AND OTHER TALES

YULINDA NOORTMAN

On a smog-filled Friday afternoon in July we loaded our three dogs into our cars and drove out of Johannesburg. In the heavy traffic I lost sight of Karen who had our highly-strung bearded collie with her. I was travelling with our Maltese and the Boston terrier. Both were lying on the front seat next to me dosed up on Rescue Remedy. Questions reflected in their eyes, which at that point I was unable to answer, and for the first two hours of the journey they never took their eyes off me.

We were relocating to the KwaZulu-Natal Midlands after being in Johannesburg for the past 25 years. We had made the impulsive decision after a recent visit to the area. During our stay we had followed the Midlands Meander route on the R103 and fallen in love with the idea of country living. A couple of weekends later we had returned to check out the housing market, with the anticipation of perhaps finding something we could buy and pay off in the meantime. We were definitely not ready to leave Jo'burg! Our house hunting exercise had ended with us putting in an offer to purchase on a house in Hilton – the personification of village living. From this point on, our lives dominoed in an apparently orchestrated way; at one point I remarked to Karen how it seemed as if it was all happening with the two of us simply looking on. We had decided to put our house on the market – just to see if there was interest. To our surprised horror we had received a great offer in the first week and had accepted. More dominoes tumbled effortlessly when the business property had sold within a week. We were moving! Was all of this a prelude to menopause?

In all fairness, several years ago a visit to a well-known Gauteng psychic had foretold of our impending move to an area "just outside of Pietermaritzburg". Karen would be working with humans, small animals, dogs and horses. At the time it made for a great party story but really, who in their right minds moved to "just outside Maritzburg"?

Well, I suppose *we* did. Thus, one could perhaps comprehend my inability to explain the surrealistic suddenness of our dream that had just materialised to the quizzical dogs in the car.

So began the second half of our lives: Unanticipated and unplanned into previously uncharted territory.

Driving into Hilton from the brown dusty Highveld created an overwhelming onslaught on our bodies. Plants spilled over the road, dripping colours onto the tarmac. Jasmine hedges in full bloom stretched from corner block to corner block. The aroma was singular in its purpose, exotic and inebriating. The pavements had long ago been invaded by an entanglement of pale pink climbing roses, bougainvillea and weeds. It was somewhat claustrophobic driving down these streets after the neatly clipped pavements of our previous suburb.

We invaded our new house armed with Handy Andy, Jayes Fluid, buckets and scrubbing brushes. Washing away the accumulated dirt, germs and grubbiness of the previous owners in order to create space for new memories. Our biggest excitement was the beauty of our garden. The water drops on the pink-orange clivias sparkled like diamonds and the delicious monster in the corner created a rain forest beneath its leaves for insects and scuttling thrushes. We smelt the pine forest close by. Every plant and tree oozed oxygen. We were intoxicated.

We converted the outbuildings into a physiotherapy practice for Karen. By January the following year we opened the doors. We chose not to entertain doubts and it was a wise decision because soon her practice was flourishing. I was uncertain of what exactly to do with my retirement status. It was a strange hat to wear at age 45 and for the briefest time I missed my previous, designer-label occupation. But not for long. I began asking people "Who are you?" rather than "What do you do?" Most were a little uncomfortable and unable to answer such a direct invasion of the carefully layered shields. When I had to fill in forms of any kind I began my own social experiment. Under the heading "occupation" I would fill in "unemployed, student, pensioner, writer, receptionist, artist, self employed, and dog-minder". No one's caught on and I am happily discovering my label-free self.

Our small village "just outside of Pietermaritzburg" embraced us, and we were overwhelmed with goodwill. We met new people through the practice and soon were invited to our first book club gathering. We both groaned, as book clubs had never been our thing. Yet we went, and in the process met some people whom we can now call friends. We didn't last too long in the book club, but it was fun while it lasted. In such a small village of course tongues wagged, and we took the decision right from the start to be completely open about our relationship. For Karen in particular this was an enormous step as she was the one who, when we met, had categorically stated that *she definitely was not gay!*

Country living was wonderful and we listened to piano concerts under big trees and the gentle winter sun. We explored the Hilton festival (a mini version of the Grahamstown festival where many of the same plays and music are performed); we had breakfast at Caversham Mill and watched the weavers dive in and out of the waterfall, and explored the Underberg and Karkloof. One delight we discovered was Kubela's General Dealer, quietly situated next to the flashier Kwikspar. It had a faded Coca Cola signboard over the door and inside you could buy anything from tyre puncture repair kits to mealie meal, Zambuk ointment to beanies and tinned sardines.

Our garden delivered avos, lemons, oranges, monster cabbages, humongous pumpkins, a Purple-crested Turaco, the crisp call of the Yellow-billed Kite, arum lilies that grew taller than our heads and the nurturing evening mist. We had no words for such abundance.

During this time the Civil Union Bill was passed and several people wanted to know if we would now get married. Initially we replied, "No; whatever for?"

Then Karen's sister called and wanted to know how in the world we had let them all sign the national petition, to fight for our right to get married, and now all we could do was rave about the twelve different types of azaleas in our garden? "It's just not right," she protested. We had created an activist monster! We owed it to her to at least contemplate the choice. Could, should marriage change our relationship? Would it though? What would it mean? We surprised ourselves with the profound discoveries we made and set a date for 27 October 2007.

At the end of July 2006 we bulldozed our lawn flat for the marquee. One year after our arrival, in the middle of August, we lay new grass for our wedding. Most people laughed and said it would never be ready in three months. We ignored them and sprinkled more fertiliser and water. What did they know; this was, after all, Hilton. Karen's patients all arrived early for their physio appointments and participated in the wedding garden project. We got free advice from many seasoned Hilton gardeners and most brought gifts from their own gardens. On more than one occasion I found a patient on hands and knees planting something *special* for this big event. We weren't sure if we had our family buy-in yet, but we certainly had community buy-in. We weren't aware of any Hilton homophobes, although there must certainly have been a few lurking amongst the foliage.

Next our attention turned to outfits. Images of two white wedding dresses made us both cringe and burst out in laughter. We needed elegant, rich in colour and most definitely comfortable outfits (yes, predictable I know!). We both leaned towards a bit of Indian *bling* to spice up the white wedding images lurking in the back of our minds. So off we went to old downtown Pietermaritzburg where the bargain is king. We walked into Fabrics Galore, an overfull little shop with fabrics piled from floor to ceiling. My initial reaction was despair – this was going to take forever. However, I spotted something shiny almost immediately and the Indian shop assistant soon draped me with it. It was exquisite and I felt like an Egyptian Queen (must have been a past life moment in an Indian shop)! When I expressed my delight there were suddenly many more women around me suggesting gold raw silk to line the *bling* jacket. I was so in love with it I did not even think to ask the price or to negotiate. It was then that Karen found the same material in a platinum and turquoise. It was so opposite to my gold and bronzes, yet the colours blended, and they suited our personalities perfectly. At this point we both noticed that our audience and interest in our shopping spree had grown.

Then the owner appeared and literally glided around the corner into our section of the shop. I stared. She was magnificent: A tall, regal Indian woman in a pale pink sari and pink turban. The troops all moved into overdrive.

"This is beautiful. Who chose it?" she asked.

"It's ours – we're getting married," we said in unison. Suddenly the ambience in the small shop changed with the collective, dreamy sigh of all five women. Nothing like a wedding to unite seven women from different cultures. They peppered us with questions about time and place. Then one asked whether we were sisters.

"No," Karen answered, "we're not."

"But are you getting married on the same day?"

"Yes," I answered.

"Oh, but at the same function, one ceremony?"

So we played along whilst we waited for our *bling* to be wrapped in silky paper. Still puzzled, the youngest dared again, asking whether it was a double wedding with us wearing the same outfits.

"Yes, that is right," I answered and was asked if we were best friends. When I answered "yes", I made sure not to catch Karen's eye.

The lady who held the door open for us when we left smiled in complete innocence and said, "You must be really good friends!"

I am not sure why neither of us explained that we were getting married to one another. Even after all the quizzing we both knew that none of them for one moment contemplated the possibility that we were both brides about to marry one another! Perhaps it was the sombre black dresses and burka headgear that kept us at bay.

In the middle of September it started raining and soon our lawn was turned into a magnificent green bog. On the Tuesday before the wedding the wedding planner decided to erect the marquee, which would hopefully give the lawn time to dry out. Later that afternoon we had four heaters and some fans on the lawn inside the tent. We felt cautiously optimistic. By six o'clock the heavens once again opened and someone came running to call me: "*Woza* Lyn, *woza!* The water, come look the water Lyn!" The electrical appliances stood ankle deep in water as the saturated water table welled up from underneath. By Thursday the wedding planner extended the wooden dance floor into the rest of the tent. We had to raise the floor off the lawn with sawdust and wood bark. The guests might all float out the door, but at least we would not sink into the marsh below!

At our age we had neither guilt nor obligation with regard to our guest list. We invited our immediate family, our gay friends and added into the mix our very straight, new Hilton friends. Some considered this a risky social experiment. Only two of the eighty invited chose not to come.

Friends and family began arriving from the Wednesday before the wedding. And the Meander absorbed and entertained them whilst we draped our house. (Actually the lovely gay boy who worked for the wedding planner did the draping.) On *the day* the sun came out and the rains waited until everybody was inside the marquee. As we were about to say "I do", the heavens opened once again and we accepted it as a blessing of our partnership.

Our blessing ceremony was an intricately woven affair and conducted by an amazing friend who was a local priest and an internationally acclaimed theologian. He understood that religion wasn't our thing, but that God (by our own unique definition) was. As part of the ceremony, my younger sister, in her role as magistrate, was able to perform the legalities. During the quiet lull whilst we signed all the papers we were entertained by Florence, our Zulu friend and employee, and her sisters, who performed the traditional Zulu wedding dance for us. My uncle composed a special song for us. Tess, our sister turned activist, was our Mistress of Ceremonies. She was seven-and-a-half months pregnant with twins and her gynaecologist strongly advised against the five-hour journey to KwaZulu-Natal. Against all common sense they made the journey to Hilton and the twins were born three weeks later. Unbeknown to us at the time, we would become the very proud godparents of these amazing little creatures.

We had a perfect day. It was a synergy of gay and straight, old and young, black and white and family and friends. We celebrated love on a floating deck in our green Hilton garden.

The next morning at nine o'clock the family gathered at one of the local churches in Hilton. We were there to christen our nephew

Josh, son of Tess and Dave, parents of unplanned, impending twins. We had made the decision to capitalise on the rare opportunity of having the whole family together in one place. The priest who performed the christening thankfully kept it short. He too was at the wedding the previous night. Back at the house the marquee doubled as a christening celebration venue. The sun shone all day long and our garden dripped with colour. Our friends all popped in to say goodbye and together we all ate wedding leftovers. By five o'clock, as the last people left, the mist rolled in and we sat in the tangible stillness so characteristic of this area. We relived every moment of this perfect weekend. The only ones glad it was all over were our dogs, the matriarch Maltese, Holly, the Boston terrier, Yoda and our bearded collie, Jinty.

This morning, almost three years since the wedding and four years since we moved to Hilton, Karen had a patient who exploded against "Jo'burgers invading the Midlands". Karen vehemently agreed with her. I could not help but laugh when she told me. I suppose we feel – *local!*

Oh yes, about the work with small animals and dogs. Karen's animal part of the practice grew weekly. She mostly treats dogs, cats and some horses, but has also been called upon to help a lame African grey Parrot. Since she treated the paralysed, three-hundred-kilogram pot bellied pig in the Karkloof, she has not again complained of the difficulties of treating her portly human patients.

It is a good life. But it was not always such. Traditionally, *to belong* was always an illusive verb in my life. Even my earliest memories were plagued by a deep-seated sense of uncertainty of being. I grew up in a Free State mining town with deep social rifts. To this day I still have dark dreams of the bridge crossing the deep donga of the Sand River that divided the town into two. Perhaps it manifests in my dreams as the metaphor for how I felt. Always having one leg on the wrong side of the river. I have one sister and we grew up with the best of everything and parents who were loving and supportive of all we did. They allowed us head and heart space to grow up. Yet no one ever grasped the notion that I felt like an alien. I am not sure that it was a mental construct for me until I hit teenager phase. Yet, looking back, it is shockingly obvious to see how little I really belonged in my town, in my world and my own skin. More so, how oblivious the significant adults in my life were to this very situation. My earliest *"alien alert!"* hailed from those early childhood days.

... SIX SHOOTERS AND PETTICOATS

Precariously balanced on the hind legs I lean the chair back onto the wall. My feet up on a wooden box. My hat tilted forward. Eyes glaring from underneath, observing the hostile world. A six shooter and holster slung around my waist. The belt riding high on the one hip, dragged down by the gun on the other. The mean, skew look. A lone cowboy in search of some unknown truth.

My serenity is shattered when my little sister wails around the corner "come, let's play dolls. In one fluid movement I kick the box away, tip the chair upright, draw, aim and fire. Six consecutive shots ring through the air and the smell of cordite burns my nose. In my mind's eye the pram filled with dolls and teddy bears is blasted to pieces. Stuffing and pink plastic scattered around us. I stare at her and say, "I don't play with dolls, okay! It's silly and stupid!" I tilt my hat at her and turn to my purple Chopper bicycle, saddle up and ride into the sunset.

...

My fantasy world was fuelled by a combination of the Western Cowboy movies at the local drive-in and reading my Dad's Louis L'Amour cowboy books. Yet, even my fondest cowboy memories were cloaked in "disgruntledness". Why were there never any female cowboys? I knew I never wanted to be a "boy" cowboy, but I had no heroine to model a female cowboy on. It was as if the possibility just did not exist. Inevitably females in movies were voiceless victims dressed in layers of petticoats. Every time I strapped on that holster and took to the veld on my purple bicycle, I rode in protest against a society that celebrated weak, witless women.

Even as a six-year-old I yearned for the independence of self-reliance. My battle was internal, and every day was a showdown between a deep subconscious "disgruntledness" and the petticoat and corset reality in which I lived. I was still too young to understand the true complexities of this battle. It was a primal screech to understand myself. Why did I feel so different? At this point I did not even have an overt consciousness that I was gay. It was not yet a sexual thing. Instead it was a profoundly genetic soul awareness that compelled me to see and experience the world in an entirely different way: The vulnerable birthing of my own self perspective, which I knew instinctively could not be voiced. There was no one to guide and nurture the dreams and aspirations of a six-year-old cowgirl. Unavoidably resisting being corseted. The *corset script* was inherent in everything I encountered in my world. Subtly disguised and permeating every breath a girl child took in the late 1960s. Nowhere else was it so deeply ingrained as in the school and church environments that served as the breeding ground for patriarchal sexism. Or, as I would come to call it: *the tyranny of penis power.*

So I grew up.

During these early teenage years being gay was a shrouded *thing*. It just did not exist within the *nurturing* folds of my community. I am not for one moment suggesting that people were oblivious or unaware of the existence of homosexuality. Rather, in my society, it was swept under the carpet with the communal broom labelled the "anti-sin morality monitor". How was it possible that there was not even one responsible, insightful adult? It was easy to recall the adults who could have or should have made a difference in my life. Ms Science, Mrs Home Economics, Ms Phys Ed; I know there was a recognition of sorts. I did not know what it was, but you recognised in me what you chose to hide so deeply for yourself – did you not? Like ghosts we passed through one another in the school passages. The only good that came from this was that I learnt very early on to become highly self reliant and self-sufficient. Even then my own gayness never made me feel like a victim. Whilst it was a deep *well of loneliness* (thank you Radclyffe Hall) I never rejected this part of myself when I was growing up. I could not because it was not something I could reject. I never felt foreign to myself, only foreign within my social context. I could only surmise that this was not the first lifetime I have chosen to be gay. It sat well with me then and has ever since. Even when I did not understand, I never got angered by my "differentness", but only by the universal injustice of being rejected because of it.

As a teenager I found myself firmly ensnared in the fairytale dreams most parents have for their young girls. These dreams were defined by expectations moulded by generations of ancestors, church dogma, ingrained yet unquestioned prejudices and the sheep-like mentality of communities that instinctively adhered to flock behaviour.

I was an uncomfortable teenager who found the whole frog kissing anticipation somewhat distasteful and unsettling. I found I had an instinctive empathy with the poor frog waiting for the insolent little princess to come and judge him and toss him aside, if found undesirable. It reminded me of a profound saying: "In fairy tales the frog is transformed into a prince. But in Buddhism the frog is crowned as a frog ... the lily pad as a royal seat."

I do not know whose quote it was, but if I had known at age twelve what a Buddhist was, I surely would have asked my parents if I could become one. Cowgirl to Buddhist would have been better than cowboy to princess. I was a princess growing up being prepared to kiss some frogs. The elusiveness of *Mr Right* was an early childhood imprint and, although unspoken, it was clear that many frogs needed to be kissed in order to find the perfect prince. It was all a little confusing because the goal was clear, but there was always a sense that one should never be caught doing the actual kissing thing: that the act in itself was fundamentally distasteful. It was assumed by all that the perfect frog would always, in the end, rise from the lily pond to honour, love and cherish the princess until death. The fairytale wedding that followed would affirm the King's power and the Queen's splendour and make the whole kingdom happy.

Weddings. Aarggh!!

When I was seven, my sister and I were flower girls at a related princess's wedding (a cousin). I was stuffed into a pale yellow chiffon dress that scratched and constricted my movement. Early that morning my hair was rolled into pink plastic rollers and pulled so tight my eyes watered. Later, amidst many tears, it was combed out into a beehive of curls and adorned with white plastic daisies.

In the late afternoon Free State heat the dominee's voice blended with the song of the sun beetles. He droned on and on, until he finally said, "Laat ons bid," and I was thankful for the chance to close my eyes. I was so caught in my own internal world trying to make sense of God and the strange rituals I saw, I didn't hear him say "Amen". So I just kept on standing with my eyes closed. The congregation saw this and thought I had fallen asleep standing up. All eyes were on me waiting for me to fall over.

It became a family joke, further alienating me in the household of God. I wove my own protective web tightly and densely and as I grew older my disbelief and frustration around weddings grew. No one could really answer me when I asked why the young princess had to vow subservience to her prince (who is after all just a frog in his previous life) in front of God and the congregation.

I left impenetrable depths unexplored because I didn't know how to access these dams of emotion. I had no role model, in fact I did not even have words to express what I was feeling. Language failed me. Thus I lived within this nebulous subconscious entity my parents called my rebellious side and never engaged these deep yearnings. In time, and out of sheer desperation, I equated this voiceless longing with something obviously irreverent. I began writing angry, horrible teenage poetry, yet I was never able to forge the metaphor to capture myself.

So when I was twelve I decided to kiss a frog.

He took my hand, told me no one would miss us. I glanced at our parents jiving the night away at the wedding reception held in the school hall. It was a night for romance, so I went with him. Both of us were chewing musk-flavoured Beechies. He was a year older, with bony knees and elbows that got in the way. After almost choking me with his tongue, I managed to push him away and ran away down the darkened school passage to find the light. The taste of his spit in my mouth lingered long after I crawled into bed. He was obviously not a prince and I wondered how many times I would have to feel this awful and guilty before I found my frog. From then on I ignored most frogs, punched a couple on the playground and won marbles and spinning tops from a couple of others.

It was in high school at age seventeen that a frog found me. He was testosterone green and desperate to do the kissing thing.

Was he hoping to win a kingdom and riches or was he just a horny teenager? Our kiss took place under the syringa tree at our front gate. His hands were sweaty and he was breathing loudly. He held me way too tight and I pushed him away. Asphyxiation! He stumbled backwards into the lower branches of the tree where two empty glass milk bottles were precariously balanced. For a moment we both stared as the bottles slowly tilted over and crashed to the cement below. The orange milk coupons that were inside were set spinning on the cement before they lost momentum and plopped face down. The noise woke the king who rushed out in his dressing gown to apprehend the perpetrators. But the frog and princess were long gone.

After Matric I went to Australia on exchange for a year. I was surprised. It was a gift offered by my parents; who trusted me in their own wisdom and released me into the big world. Here I would kiss the last hopeful frog.

High on cheap wine and good ganja I took the step to lose my virginity. The rush of blood and adrenaline lifted the dagga fog to bring clarity. From deep within a voice screamed out wells of revulsion against the intrusion, which was not only physical. He looked puzzled when I moved away. His face a question mark as he took my rejection as personal. I did not know how to make him feel better or how to make him understand.

During that year away from home I grew, explored and discovered many parts of myself. I travelled through the vast Northern Territory Desert and climbed Ayers Rock where I felt the poignant presence of spirits moving around this wonder of the world. For two weeks I explored Sydney with another student and discovered Kings Cross, blue movies and sex for sale. We saw *Evita* performed in the Sydney Opera House. The highlight of the year was the month long skiing trip in the Australian Alps (I kid you not). Never once did I meet another lesbian. In retrospect, some of the people I met were gay, but at the time we were all *straight!*

When I got back I had to decide within a week which university I wanted to go to.

I had bursaries at Wits, RAU and UCT but somehow, in a conspiring move of the universe, I ended up at Potchefstroom University (vir Christelike Hoër Onderwys/Christian Higher

Education). After I had fallen around for three months I finally decided on International Politics. I was once again a fish out of water. I didn't fit. Not in the classes, nor the res, nor the community. I stayed for five years perfecting the art of introverting. One Sunday morning, whilst the rest of Potchefstroom was in church, I picked up a newspaper and found a job.

I started working in Sandton at a financial institution. I got a title, an office, a secretary, and I bought a house and a car. At work I met interesting, vibrant, professional women. Women with opinions, questions, bold voices. Slowly they let me into their world where I was welcomed and nurtured. One partying night I travelled between fairytales and entered a Sapphic parallel universe. I was surrounded by women. Magnificent creatures who celebrated who they were. One of them kissed me. The next day I took time off work, time to think. I drove home and sat under the familiar old syringa tree where I had previously kissed a frog. I compared the last kiss to all the previously aborted attempts and I wondered if the syringa tree had known all along? Over the next few days my self-spun cocoon unravelled and understanding began to dawn. In my child time and place, the word lesbian did not exist. That is why I could not find it: That as a lesbian in a conservative Free State mining town in the mid 1970s, I did not exist. Now I had found language. Lesbian!

I drove back to Johannesburg. And as I walked into my house, I knew I was home. In time I grew into my own gayness and I explored my new world. I became part of a family of people who all knew and shared the world of warped fairly tales. I grew a little wild and kissed many more women in the process. I enjoyed all of them but they remained passing ships. I was happy but I wanted my own lily pad and pond. I turned once again to writing poetry.

> I feel that familiar yearning
> Like the tug of the tide
> Calling like a whale song
>
> I ache with yearning
> As the song intensifies
> Reminding me of who I am

The song grows into a symphony
Filling the universe
Until the notes spill over
Into galaxies yet undiscovered

I embrace that familiar yearning
As the symphony calls
Challenging me to comprehend its
Complexity, its simplicity and its beauty.

All the while the sea nymph
dances the whale symphony
and smiles at me.

At times I despaired that I might never ensnare the sea nymph. In my disillusionment I grew even wilder and began pushing more risky boundaries whilst at the same time feeling more and more lonely. On the outside I lived the glamour life. At the age of 32 it all imploded.

... I SEE YOU

One night I sat in the bath and watched as the water ran out. I saw my life in the outlet eddy, spiralling out into the sewer system. I was exhausted and so tired. I sat in that bath for a long time. The next day I visited my local GP and explained my strange symptoms and exhaustion.

Two weeks later I woke up in the ICU at Parklane Clinic. I was almost a complete quadriplegic. It was the result of ten years of misdiagnoses by the medical profession and a butcher of a neurosurgeon. They removed a nasty tumour from my spinal cord and I spent two weeks in morphine-induced nether worlds in the ICU. During this time I experienced Death as an entity. I heard everything everyone around me said. I knew who was there. At the same time I saw Death, adorned in magnificent robes, move between the people: Claiming some and passing others by. As the dead and Death left the ICU, strange lights distorted their images and Death looked a lot like Birth. After a month in that hospital I moved to a rehabilitation facility. It was during this time that I sat over the edge of the bed waiting for someone to help me get into the wheelchair, and for no apparent reason I passed out.

I was in an old familiar place that reminded me of the time in ICU. I gave up trying to figure out where exactly it was. My first effort at constructive thought in this place was that a lot of time had passed again. I wondered where all this time was going. I was in a new space-nameless-place. It was quite still.

I just was and yet I was not. Even cognition was strangely fluid and devoid of unnecessary noise. I dissolved into the stillness. My parts and particles were taken up into a dance of profound beauty. In slow gracefulness the dance stopped. I was reassembled into being.

I then knew. God was unlike anything I had ever been told, or asked to believe. Tears ran down my cheeks. Oh, I had cheeks again. I was disappointed and relieved at the same time when I opened my eyes to the faffing of the nursing staff around me.

I spent four months in this rehabilitation hospital where I learned to walk again. Physically, emotionally, mentally and spiritually. I learned dependence. A strange and foreign concept. I learned patience.

My friends and family were there but I was deep inside. Where I fought for survival. There was no fairly tale there. Only rawness contrasted with a couple of seconds of profound beauty.

In this strange place I met Karen. She was a rare human being and gifted healer and she was assigned as my physiotherapist. At times she pushed me, encouraged me and when I just could not do it by myself, she carried me. She refused to hear the medical verdict. She just believed that it could be better. I began to believe her and started taking bigger and bolder steps. We built an intimate working relationship that existed in a parallel universe: a connection that surpassed all things mundane and physical. When it was time to leave I felt a deep sadness.

I returned to my job and once again I felt like an alien. Nothing felt familiar. My own gayness was no longer hidden but now I had a new label to deal with. Disabled. I was on crutches. I sold my brand new red Golf GTi 16 V, which I could not drive, and bought an automatic white Audi, which I called my "ship". It was a huge step in the fight to regain my own independence.

At this point Karen went to America for six weeks on a holiday. Upon her return we saw one another sporadically. She started a new job and I tried to find a rhythm in my old job. In the far distance, like an erratic dust devil, I heard the whale symphony again. It had dried up for almost a year. I dared to look if the illusive sea nymph still danced for me. She was there and it was Karen's face I saw. Slowly we were enticed into the rhythm of the ocean. Warring emotions raged through me. Why now when nothing was as it should be?

When I kissed her for the first time, I kept my eyes open, unwilling to entertain the brutality of any more fairytales. I froze our image into my mind so that she might stay true to all she was, and in doing so denied any form of societal transformation that dictated who we would be or become.

THE BEGINNING

So began the journey which finally, fifteen years later, brought us to the Natal Midlands. We both sold our properties and with a little trepidation rented a house together. We were both fiercely independent and a little fearful to be living with someone in our personal space. But on a tsunami of love we stayed for only three months before we bought a house that we registered in both our names. We began our family when I gave Karen a "pet shop special white fluffy sort of Maltese" puppy for Christmas. We christened her Holly. She became the matriarch of our household. In 2000 we decided that it was time for Karen to open her own practice. We sold our house in Randburg and moved to Fourways. Just before we moved our friend Sharon blessed us with an amazing gift: a Boston terrier puppy that we called Yoda as she is the personification of the Jedi Master Yoda in *Star Wars*. Even as a puppy she was wise and expressive.

Karen opened her practice and I still worked in Midrand and hated every moment of it. The corporate world was not a place for disabled persons. After 1994 many things changed on this front and at one point I thought they might offer me the CEO position as, according to our new Constitution, I now qualified on so many levels for special consideration. I fell into several affirmative categories – being gay, disabled and female! To keep my sense of humour going I began studying.

I studied psychology and branched out into side disciplines that caught my attention. Later I did some lateral moves and studied meditation and mysticism, languages and literature and creative writing. The study bug bit Karen too and together we explored love, life and the universe. Her practice flourished. I hung in with my job. I realised that being a white forty-year-old disabled lesbian would not open doors for me if I resigned. Around this time we met a bearded collie for the first time, a breed of dog we knew nothing about, but fell madly in love with. We placed our names on the waiting list and had three interviews before we passed the grade to get a puppy. She was Milo brown and white and we called her Jinty. Everything was as it should be. We talked about "one day" when we moved out of Johannesburg.

We have been in the Midlands for almost four years. Our family once again grew by one: a little Boston terrier pup called Nala Moonbeam. She only grew to half her potential size, but she is a terrier at heart and is fondly called Sample Size by our friends. Our first Bostie, Yoda, sadly passed away this year. Karen and I too are older, a little slower, but we like to think a lot wiser. We strive to live each day with intention and awareness. We are coming to understand that the only constant is the inevitability of change. The whale symphony still provides background music to our lives and we are solid in our knowledge that neither of us ever need magically transform. We are constantly reminded that our lily pad is our throne. A throne on which there sits two queens.

In true courage there is always an element of choice …
And of anguish, and also of action and deed.
There is always a flame of spirit in it,
a vision of some necessity higher than oneself.

– Brenda Ueland

MAVOURNEEN FINLAYSON is a self employed Holistic Practitioner and Yoga teacher in Pietermaritzburg. Her practice, Body Balance, has been running successfully for eleven years. She has been published in *Journeys – A World Anthology of Poetry*, *Murmuring Memoirs – Anthology of African Verse*, and her own poetry book, *Verity* (Alexander House, 2009). She draws inspiration from working intimately with people and believes passionately in self expression through creative mediums.

1ˢᵗ March

Wine glass next to my bed,
silent upon wooden top
whispering memories of your lips.

Your feminine shape on crumpled bedding,
far as the stars you have gone,
scents linger warm and heady.

Pillows scattered near wet towels,
cold incense ash and candle drippings,
glowed once with fire also.

JANET SHAPIRO and partner Marian Nell are both of Ashkenazi descent and have two sons who they have brought up in the Jewish tradition.

A COMFORTABLE FIT
JANET SHAPIRO

I was born in 1949 in East London. My partner, Marian Nell was born in Johannesburg in 1945, the year World War II ended. We are both of Ashkenazi (East European) descent, second generation Jewesses, born in South Africa. Our grandparents were part of one of the many exoduses from Eastern Europe, Lithuania, in the wake of waves of pogroms and anti-Jewish activity. As was often the case at that time, our grandparents ended up in South Africa more by accident than design. Someone in the family put down some tentative roots here and others followed. Marian's family migrated to the Western Cape and mine to the Eastern Cape.

Marian's mother grew up on a farm in Ceres and her father in Cape Town. Both my maternal grandmother and my grandfather ended up in King Williams Town where they met and married. My paternal grandfather was a *chazan* (singer in a synagogue) and, as there were not enough rabbis to go round, ended up as the acting rabbi in a series of small towns in the Eastern Cape. He died before my parents married and was, according to my mother, not a religious man at all – he could sing, a talent none of his grandchildren inherited, and earned his living by doing so. Both my father and Marian's were attorneys and our mothers were housewives. Our fathers were quite conservative and our mothers liberal.

I was the third of three children and have an older brother and sister. My sister emigrated to Israel, with her husband and three children, all of whom are now married and have their own children. My brother married a woman who isn't Jewish and has two children who were not brought up as Jewish. They have a warm and loving relationship. Marian was the third of four children. Her older brother, Paul, was born with Down's Syndrome and later institutionalised. He died some years ago. He was followed by Josephine, Marian and Matthew. Matthew also married a woman who is not Jewish, but his children have been brought up Jewish and are roughly the same age as ours. Josephine is married to a Jewish man and has two sons, one of whom is married to "a nice Jewish girl" and they have two lovely children. We often share Jewish holidays with all of them.

We both grew up in what were then traditional, largely non-practising, orthodox Jewish families – they celebrated the holidays, and, in my case, had Friday night suppers. We were both from "liberal" white homes: our parents voted for the Progressive Party and probably had friends who were to the left of them, but most of their friends were to the right of them, as was most of the Jewish community.

My father died when I was fourteen and we moved to Cape Town where my sister was already married with a child. I went to the University of Cape Town (UCT), where I received a BA in English and philosophy and, after a brief stint of work at the then Progressive Party, travelled overseas for two years. During this time I spent a year in Israel, where I was teaching English in schools in the far north when the Yom Kippur War broke out in 1973. Marian went to the University of the Witwatersrand (Wits), where she edited the student newspaper and also got a BA – in English and history and politics. She volunteered for six months after the Six Day War and worked on a kibbutz. She then went on to do her honours in psychology through the University of South Africa (Unisa) and subsequently an MBA at Wits. I did various Unisa courses while I worked in a children's bookshop in Cape Town. Marian worked for the Zionist Federation and then for the Union of Jewish Women before, at the behest of the Institute of Race Relations, she set up an initiative called the Human Awareness Programme (HAP) in response to the student uprising of 1976.

Neither of us had great relations with our fathers – nor our mothers! Marian was close to her brother, Matthew, and I to mine. We both had some boyfriends – were even in love – but these relationships never came to anything. Our subsequent "coming out" seemed to cause our sisters more problems than our brothers, but they have learned to live with it. Indeed, my whole family regards Marian with love and respect and they are all very happy that we are together.

In the Seventies I went to Rhodes University where I did an honours degree in sociology and discovered my political home, far to the left of anything my family had ever espoused, and made friends accordingly. I had my first two relationships with women, neither of them Jewish (nor had mine with men been). In the early 1980s I went to live and work in Johannesburg. I ended up working for HAP where Marian was the Director. I cried on her shoulder when I fell in love with a woman who dumped me and, although Marian claimed that she "didn't go for women", I seduced her on a rare snowy Johannesburg afternoon in September 1981. We fell in love, found we had much in common (age, Jewish, lawyer fathers, iconoclastic, shared senses of humour and values) and started living together at the end of 1981. We were rich by South African standards, but poor by our families' standards. Marian had a house (bought with a deposit of R2,000 after she had had a robbery in her previous, rented house). I brought no dowry except a Jack Russell dog that spread her white hairs all over Marian's house and was the first in a long line of dogs (and some cats).

I made it clear from day one that I intended to have a child. I don't know why it was such a strong drive in me, but I wanted a baby in my arms and knew I wouldn't be satisfied until I had one. After many false starts and stops, we finally decided to use a double blind system: we found a go-between, who found a go-between, who found a donor. No one in the line knew anyone else as we did not want a "donor" laying claim to the child. Today we would have adopted.

Benjamin (named from Marian's father) was born on 22 December 1984 – as it happened that was Marian's father's birthday. He called me Mommy and Marian, Mina (a contraction of a nickname). At Marian's suggestion, we had another baby (also mine biologically), named Samuel David after Marian's mother, on 16 June 1988. In between there was a miscarriage, so having Sam is most fortuitous. At the time of Sam's birth the Tissues Act made it illegal for a doctor to give an unmarried woman artificial insemination, so we did it the same way as we had done for Ben, although we don't know if the donor is the same. The children have brought us both great joy – Marian was, initially, nervous because they were conceived during the very dark Eighties, when the struggle was at its height and the society very conservative. She had no legal rights with regard to them but, after taking one look at Ben, she was enchanted and has never had any regrets. Motherhood has been everything I ever wanted it to be. When the law changed, much later, Marian adopted Sam, but Ben was already too old.

The children were brought up knowing how they were conceived and that their conception was an act of great love. The relative uniqueness of their conception has never been a great issue for them, although we have offered and paid for psychotherapy whenever we thought it necessary, as we would have with any children. They have never had any trouble discussing the situation with their friends, on the whole with few repercussions. Our families accepted their births with surprising ease and, in some cases, delight, and we made it clear that our family came as a whole and that we would not accept anything less. While both our fathers had died before we met, our mothers lived to see Ben born. Marian's mother died before Sam was born and my mother died when he was a baby, so the children have never known grandparents.

Both boys had proper *brith milahs* (ceremony of circumcision), although, as Sam was born with serious heart defects and had two operations in the first five months of this life, his had to be delayed. We joined a Reform *Shul* when Ben was seven and both boys had wonderful barmitzvahs there, although they now declare themselves atheists. The congregation was warm and caring and accepted us as a family. Again, we would not have stayed members on any other terms. Ben and Sam were called up to read the Torah on their barmitzvahs as "sons of Miriam and Johanna", our Hebrew names. Our expectation is that Sam, if he marries a Jewish girl, will bring his children up Jewish. Ben is gay – he may adopt and then we will have to see.

Marian and I were married in terms of the new legislation in 2008, in our garden, with the boys as our witnesses and their and our friends present. It was a beautiful spring day and, although the service was secular, it was done by a young, gay Jewish lawyer, who is a registered marriage officer in terms of the Civil Union Act. During the ceremony, he quoted Martin Buber extensively. Friends and family came from the country – even some from out of the country – and my brother, who flew up from Cape Town with his wife, wept throughout the ceremony! The wedding invitation read:

> *The passing of the Civil Union Act of 2006 was the result of the efforts of many people. Whatever the legal and political implications of the Act, for us it is a personal opportunity to affirm publicly the love that has united us over the past 27 years.*

We have little to say about our sexuality – we love each other and that is as good as it gets. I don't even know that Marian would call herself a lesbian – she fell in love with me and there is space along the continuum of sexuality for just such a relationship.

We are no longer members of a Jewish community although we regard ourselves as Jewish and so do the boys. Certainly we would not link our sexuality to our Jewishness, although the fact that we are both Jewish has bound us even more closely together. At the wedding, I read the following (Marian is too shy to voice her feelings publicly but is happy for me to do it for us both):

> *A long time ago, with no one to witness it, we made vows to each other, vows of love and vows of friendship, vows to be there in the hard times, vows to cry together and to laugh together, vows to say sorry when we were wrong and to remember to say I love you as often as we felt it, which has been often. We have kept those vows. There have been happy days and angry days but there has never been a day that we have been sorry that we made our commitment.*
>
> *And so all we want to do now is to confirm those vows, to be thankful for the opportunity to have lived them, to commit ourselves to living them for as long as our "always" will be, and say that we believe that long after we are gone the tears and laughter will echo in the walls of our shared homes and bring happy dreams to all who live in them. We hope that they will echo in the lives of our boys and they will remember our life together as the gift we always wanted it to be for them. They have made the circle of our love so much bigger. It is wonderful to have them here to witness this moment.*

Marian and I now run our own organisational development consultancy (doing mostly development work) from home and have moved from Judith's Paarl, to Bez Valley, to Parkmore. I am currently doing some writing for The Atlantic Philanthropies on the lesbian/gay/bisexual/transgender and intersex (LGBTI) sector and, as part of this, I am writing a kind of retrospective about how queer rights came to be woven into the fabric of South African life, what various people think about the current situation, and what the future might hold.

On the whole, our sexual preferences have been treated with respect by others, and we have never seen them as a handicap in any way. Our families have come to accept our relationship even when there were initial doubts; some do it with more grace than others. As members of a progressive Jewish community we received nothing but respect. There would have been no place for us in an orthodox Jewish community, but this is not something we regret.

We believe that the current situation with regard to homosexuality in South Africa is beset with fragility and we watch it carefully. We consider it an honour and a privilege to have lived through exciting times in South Africa and we look forward to finding out what happens next. We have never regretted any of our decisions.

We are still very much in love.

Dream

Mavourneen Finlayson

Soft nightly pillow holds
dreaming mind,
head on your breasts bringing
light into sound.

MARCO P. NDLOVU "How you want to be described." This story is one of the "I" Stories produced by the Gender Link Opinion and Commentary Service for the Sixteen Days of Activism on Gender Violence, held in November, 2009. On the first of the sixteen days women who had decided to break the silence headed a march through Hillbrow to Constitution Hill in Johannesburg, where a rally was held. Twenty women wrote stories about their experiences of gender violence in an attempt to reclaim the lives which have suffered so much, and to demand their right to safety at all times of the day and night.

FINDING THE REAL ME IN A STORM OF VIOLENCE

MARCO P. NDLOVU

My name is Marco and I come from Pietermaritzburg, South Africa. I am a 39-year old black lesbian born into a family of eight, of whom only five survived. Gender violence has been so much a part of my life that at times I wonder if there is such a thing as a life free of violence.

As a lesbian, hate, violence and misogyny follow me wherever I go. I became pregnant as a result of being raped by a man I believed to be a friend. I have been beaten almost to a pulp because of my sexual orientation, at the instigation of none other than my mother.

Yet the vicious cycle of violence that has left such deep scars in my life began from the moment of my birth, in my family: with the uncle who raised me, and with the death of my three brothers. One was stillborn, my drunken mother accidentally squashed the other to death and the third brother suffered from mental disorders after he was gang-raped by monsters in a nightclub. He committed suicide at a tender age.

When I was five, my mother married another man after she had broken up with my dad, whom she accused of being a womaniser. I was taken to my uncle's place where I lived a miserable life. My uncle used to abuse his wife and on the many occasions when my aunt almost died in front of us, he punished us severely for screaming. He would try to force us to tell him who had called the ambulance for his wife, but we didn't dare tell him since we knew exactly what he would have done.

When I was twelve, my cousin became pregnant from the guy she went out with for seven years. He denied being the father of the child, but later claimed the child, after my cousin had endured the hardship of giving birth without him. I vowed then never to marry or have a relationship with a man. I said I would prefer marrying a woman: that was the start of me discovering my sexual orientation.

For a time, I got involved in politics. In the heat of the anti-apartheid struggle, I joined the United Democratic Front (UDF), but withdrew from politics after being tortured and left for dead, in a ditch somewhere near Howick, by the police.

I earned a reputation as a tomboy because I chose to dress like a boy, and play games like soccer with boys. To this day there are people who ask me if I am a boy or a girl. I enjoy this power I have over them: the power of not fitting easily into anyone's idea of whom I should be.

At seventeen I started dating Nonhlanhla, a woman who stole my heart with her inner beauty. Oh! she had the most amazing personality! Nobody knew about our relationship. Everybody thought we were just friends.

Then, out of the blue, my mother decided I should get married to a man older than my daddy: a priest whose wife had died. I ran away from home, wondering how much money he had promised her, because my mother has no scruples when it comes to money. I went to stay with my cousin in Durban, who was married to a doctor. She had a friend called Theophilus, to whom I became very close. Even though I loved Nonhlanhla, I could not tell anyone, so, for the sake of everyone around me, I hung out with Theophilus. Then, one fateful day, he shattered my dreams: he flung himself on me and raped me. The whole act took less than five minutes. I screamed and kicked, but nobody came to my rescue.

When I threatened to lay charges against him, Theophilus apologised and asked for my forgiveness. He compelled me to take a bath, threatening to not let me go if I refused to do so. I was bleeding. I wanted to take my panties that he had torn and hidden away. In those days, when no one, least of all your parents, talked about sex, rape or abuse, I had no idea that he had torn them to destroy the evidence.

Soon after this ordeal my cousin took me to the doctor for a pregnancy test. To my horror, I discovered I had become pregnant as a result of the rape. Theophilus wanted me to terminate the pregnancy, but in those days it was not the done thing and it was illegal. Theophilus tried to contain the situation by paying two cattle as "damages" to my mother. We agreed that he would pay child maintenance voluntarily. I delivered the baby – now my beautiful 21-year old daughter who I love dearly, though I will never forgive her father for ruining my life.

After two years, I moved to Johannesburg and found a nanny for my daughter. I got a job as a security guard and eventually started a relationship with Bob, a charming guy who proposed marriage to me. However, I could not get sexually interested in him. Our relationship came to a crashing halt when I found him with another girl. I told him I would leave him peacefully with his new lover. The next day he refused to go to work and that night he tried to strangle me, stripping me naked and tying my arms and legs. The following morning he freed me and apologised. Even though I was two months pregnant with his child, I decided to leave. My second daughter, who is now fourteen years old, doesn't know her daddy since I also do not know his whereabouts.

I started dating Sheila, one of the most loving people I ever knew. We raised my children together for some time and I owe her a lot even though we parted after she developed a drinking habit.

In the meanwhile, after I parted with Bob, my relationship with my mother took another turn for the worse, as he used to spoil her with money. She called the street committee and told them that I was a lesbian and she did not want anything to do with me. The street thugs almost beat me to death and I was told not to go back home. I opened an assault case against them, but the courts dismissed the case, supposedly for lack of evidence, and despite all the scars I have to show for the assault.

I live in a shelter – I am like a refugee in my own country. I am undergoing counselling.

I have a female lover, but since she is not ready to be open about our relationship, we have to keep it secret. While I look for whatever job I can get so that I can build a home for my children and grandchildren, I write poetry and create the world of my dreams with the words that flow from my pen.

Each day I pray for my mother, the woman who brought me into this life and yet who has added so much to my misery. I forgive her and hope that one day she, and all South Africans, will accept me for who I am.

I am Marco, a proud woman; a woman who loves her two daughters; a woman who loves other women. And, despite the pain and suffering that I have endured, am finally finding the real me.

Left hand lesbian

Mavourneen Finlayson

Awkward
descriptions of sex
to probing heterosexual.
Anger at justifying
to prove worthy.

Charges with fear
of not being felt as real,
the ache of lovers in public,
strain not to be spotted
yet desperate for identity.

Finding a comfortable language,
inside that glass wall
we spend lifetimes breaking,
checking over our shoulders
for safety outside the box.

Through our creative survival,
our magnificent kind
should not be locked
in – or out,
unhurt, we are teachers of love.

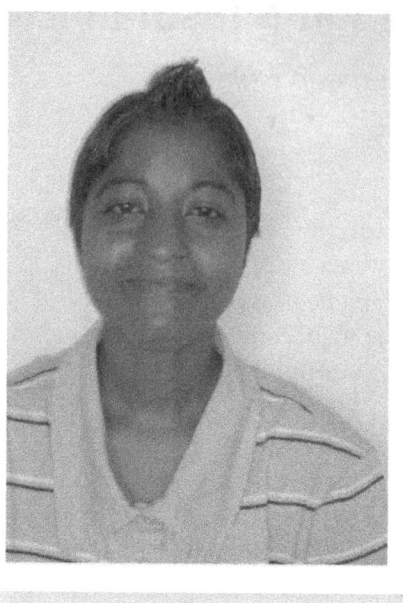

ASHIKA MAHARAJ is the Health Coordinator for the Gay and Lesbian Network in Pietermaritzburg, KwaZulu-Natal, an organisation that caters for the specific and particular health needs of the Lesbian, Gay, Bisexual, Transgender & Intersex community.

MY JOURNEY
ASHIKA MAHARAJ

I was born and brought up in Ladysmith, and attended the Ladysmith Secondary School, a public school which comprised mainly Indian pupils, although there were a few black and coloured kids as well. After finishing Matric there I came to Pietermaritzburg, to the university of KwaZulu-Natal to study Social Science. I completed my bachelor's degree in 2003, majoring in psychology, sociology and politics, and am presently finishing off my Masters, with just the dissertation to complete.

In terms of my sexuality, at about the age of ten or eleven I began to realise that there was something different about me – not quite "normal". I couldn't understand what the difference was all about, because when I compared myself to my three sisters, who were older than me, they wanted to do all these "girl" things that just didn't interest me at all. I was much more interested in changing a car tyre, or something like that. But it didn't faze me too much because I was still young, and one just lets things slip by. What I did know was that I was attracted to girls, especially to my female teachers, which didn't make too much sense at that point. However, I just continued to be myself and focused on finishing school and going off to study somewhere. So my sexuality didn't impact too much at that point.

When I came to Pietermaritzburg to University things took a change. I started meeting gay people, specifically a couple of gay guys who became friends, and I noticed that they were different. At first I couldn't quite work out exactly what was different, but after a while, just hanging out with them and socialising, I began to see the difference. I had heard of people who were gay or lesbian, but at that point didn't know how to define it. I got into a relationship with a guy because I was still not sure what was going on, and I thought I had better go down that road and see what it was all about. I was searching for some clarity. Things seemed to be working out, until some friends said they had a lesbian friend for me, and I was, like, "No, I'm not interested in women." So, that was my stage of denial.

But anyway, they gave this girl my number; she got hold of me, and the very next day she was there to see me, wanting to pursue a relationship. We ended up going out for five years, which was fairly amazing for somebody who had said she wasn't interested! Because it was my first relationship I wasn't sure what to expect, but it turned out to be very nice. Eventually it didn't work out, because she was a Christian and had this feeling that it was sinful. It was her problem, not mine, but although we broke up we still keep in contact.

So, that's how I got to know more about the "other side". From then on I had other relationships with women and I enjoyed them. At one stage I thought I could identify myself as bisexual, as I had had one sexual relationship with a guy. However, I slowly came to the realisation that I must accept myself for who I am, and that I'm not interested in guys. It wasn't for me. The more I socialised with my friends, the more I came to accept who I was.

At one stage, because I was confused about my sexuality, I decided to go to the campus student counselling centre and speak to a psychologist, as I thought it might help to clear up my thinking. Also, I wanted to be more informed as a lesbian and I thought that, when I spoke to my family about my sexuality, I could say that I had spoken to a psychologist about it. It did help in a hazy kind of way, but what really helped me was finally finding out about the gay and lesbian community and the organisation. Then I met other lesbian people and found out about what other people were going through. I began to feel at ease and that I was no longer an outcast, and this made me feel much more empowered.

At this time, while I was in Pietermaritzburg, I started coming out and being open about my sexuality, and decided that I needed to tell my family in Ladysmith that I was not straight: that I was a lesbian. The first person whom I actually told was my sister-in-law, and then my sister, because she was also studying on campus and word was beginning to go around that I was not straight. They were both quite tolerant of it, but not really comfortable with it. My sister had always told me that I should not cut my hair so short, and she now said I should just keep a low profile about the whole situation. But, I didn't really care what they thought. Eventually I told my other siblings, and they were also OK about it, but not really comfortable, and they asked me not to bring any of my girlfriends home with me. So whenever I took one of my girlfriends home, I just said she was one of my friends. I don't know if they believed me or not, but they seemed to take it at face value.

A few years later, after my mother had passed away from cancer, my siblings asked me to tell my father that I was a lesbian. Although I didn't ever get a chance to tell my mother, I think she always knew; I think every parent always knows. So, I told my Dad and his first reaction was, "Have you seen a doctor?"

I said, "Well, I have been to a psychologist, but it's not something that we can actually change."

He apparently thought it was a medical condition that you could fix. After that he was sort-of OK, but he still had expectations of me being married some day, and that's never going to happen.

My family kept trying to persuade me to keep a low profile and not say anything about it, and not put it out in public because people would talk and whatever. Indian communities are very conscious of things that are different being an embarrassment – even smoking. And sexuality is a much bigger thing to deal with.

Obviously, because of who I am and because I consider myself to be a lesbian activist, I couldn't keep it private, and I was interviewed by the *Post* newspaper, an Indian publication. I spoke about breaking the stereotypes of sexual orientation, especially in Indian communities. And, wow, there was my photo in the paper, and my family saw it there. I had been in newspapers previously, but they had never seen the articles, so I just thought, well I'll do it anyway and probably they won't see it. But this time they actually saw it, and they phoned me. They were very shocked and asked the reason for me going to the paper. I tried to explain, but they were very upset and they disowned me, telling me to make my own way in life because I was an embarrassment and a disgrace to the family. They said every bad thing you could think of. So I decided I would have to live my life my own way, because they had said I was not to contact them at all.

However, later they seemed to realise that they had made a mistake, and my relationship with the family is actually improving now, and they have come to accept that I will bring a partner home and that I might even get married to a woman. But it will never be seen in the same light as a heterosexual relationship. Still today most of the focus is on heterosexual relationships, and it's like mine is non-existent.

How I got to be at the Gay and Lesbian Network, is that I met Anthony Waldhausen when I was studying on campus. He had just started a support group there. I decided to join, as it seemed to be another avenue to meet people; it's very difficult to find gay and lesbian people. Anthony directed me to the organisation, and I became a volunteer in 2004. I worked there as a volunteer until 2007, and I really am passionate about lesbian/gay/bisexual/ transsexual/intersex (LGBTI) issues – not just because I am a lesbian, but because I want to help change people's attitudes about gay and lesbian people. Also, because of the hardship that I went through myself, I'd like to help others to make an easier transition to accepting themselves.

Last year I started working for the organisation as a salaried intern, and this year I was asked to be the coordinator of the health programme, which is a great improvement on being an intern. The health programme deals with the emotional, psychosocial, and physical wellbeing of LGBTI people. We do a lot of counselling, telephone and face-to-face, and run workshops on sexual awareness, positive living and treatment literacy. Much of the focus is on HIV/Aids. We also have support groups for those who are HIV positive, and an open group for anybody who is infected or affected by HIV. There is also a group for both men and women who have been abused in some way, and there are support groups for parents of LGBTI children. In 2010 a new group was started for gays and lesbians on campus. Members of the Gay and Lesbian Network sit on councils for HIV to make sure that LGBTI issues are mainstreamed, as often only the needs of heterosexual people are addressed. All this experience has made me passionate about being an activist for LGBTI issues.

I am very open about my sexuality, but because my family is so closeted I am happier in Pietermaritzburg. I know that if I go back home again I am going to be trapped: put in a box. At this point in my life I am very happy because I have dealt with a whole lot of issues that I had about my sexual orientation. I feel I know who I am and I'm comfortable with myself, and that makes me confident. The only thing that worries me about being a lesbian is the issue of hate crimes. Considering that I am quite petite, I think I'm an easy target. If people recognise you – and lots of people know I'm working for the Network – you can become the focus of homophobia, and there's lots of homophobia out there. There have been a few lesbian attacks in Pietermaritzburg: assault rather than anything worse.

I have recently had a partner who is just a year older than me, is white and works in town. We only started dating after we had known each other for about three years. Sometimes her being of a different race group made things a bit tricky, because, first, people have to deal with the fact that you're lesbian and then, second, they see that she's of a different race group – so there are two issues to be dealt with. We are both quite open about our sexuality, not minding holding hands in public, which sometimes seems to confuse some people.

In 2004 I had the experience of going to a nightclub in central Pietermaritzburg with my partner and some friends who are black. We decided that, for reasons of safety, we should not go to the toilets alone but together. Some guys who had been watching us, and who we knew had identified us as a lesbian couple, followed us into the toilets and they started banging on the door so hard that we thought they were going to break it down, and yelling that we should get out of there. We were very shocked and scared and felt that we were on the point of being raped if they managed to break down that door. They put their arms under the bottom of the door and tried to grab our legs. So we used our cell phone and called our friends who were in the club, and told them to come and rescue us. We decided that the best thing was to leave the club as soon as we could. We thought we should go to the police to report it, but they treated the whole thing as a joke and we didn't have the energy to try and pursue it any further.

At some point I would like to get married, which leads me to the question of the Civil Union Bill. As an organisation, the Network was involved in the process leading up to the passing of the Civil Union Bill. We were involved in signing petitions and we marched. I feel proud that I contributed towards something like that but, although it's there for the gay and lesbian community, for some people, especially in the Indian culture, it's very difficult. What it means is that, if I want to get married, I'm not going to find a Hindu priest who is prepared to marry me in a religious way. So, although the Constitution allows for it, it's still difficult at a traditional level. To some extent Hinduism is very tolerant, but we have lots of things that are taboo and are swept under the carpet, and one of these is homosexuality. So religion limits and constrains you; for example, I don't like wearing a dress, but if I want to go to a place of worship I would have to wear a dress or a skirt, and that's not OK for me. For this reason I'm not really too much into religion, because they don't cater for LGBTI people. I know many think it's a matter of respect, how you dress, but it's just fitting into society's construct of what is a male and a female, a stereotype, and it totally sucks. I don't think that most people understand that gender is a complex matter. They just think that men do this and women do that, and it's a very narrow-minded view.

One of the problems with the Civil Union Bill is that I have heard that some people complain that it is too difficult to make a date with Home Affairs, as they are always told that it is fully booked, so you wonder whether there is a reluctance there to perform this function. And others have complained of being rudely treated when they go there. So there still needs to be lots of sensitisation to gay and lesbian issues, also in health centres and police stations. Often when gay and lesbian people go to report rape, the police laugh and say how is it possible that a man can rape another man, or a woman beat up a woman, and they won't take a statement.

In terms of the laws passed recently, I don't think that LGBTI rights are sufficiently protected. For instance, there is no legislation dealing with hate crimes, so that is another challenge that has to be met. Apart from that, the media tends to be very heterosexist, and little is reported about gay and lesbian concerns. Even the HIV/Aids reporting is very directed towards the heterosexual community, with little concentration on the involvement of LGBTI people in the pandemic. There is still much discrimination about gay and lesbian people adopting children, and considerable negative feeling about same-sex couples raising children, while generally the existence of single-head, all female households is overlooked, and there is no sense of prejudice against them.

I've gained valuable experience with the Network, and I've really loved working here and am passionate about the issues. However, I would like to look for some other employment that is more related to my sociology training – something like research or communications. Working for a non-profit organisation does have constraints, and there are many more things I want to do. And, as you get older, there are other things you want from life. So, yes, money is a consideration, and I would also like to better my life and have new challenges. I have applied for jobs and have listed my time in the Gay and Lesbian Network as part of my previous experience. But, because I haven't had much interest shown in the sense of anyone wanting to interview me, my friends have said that perhaps I should leave that out as it might put people off. Interestingly, when I took it out of my CV I actually got some interviews, so I wonder if it was seen as a problem. Some people who saw it on my CV would ask: "So, what is your sexual orientation?" I found this quite offensive because you're not supposed to be judged on your sexual orientation, but on the quality of your work, and, in fact it's against the Constitution to use that against you. It's at times like this that I really get the strong feeling that we are not well protected, as there is still so much discrimination going on. It's all very well for the Constitution to demand all these good laws, but at the ground level they don't work very well.

There is just so much more that needs to be done, especially in terms of sensitising people, creating awareness, and learning not to categorise people. Why do we always have to put people in boxes? Some day there should come a point when we will no longer need to fight for LGBTI rights any more. When that time comes, we will all be treated equally, and it will not matter whether you are gay, lesbian, or whatever. Because, in the end, being homosexual is just a small part of your life, who you are and what you have to offer.

LIESL THERON is the founder of Gender DynamiX, a human rights organisation promoting freedom of expression of gender identity, focusing on transgender, transsexual and gender non-conforming persons. As a gender activist she is involved in the organised LGBT sector of South Africa. Her work focuses on the intersectionality of gender and other bodies. Her research, as part of her Honours degree at the University of Cape Town, explores the struggles, support and forming of identity of SOFFAs (Significant Others, Family, Friends and Allies) of trans people. She was selected by the African Regional Sexuality Resource Centre (ARSRC) based in Lagos, Nigeria for the fourth annual Sexuality Leadership Development Fellowship in July 2007. Her research topic, "[Un]accessible shelters for LGBT people in Cape Town" was completed in December 2007 and accepted by the Resource Centre for publication. The book was launched in February 2010 in Ethiopia during the fourth Africa Conference on Sexual Health and Rights, and Fanele, an imprint of Jacana media, published the book under the title: *Tapestry of Human Sexuality in Africa*.Gender DynamiX published its first book, an anthology, *TRANS: Transgender Life Stories from South Africa* (Fanele an imprint of Jacana media) in 2009. Liesl was part of the process from interviewing and conceptualising, as well as being part of the focus group, and contributed a chapter, "The SOFFA Perspective".

ORIENTATION QUIZ

LIESL THERON

I think it is a fair remark to say I have a little bit of a rebellious streak in me. If there is a general expectation that something can be done only in a prescribed manner, I will always try to do it differently, to prove the opposite. In Afrikaans there is an old wive's tale that says: *'n meisie wat op tafels sit, sal nie 'n man kry nie* (a girl who sits on tables will not get a husband). Needless to say I always sat on tables. And that was long before I knew I would one day come out as a lesbian!

Combine this with a bit of activist blood flowing in my veins, and the fact that I am a "go-getter", and throw into the mixing pot the fact that I have dated a trans man twice in my life, and you will understand why Gender DynamiX was formed, the only organisation in South Africa catering for transgender, transsexual and gender non-conforming people. But more about that later …

I came out as lesbian in my second year of studies after Matric, or should I rather say, I was yanked out of the closet while I was still contemplating my new two-week-old lesbian relationship. Still living in my parent's house, my mother suspected what was going on, long before I was near ready to tell her. What followed was five years of cat and mouse games between my mother and I. The cycle would start with me being in a relationship, my mother finding out, questioning and trying to deal with it all, and the relationship not lasting long – sometimes because of this, and sometimes because it was a typical relationship of a twenty-year-old person. After the end of each relationship, or perhaps one could rather call it a fling, I would swear celibacy which would please my mother as this compromise sounded like the "logical" thing to do: "I can keep my lesbian status, alas without a relationship" so each party involved is "happy". After a while I happened to find myself falling in love again with another woman and everything started all over again. This continuous bargaining with myself and my mother

69

also included visits to the pastor and a psychologist – which also ended up in a bargaining session, as I agreed to visit one on the condition that it was one of my choice. Since the "outcome" of the psychologist of my choice was favourable towards me, my mother believed that I had somehow informed him in advance to tell her that I was a perfectly healthy (minded) young adult, even if I was a lesbian.

Today, thinking back to all of this, it is actually quite laughable. Firstly, because those years when one believed that a person might not be well adjusted to society because of their sexual orientation are long gone (remember my coming out was in 1992). And also, to my relief, my mother came to terms with my sexual orientation long ago! You might wonder why I speak predominantly about my mother. Well, it was she who grappled the most with my coming out. In fact, I was long out and trying to make sense of my young adulthood, while she was still in her own bubble and trying to object. I only have one sibling, my sister, who is about two and a half years younger than me. She was initially shocked, in denial and "hating" all my new ho-mo-sex-u-al friends (with an emphasis on each syllable). This stage did not last too long. At the outset, my dad was disappointed – he had all his dreams of his eldest blue-eyed-blonde girl shattered – but, in not too long a time, in his own way, he accepted the new status quo.

I still remember one incident clearly. I inherited a love of gardening from my dad's side of the family. I cherish the memories of working in the garden on Saturdays alongside my dad. A short while after I came out, I think round about the time my dad had just started accepting my sexual orientation, we worked in the garden again together one Saturday. We had a few shrubs and trees to plant. Chuffed with ourselves, we stood and admired our handiwork, and called my mother to come out of the house and comment on our gardening. She took one look at the trees and her only comment, pointing out one tree, was: "This one is skew." As she turned around to walk back into the house, my dad commented: "Not everything [one] in life is straight!" My mom was absolutely not impressed and my dad and I shared a good laugh. That incident will always stay with me as the confirmation that he accepted me.

As I said earlier, it took my mom about five years to come to terms with me being lesbian, and by that time, when she was just comfortable to readily welcome my partners into their house, she was yet again challenged by my life partner/s. I introduced the first of my trans partners to my parents. At that stage I was not living in their house any more. I was newly in love and had a coffee date with my mother and could not wipe the smile from my face, so she quickly learned of my new love. I was a bit ambiguous with the information, not saying too much, so she clearly thought it was a woman/lesbian we spoke about, and I left her for a while with her assumptions. So, now she knew there was a new person in my life.

Not long after this revelation, I had to quickly pop in at my parent's house one weekend to fetch a few things, and my partner went along. My dad opened the door and I introduced the two to each other. My dad asked if this young chap was my boyfriend (completely reading my trans partner as male, which served as a big compliment to him since he was not even on hormones yet). With a big smile I replied, "Yes." This was easier than I thought it would be. Then I ran into the house like a whirlwind to fetch what I had come for, found my mother in the passage and she asked if this was my new girlfriend (of whom we spoke the other day) to which I also answered, "Yes." We left with me knowing that I left behind parents who would compare notes afterwards and be totally confused: the one would insist he'd met my new boyfriend and the other one would be certain it was my new girlfriend.

This served as the dawn of a new confused era for my parents. I left everything unexplained for about two weeks, after which time I sent a letter to them with my initial explanation of transgender, FTM[1], trans man, transsexual, and transitioning.

Eventually, years later, my mother wrote a book[2], sharing experiences and breaking silences of parents who face the challenge of when their child comes out as gay or lesbian. She shared her feelings of isolation and inner struggles and in general, until today, her book is well accepted and highly praised by people who read it. Unfortunately it is only available in Afrikaans, as translation costs

---

1   FTM: Female to Male.

2   Book title: *Jy bly my kind* – Hemel en See Publikasie.

are extremely high. However, this may change, as somebody has volunteered and is busy translating the book into English.

Being a lesbian and involved with a trans man/FTM brings a whole new dynamic into a relationship. Like many other gender and transgender activists, I promote and firmly believe that gender and sexual orientation is fluid. But it also creates a slippery slope for the person who lives in a relationship and who maybe has to deal with redefining, repositioning and re-deciding. Challenges abound, varying from inner questions to questions and criticism from friends, family and the lesbian and gay community. Sometimes in gay and lesbian social circles trans people and their partners are rejected, frowned upon and not accepted. In my opinion it is mainly due to ignorance, as not many people in life are challenged to think about gender, let alone transgender. Lack of information is usually the biggest enemy of any minority group.

When I said slippery slope – well, it is a bit more difficult for the female partner who exclusively identifies as lesbian as opposed to female partners who identify as heterosexual, seeing that the FTM partner transition is from female-bodied person to male. This difficulty in coming to terms with, or getting your head around the fact that you are now in a relationship with a person who predominantly identifies as male, is a very complex situation. There are little irritating voices in your mind, asking uncomfortable questions, such as: *He looks more and more like the guy he wants to be presented as – what does that make me, being his partner?*

I still remember clearly an incident in 2004, which most probably neither of us will easily forget, as it was one of those turning-point moments in both of our lives. I was in my second trans relationship, and he had been on hormones for a few months. We strolled into a rainbow-flagged travel agency in Sea Point, looking for ideas for a planned weekend away. Now, knowing "queer shopping", the politics behind deliberately selecting a rainbow-flag establishment is no doubt to support the "family". Being part of that community, which knows what the struggles are all about, how difficult it is sometimes to gain a "pink-only" space or vibe, I well understood the "slow attitude" (slow beyond the usual Cape Town laid back slow). To put it bluntly, I could translate the expression on their faces as, *Oh well, when will those straights realise they are in a gay shop?* After about thirty minutes of no service attendant coming our way to offer their services to us, we walked out. There was a long dense silence. He was firmly recognised and finally "passed" as the man he wanted to be. And me? I was firmly dismissed, overlooked, not seen any more as the lesbian I knew I was.

In 2006 I gave a presentation at a national lesbian conference in Johannesburg. I challenged the audience by saying I had read about the term trisexual, where the "tr" indicates trans and the "i" more in the sense of bisexual. I stated, tongue in cheek, that seeing I was (at that stage) in my second relationship with a trans man I thought I might be trisexual, meaning having an interest in trans people, relationship-wise. Not long after that, the relationship ended. I was single for a long time and "declared" openly my lesbian status again. Trans people are often, due to ignorance, stigmatised as "weird" or "freaky". One must not underestimate the amount of stigmatisation and difficulty the partners of trans people experience. And if you are, for example, lesbian-identified, and enter into a relationship with a trans person, it is extremely difficult to attempt to "re-enter" the lesbian circle once you have stepped outside the expected norm.

Two years after that relationship ended, there were still lesbian activists and friends who did not accept me back as a lesbian; even after I started dating my current partner, we had many questions to answer and explaining to do about her not being trans and me being "actually" a lesbian.

So let me recap at this stage: maybe I am jumping around quite a lot. I am a femme lesbian, who came out in 1992, to everyone's surprise, including my own, as a lesbian. The first five years of my lesbian life were quite bumpy as I kept on bargaining between being a lesbian and swearing celibacy to please "those I hurt" with my "lesbian nature". Then in 1996 or 1997 I met my first trans partner, knowing basically, right from the start, that he was trans and was going to transition from female to male. That relationship lasted for nearly three years. After that I again dated women/lesbians. Later, in 2004, I met my second trans partner and it was during that relationship that Gender DynamiX was born. The relationship lasted about two and a half years and, after being single for quite a while, I am now in a committed relationship with my current lesbian partner.

One might ask, how does it happen that a lesbian falls in love, twice, with a trans man? As I mentioned before, I think at times I am fairly femme – maybe that is also the reason why family and people were so surprised with my coming out as lesbian in the first place. There were no "early childhood tomboy warning signs". When I first came out as a lesbian, people asked me why I was attracted to women. My answer consistently was: "I am not in a relationship with a body. I am in a relationship with a person, with a personality and everything that goes with it. The whole package."

I have always felt more attracted to a more masculine-identifying person – some call it butch. I think that potentially led to why I was twice in a relationship with a trans man.

At the age of 25 I met someone I really was attracted to. At that stage I thought I had fallen in love with a very butch lesbian. When he[3] realised I really liked him a lot he said he would like to tell me something; that there was something we would need to talk about before anything further happened. In his voice over the phone I could just sense there was something troubling his mind. He sounded nervous, worried and very stressed. He asked if we could meet that afternoon at his friend's flat. He didn't even want to let me be at his place. I realised it was a "self protecting" strategy.

The whole day I spent wondering what could be so bad. I kept asking myself what this was all about. Did he kill someone and expect to be sentenced? Or was he already in jail for some major stuff? I really couldn't figure out what would make a person stress like that.

---

3   It is trans etiquette to refer to a trans person in the pronoun of the gender *they perceive themselves to be.* Trans positive people will also honour this when making references to the trans person prior to this knowledge, as we are not speaking of sex and genitals here, but perceived gender or *gender of preference.* You will find thus, that I will speak of both my male identified trans partners using "him" and "he", *regardless of their transitional status or time in their lives.*

Then, that afternoon, he told me in his friend's apartment: "I am about to start transitioning to male. I am not going to look like this for much longer."

I had heard the term "sex-change" before, so I knew what he was talking about, but I just didn't expect this to be the "big secret" he needed so desperately to reveal to me. One does not know how to react, because we are not prepared for that. As though it is something that only happens overseas.

Now, to add to the Liesl-dimension, I absolutely hate hypocrisy. I was challenged with my own theory: "I am not in a relationship with a body. I am in a relationship with a person, with a personality and everything that goes with it. The whole package." Or would I be, for the first time in my life, a hypocrite and use some lame excuse as a cop-out? After a long tense silence, my first reply to him was: "I am not in a relationship with a body, but with a whole person, the mind, the personality, the whole package. So yes, let's give it a try!"

Very shortly after we started our relationship – in true "lesbian style" – I moved in with him. Thinking back to all of that now, I also think my moving in with him so quickly was not only the traditional "lesbian meets partner and arrives after second date with bakkie loaded with furniture" thing – there was another reason for my quick move. At that stage I shared a flat with a gay guy and had very quickly realised the animosity from the gay community towards trans people (and those who chose to be with them). I think we became the topic of discussion for a while amongst previous friends; invites to socials became fewer, and in general there was just an unfriendly vibe. All under the pretence that they were "concerned about my happiness and maybe he would just use me"! For what? And why not the same concern when I was dating a lesbian?

I must honestly say I think I lost most of my friends and, sad to say, the ones I lost were mostly gays and lesbians. I don't deny that I gained a few new friendships – including a couple (two lesbians) who were for a number of years his best friends. So maybe it is a case of some you win, some you lose.

With the little information I had, and what was available, I confidently embarked on the journey to educate and reassure my closest family members on transgenderism. I always made sure that it was, to the best of my knowledge, in support of my partner of choice. That being said, having to go through the loss of my own best friend and confidant, and having to reassure my mother and sister with whom I happen to have a good and close relationship, I had nowhere to turn when I was in doubt, had questions or just wanted to have typical girl-talk and compare notes. I think such situations lead to many partners of trans people being very isolated. How dare you try all your efforts to "convince" your sister, mother or a close friend that this relationship is just like any other, everything is fine (and in fact it is), but at the same time know that you also have your own questions and insecurities? Maybe I was too proud, imagining myself in a situation where I was just like any other women in a relationship who feels the need, from time to time, to vent in front of her mother, sister or long-time best girlfriend about the small "nitty-gritties" of the relationship. I did not want to be in the situation where I, for example, told a person what my own concerns were, and showed signs of not knowing how to deal with this "newly-perceived heterosexual vibe" that all of a sudden clung to me. I didn't want to hear something like: "Hi, shame, ja, I am happy for you if you say you love each other, but I was wondering myself how long it will last?"

I ended up in a very isolated space: not able to share things with my mother or sister, without my best friend, and not always able to share everything with my partner. I didn't want him to think I loved him any less, just because I really struggled with fitting into a heterosexual mould: A mould which seemed to automatically be assigned to me, just because he started to pass well as male. Rebellious Liesl had not realised before how gender and sometimes sexual orientation were taken for granted. Just because people saw me with a guy, they assumed I was heterosexual! I suppose I can't blame them – at that stage in my life I would also make the same assumptions about other hetero-looking couples I encountered.

It was these assumptions of being heterosexual – this hetero-norm I lived with – which eventually became the overall reason for the ending of that relationship. But more about that later, I am again running ahead of the story …

About a year after we were together he was scheduled for his hysterectomy. I was thinking I should be the good and sensible girlfriend, so when he was booked to see the surgeon the final time before surgery, I requested to go with him. I would also have a chance to ask what I wanted to ask. In principle that is all fine – but hell, we don't know what it is we need to know. How could I have known what to ask? Besides, since my partner was in the medical field (being a staff nurse), the doctor and he spoke mostly in medical terms. I heard words such as *hysterectomy*, *oophorectomy*, *vaginectomy* and all sorts of things. To me all of those sounded like different parts that would be taken out – but to me a hysterectomy simply meant no more babies, no more blood. I was ignorant, uninformed and not aware of my own body and its workings – or that of the female body generally. Maybe I didn't pay enough attention in biology class, or maybe back in that day they did not give so much attention to teaching us in school what we really needed to know later in life. The point is, I didn't know much more walking out of the consultation room than before I walked in. I just asked some questions such as, "How long will he be in theatre? How long will he be in hospital? How long will recovery time be?" Just some fluffy questions.

He was indeed in hospital for a very short time, and soon after arriving home we realised there were small complications. He really struggled with what he thought he could do himself, because of being a nurse. He didn't manage to catheterize himself, and I had to receive a crash course on doing it for him. By the time he became so desperate with struggling to ask me for help, the fresh wound was sore from all the fiddling around. So not only did I have to learn very quickly how to catheterize my partner, but also to be very good at it, as it was already very painful.

About a month and a half later, the time came when we wanted to be intimate again. I am going to speak very candidly and openly now; it is still hurtful, and the information is fairly explicit, but I need to tell it as it is.

Now I know how many FTMs don't allow their partner to touch them in their genital areas. In love making with a trans man there are many "off-limits", and many negotiations form part of the intimate relationship. So, yes, I never inserted my fingers when we made love – but I was "allowed" to touch him around his genital area.

I think the very first time we made love after he healed from surgery, he had some personal expectations (other than the usual arousal he felt). We were getting on quite well, and he encouraged me, saying it was not sore any more, and I could touch him. My hand went down, I wanted to feel him; I wanted to feel his wetness again … To me it is part of lovemaking, to touch him there, to feel the wet, you know. But this time when my fingers played around I discovered he was not wet, there was nothing to be wet any more. I realised that I would never be able to use his wetness as lube again. There was nothing. I discovered the meaning of a vaginectomy in a very real way for the first time. They closed him. There was no more. In the middle of an intimate situation it was very hard to hold back the shock of my discovery!

Personally I think from then onwards things just started sliding. I still loved him very much, we had a good relationship and I supported him a lot, but on the intimacy front not much was happening. Anyway, a while after that I took up employment just outside Warmbaths (now known as Bela-Bela) at a private game reserve. At first we managed our relationship, with me staying at the game reserve while he still stayed in our flat in Pretoria. The distance was not too far and we managed to see each other most weekends, depending on the shifts he worked at the hospital. And working nightshift – with the typical seven days on, seven days off – was an ideal situation; he spent many of his off-shift weeks at the game reserve with me.

Eventually a position at the nature reserve became open in the household department and he was also employed there. Since the owners and management of the resort preferred couples to work there – as "it would ensure commitment and discourage single staff to sleep around" – it was welcomed that he could start working there. This also led to a move from single staff quarters to a house. Now here already one must read between the lines and see the red light: not just a flicker, but glaring. Working on a game reserve outside Warmbaths, on its positive side does mean you are closer to nature, but also without fail spells out: C-O-N-S-E-R-V-A-T-I-V-E! In every way you can imagine:

politically and racially as well as any sexual orientation outside the scope of being one hundred per cent heterosexual – if there is such a thing. With permission (I don't know whose) it was perfectly accepted, especially for the males working on the game farm, to prove their heterosexuality by having more than one bed fellow – whether with a marriage certificate or without. Given the dynamics or quota of staff working there, it is logical to imagine that many heterosexual female staff also had to be unfaithful to their partners. It is also typical of the scenario, that this was not spoken about, and the few women who "did it" openly were "sluts".

I think what seemed from the outside idyllic and inviting to us, turned out to be something completely different. Living and working on a game farm, having full range of so many hectares of wildlife around us, sharing the veld with four of the big five, could not make up for the extremely conservative environment we had to live in. It became the reason that I just withdrew more and more into myself. I ended up in the deepest depression. Prior to this I was fairly unsympathetic towards people who said they were in a depression. I thought they just had to change to a positive attitude, and it would all go away. I also heard people refer to depression as a black hole. I did not understand the full meaning of this until I was there. Days went by that I could not account for. I really do not know how I got through that period in my life. I was twice in a very bad spell of depression. The second time, years later (by the way, when I also tried to live in the closet) was not as severe as this first spell of depression. I think this was because my mother and I could see the signs, and saw that I was heading in the same direction as my first deep depression. So I was able to act more promptly to get myself out of it.

Eventually our relationship broke up; I could not continue this closeted life, trying to be heterosexual. Maybe in a city, heteronormativity is a bit different, distanced: you don't necessarily know the person you serve food to in the restaurant you manage, you don't know your neighbours, you don't know the staff of the only shop within a fifteen-kilometre radius where you can buy cold drinks and magazines. Living, working and sharing everything with everyone on the game farm took its toll. It just did not work out for me. We surely had our good times, and we are still friends. Today he is happily married and he and his wife have a beautiful son.

My life also went on and I moved to the Cape. At first I was employed in Mossel Bay and had it in my mind that closet life would equal better positioning on the corporate ladder! Obviously that was a pot of nonsense, and yet again led to me being extremely lonely, so that I became depressive. At the end of 2001, I moved to Betty's Bay. On my way to Betty's Bay, where my parents lived, I passed the Gouritz bungee jump bridge. As much as I am extremely scared of heights (I even struggle to find the right step down on a rolling escalator) I decided to jump off the bridge. Don't get me wrong – not in any adrenaline-chasing way. No! I was too scared for that. But I had thought about it for two weeks before I did it. I made a pact with myself: from that moment on, I would always be true to myself. I left all negativity at the top of the bridge and, as horrible as the jump was, I brought only the positive with me.

I worked as a *chef de partie* at a very renowned restaurant in Betty's. It was a small family business with a chef patron – meaning the owner of the restaurant was the main chef. I quickly worked myself up to be "second in charge" so to speak. During that time the owner and I embarked on a side business and started a *chocolaterie*. We did well and made some really good truffles. I was open and out of the closet at my new work, and the restaurant's family all knew about me being lesbian. I came up with the idea that we should develop a range of rainbow truffles. The gay rainbow, that is. The owner of the restaurant encouraged me to explore with flavours: the red included cherry liqueur; orange had Van Der Hum; yellow was flavoured with banana liqueur; green was mint liqueur; blue graced with Blue Curaçao; and purple had violet liqueur. We were happy with our rainbow truffles and I happened to discover the Pink Loerie Festival. That is how I ended up finding myself in Knysna, in May 2003, selling rainbow truffles – which is, by the way, also where I met my current partner for the first time. But, more about that later, as I am yet again running ahead with my story!

Anyway, eventually I moved to Cape Town where I attended the Good Hope Metropolitan Community Church (GHMCC) situated in Zonnebloem, previously known as District Six. I had

had a few short lesbian flings, alternating with periods of being single, since the time my relationship had ended in Warmbaths. In Cape Town, through a mutual friend who also attended GHMCC, I was introduced to my second trans partner. Through this friend he heard that I was previously in a relationship with an FTM, and in South Africa information about transgenderism, transitioning and related topics was still scarce in 2003. What was meant as an advice-giving session ended up being the beginning of a new relationship. So I fell in love, again, with a trans man, and again knowing right from the onset of the relationship that he was trans. I mention this because I think that, if one were to be in a relationship with a person for a substantial time, and only later discover your partner is trans, it must be more of a challenge to come to terms with, and understand and support your partner.

Bravely, I thought I knew exactly what to expect from being in a relationship with an FTM since I had that experience from my first trans relationship. But there were quite a few logistical differences to start with. The first relationship took place in Pretoria, the second in Cape Town. I think that is the root of one of the reasons why Gender DynamiX exists today. At that stage Pretoria was considered to be the only city in our country where the State hospital system provided opportunities for surgical transition. If I had still been living in Pretoria and had met my new partner there, we would simply have accessed that same medical care and there would probably be no Gender DynamiX.

So, thinking this was going to be a self-navigating journey, with map in hand, I entered into this new relationship. The first stumbling block was when I suggested to him to phone the Government hospitals in the area, in this case Groote Schuur and Tygerberg, and ask them about their procedures and appointment days of their gender clinics. We might just as well have asked any random question, such as, "do you know how many ants are living in a standard size ant heap in high summer time?" or "how many spots does a Dalmatian have at birth?" Then we started approaching LGBT organisations and they were equally uninformed about any of the questions we had.

We quickly learnt that "Google is your friend", but also discovered that some information is helpful, while some is less helpful. For example, when you read somebody else's life story and it was not country-specific, you could identify to a degree with another person's experiences. But it became challenging to only read information from abroad.

Here my go-getter streak and activism stepped in. I kept on saying to him, "Transitioning in South Africa is possible." It has happened before – but where is the information? It started making sense that *stealth*[4] plays a much bigger role in South Africa than one could imagine. Not only does each and every trans person "disappear" after surgery, but also the information they gathered along the way. It was when I presented a workshop in May 2005 at GHMCC that I realised that, beyond the workshop, there was more work to be done than was possible for a person who was employed and only able to do trans-related activism, education and awareness-raising in the evenings and weekends. And a new organisation emerged: Gender DynamiX was formally founded in July 2005.

How does the forming of Gender DynamiX bring us back to my story about myself and being a lesbian? First off, it is extremely difficult to be part of a lesbian community – especially if one is a little bit on the proactive, activist side – and out as a lesbian, but hope to still be fully accepted within the lesbian community if one dares to start dating a trans man. What puzzles me more is the lack of acceptance. When lesbians, feminists and sexually liberal, open-minded activists do what they do best: claiming spaces, educating, raising awareness and in general challenging everything there is to be challenged about sexual orientation and gender-identity, and exactly how fluid it is, they are not only fighting for tolerance, but must at least aim to settle for acceptance (worst case scenario). What happens then if one of the sisters starts dating a trans man? Where did all the progressive talk of gender fluidity disappear to? All of a sudden this fluid space becomes as solid as Table Mountain.

I absolutely cannot understand why my own lesbianism was under scrutiny by other queer people. Why did I, all of a sudden, have to prove that I was a lesbian? Even worse was the fact that

---

4   Stealth is a term widely known in the trans community at large, referring
     to a person who *chooses to* keep their trans status a secret.

when I did, the proof was not good enough. I wonder how the world would be and, on a more personal level, how trans relationships would have a stronger chance of surviving, if the supporting partner (or, as in many cases, the lesbian partners of FTMs) were given support and safe spaces in their "previous" lesbian circles. Then the meaning of *acceptance* would come into its full right.

Speaking of the lesbian "club membership" scrutiny I experienced each time I was with a trans partner, as I mentioned, I was single for quite a while before I entered my current relationship, and this new lesbian relationship was yet again held under some sort of queer societal magnifying glass. I suspect there might be quite a number of layers to this. The comments varied from: "So when will the transition start?" (pointing to my partner), to "But are you really a lesbian?" (referring to me). It is almost as if being in a relationship with a trans person in your past nullifies your previous lesbian experiences on your lesbian CV. As a new couple, our relationship was obviously also for other reasons under the lens, and I would like to think in some circles the "talk of the town". Cross-racial relationships are not entirely a new concept; also not unheard of. I do think, though, that there are not too many Zulu-Afrikaans lesbian couples. If one could place all the South African ethnic groups on a cultural continuum, with their customs, traditions and all relevant traits that make a culture what it is, I would imagine that Zulu and Afrikaans are not only alphabetically on the two extreme ends of this cultural continuum.

I like using the term "cross-racial" instead of "inter-racial". "Inter" sounds and feels to me like interlinked, like between, like it really is just so easy-peasy, a hyphen between any two things. "Cross" indicates to me that there is a difference – to cross something you have to "step over the line", something has to be achieved to cross towards the other side; some action has to take place to arrive at the point of crossing. To be in a cross-racial relationship involves negotiations – constantly. It takes work. We are in an ongoing process of challenges, from within and from outside. To be in a cross-racial relationship leads to facing questions, sometimes from ourselves, sometimes from each other and sometimes together, facing the scars apartheid left on all of us as human beings.

We met each other briefly in 2003 at the Pink Loerie Festival. I was selling chocolates and she was there with her partner of the time. We lost contact. I was not even in activism yet, but somehow she made a huge impression on me. Huge enough so that in 2005, when Gender DynamiX was founded, I looked her up again, to introduce the organisation. Gradually we became friends and later on, when she visited Cape Town we would see each other, and the same when I was in Johannesburg. We started staying over at each other's place. At that stage she was involved with somebody else and always told me that she didn't mix work with pleasure, and besides I was not going to *krap in iemand anders se slaai* (toss somebody else's salad), so I was not prepared to show her, or talk about, the feelings I had started to develop. When staying over at each other's place, we usually shared a bed. Sometimes we slept head to toe, but sometimes both of us with our heads the same side of the bed. Yet nothing ever happened. I liked her (and her work) too much; I respected her professionalism and was not going to put our friendship at stake and jeopardise the times I saw her.

In 2007 she left to study abroad, and I sulked for days when she left. I did not even wish her, in person or via email, good luck or a safe trip – nothing. At that stage only three of my closer friends knew I liked her, but she was unaware of the fact. Then, during the 2008 opening evening of the Out in Africa national Gay and Lesbian Film Festival in Cape Town, there she stood, right in front of me! And we kissed hello. Until today I tell her she gave me an extra nice, special kiss: a few seconds longer than a platonic kiss should be, or anyway, at least an extra emotional-feeling kiss. She "can't recall". I was overwhelmed and surprised. I did not expect to see her there; in my mind she was not in South Africa, and if she was, she was synonymous with Johannesburg. Since the festival had already opened a week and a half before in Johannesburg, Cape Town was the last place I expected to see her. It was a Thursday evening and she gave me her new cell number and said I must call her on Saturday so that we could link up. She would be at the gallery in the morning, and free in the afternoon.

Saturday morning came, and I plotted the time of the phone call. I thought that if I called too early, I would look suspiciously over-eager to see her, and if I called too late it would look as if I almost forgot, or was not necessarily in the mood to see her. So half past ten was the agreed time I made with all the conversations in my head. I phoned the number to hear: "the number you have called is not available in the MTN network". I frantically tried again, and again, and again. I realised that, if I didn't make a plan soon, I may well miss her; she had said on Thursday evening that she would be here only for a week before leaving for Italy! I looked up the number of the Michael Stevenson Gallery and phoned, hoping they would be willing to help me by verifying the number. The woman who answered the phone instead offered that I could talk to her!

In the few seconds I waited as the receiver was handed over to her, I tried to get my heartbeat down. So, when she answered, we just calmly arranged when and where we would meet. She was with two other friends and we went to Nando's in Long Street. Just like old times, we had a good activist conversation. I told her that, on that specific evening, the film festival was screening one of the transgender movies and Gender DynamiX was hosting a panel discussion afterwards, and that it would be nice if she wanted to join me. She agreed.

Afterwards we all went to a coffee shop and debriefed, socialised and generally had a good time. We sat there until "pumpkin time", and then she asked me if she could "crash" at my place – just like the old times. I said yes. We sat for a while a bit awkwardly in the lounge and then I asked her if she wanted to sleep in my bed, saying I would sleep in the lounge.

"Why would you want to do that?" she asked.

I said, "Because maybe I snore and will keep you awake if you are sleeping light?"

She insisted that I did not offer my bed; we could both sleep in my bed (just like always). I think she slept well that night. I spent the night lying awake, on the edge of the bed, like a stick; in fact I was lying so far from her, I had to stick my arm out to the ground to prevent myself from falling off.

The next day Out in Africa had their usual annual sponsored lunch for invites-only guests and I told her I was to go to that, and invited her to join me. She replied that she would, but only if I was then willing to go with her to Gugulethu to meet with people afterwards. We agreed we would go first to the lunch, and then leave at about two for the other appointment. We went first via her friend's apartment where her luggage was, so that she could change outfits. Her friend was very welcoming, and thinking back to it now, was maybe pre-SMSed with some information because she greeted me with that smug smile, you know that expression of nodding head and checking me out, maybe approving of what she was seeing? I don't know. They spoke in Zulu and I have an idea it was not only arranging logistics. Anyway, when we left the friend gave us a bag of oranges that we decided we would take with us to the township.

We arrived at the lunch and were met with curious stares, yet there was "nothing between us". One of my best friends who knew for so long, about two years, that I liked her was also there, elbowing me when we sat down with that look of "… and?" Playfully, one of the other women there flirted with her, and playfully I flirted back, saying, "Hey hands off, she's with me" – all in good spirits. I mean the other woman was involved, and sat next to her partner, and I was coy and "just joking". Two o'clock arrived before dessert came, but she asked me if we could please leave for the other appointment.

In the car she asked me to stop at the 7-Eleven to buy newspapers. She came back to the car, and handed me a P.S. chocolate bar: "This is to make up for the dessert you are missing out on."

The purple P.S. wrapper's message was: "u mean the world 2 me" – I took it, and thought to myself, "Ag, you know these butches – maybe she just grabbed whichever chocolate was closest at the pay point". So I thanked her, and we drove to Gugulethu. On our way back in the car we had two or three of those oranges she kept for us, having given the remaining ones to the friends we visited.

Now here you see how fixated I was on the previous mindset I had – I mean, we had discussed long ago how we are both professionally involved in the work we were doing, we didn't mix work and pleasure. As a photographer she couldn't afford to jump into bed with just anyone – her name was at stake and word would go around and she would lose respect. Likewise, I always agreed, and due to my position in the organisation I worked for, I also couldn't afford to just have random sexcapades, especially with people in the same work field. So, my mind was so stuck on those conversations, that I did not see the previous evening's awkward discussion of sleep arrangements for what it was, and I dismissed the P.S. chocolate's meaning, too. As we drove back from Gugulethu, on our way to the Waterfront to see another Out in Africa movie, she started peeling an orange and asked me if I also wanted some. I replied, yes please. While I was driving she would eat every other orange segment, alternating by putting a segment at a time into my mouth. Most sensually, as Nan fed her lover in *Tipping the Velvet*. But I still dismissed this juicy sensual act, and thought maybe over-zealous-Liesl's mind was running away with her.

We went to the movie, and went out afterwards again with a group of women who were in the audience, to a coffee shop, and eventually ended up again in my apartment. When we were finished eating she asked me out of the blue, catching me unawares: "So why were you willing last night to offer your bed and sleep in the lounge of your own place?"

I thought to myself, well I thought we sorted that out last night! I replied again that I was scared that, if she was a light sleeper, I might keep her awake with my snoring and tossing and turning because I am a restless sleeper.

She looked at me and said, "That is nonsense."

Now I had to think hard and quick, and defended my point by saying, "Well, I can remember the laaaast time I slept over at your place in Johannesburg before you left for Canada in 2007, you got up in the middle of the night to go and sleep on the couch in the lounge."

To which she replied, "Yes, because I realised if I did not leave the bed right now, I would not be able to keep my hands off you any longer!"

We kissed, passionately. Through the kisses we managed to find our way to the kitchen to put the plates down, we worked our way via the stove top, to the kitchen counter, to the bed …

We are still together. The time from the opening of the film festival in September 2008 until she had to leave for Canada on the second of January 2009 to complete her studies is the few months in my life I treasure the most. We learned so much about each other, we did so many exciting things together, I explored so much about my own body and loving myself sensually, which leads to loving my partner, loving us – sensually. We discovered so much together about our bodies and sensual, passionate love.

Being – *sometimes* – in a long-distance relationship brings its own challenges, but it also gives a unique kind of freedom. We are both very individualistic, independent people and the time away from each other also creates space and freedom.

We are passionately engaging in our activist work, which is mostly concerned with sexuality issues, whether it be queer people, lesbians, transgender, intersex, rights for women, or any marginalised people. Needless to say, we are also focusing on how this intersects with racial, class and socio-economic matters. Our own histories, past experiences, and our parents' influence inform our work. In our reading, researching, our collaborating in photo projects, and many of our discussions we focus on cross-racial relationships and, more specifically, on lesbian cross-racial relations. We will continue our discussions and work with this topic.

One day she came home, saying she saw a T-shirt with "Swart gevaar" printed on it, and was wondering how I would feel if she wears it. I will love it! I wish I could find a T-shirt I can wear to the same occasions saying, "There's a Zulu on my stoep!"

Morning

Mavourneen Finalyson

Morning undercover warmth
floating as mist does,
tender moisture remaining,
deep with resting quietness.

You stir – I have waited
first conscious awakening,
lips warm and desirous
reaching, I pull you in.

KEBA SEBETOANE This story is one of the "I" Stories produced by the Gender Link Opinion and Commentary Service for the Sixteen Days of Activism on Gender Violence, held in November, 2009. On the first of the sixteen days women who had decided to break the silence headed a march through Hillbrow to Constitution Hill in Johannesburg, where a rally was held. Twenty women wrote stories about their experiences of gender violence in an attempt to reclaim the lives which have suffered so much, and to demand their right to safety at all times of the day and night.

WHO ARE YOU TO TELL ME WHO I AM?

KEBA SEBETOANE

On the 7 March 2004 when I was seventeen years old I started hating all men. It took one man to make me hate all men. I hated him so much. The only thing I could think of was killing him. On that night I made a promise to myself that I'd never associate myself with any other man. I blamed myself. The thought of him on top of me, unable to defend myself, made facing tomorrow impossible. I saw no hope and lost faith. My dreams were shattered, and the freedom to say "I am me" was lost.

Kingsley[1] and I were friends, more like a brother and sister. I was on my way from the Forum for the Empowerment of Women (FEW) offices, where I attended life-skills and computer training, when I first met him. He introduced himself as a gay man, but not many people knew about his sexuality, so he said. He warned me not to tell anybody, especially his friends because he was not "out" to everyone. We'd spend most of our days together if I was not with my girlfriend or my other friends, and it would feel odd if a day passed without us seeing each other.

One evening we went out to a "club" near his home. It was nice there because I met some of my friends from high school. I started dancing with other people and was really enjoying myself until suddenly his mood changed. He complained that I was spending too much time with other people and I didn't want to upset him, so I sat with him. It got really late, and I had the only key for the house so I insisted on going home. It was a bit chilly and he wanted to get something warm to wear; we went to his place since it was close by. I went to the outside toilet and I thought he was getting a jacket. He was standing right in front of the toilet. I was shocked to see him. He did not look happy, so I asked him what was wrong. He did not

---

1   Not his real name.

reply, but he went to his room and I followed him in the hope of finding out. That was the worst mistake I ever made.

I got a bit tense when he started giving me the "you make me sick" look. He locked the door. I was really confused as he was swearing at me and saying how much he hated people who pretend. I then asked him what he was talking about. He was furious with the lesbian life I was living. He said that I should stop taking other people's girlfriends, and that I was beautiful and capable of getting myself a boyfriend. I got angry and started arguing back. He slapped me on the face, and warned me not to shout at him or I would regret it. He said: "Tonight I'm going to change you, and from now on you are my girlfriend."

I got angry and told him that I knew my rights. I started to leave. He got up holding a screwdriver and threatened to stab me if I didn't cooperate. I became quiet, trying to calm him down and think of a way to leave his place without anyone getting hurt. He ordered me to take off my clothes while he hit me with anything he came across. No matter how hard I cried or how loud I screamed, he told me it wouldn't help because he was not scared of anyone or anything. He punched me and I thought he was going to kill me if I fought back.

He raped me repeatedly for over an hour. I was quiet with tears streaming down my face. He continued to beat me even though he had succeeded. He kept asking me if I loved him and when I said no, then the beating got worse. "You go about pretending you are attending classes in Jo'burg while you hook up with your Nigerian boyfriends, and then you come pretending to be something you are not," he said.

A little after midnight he fell into a deep sleep. I dressed silently and left. I went straight home. I cried the whole night. I couldn't sleep. My face was bruised. When my family asked what had happened I lied and said I was in a fight with a friend. His smell was all over my clothes and body, and it felt like he was still with me. I took a bath three times.

I called Zanele Muholi; she was the only person I could relate to, and someone who'd come up with a way to deal with the mess I'd got myself into. I took a train and we met in town. We went to People Opposing Women Abuse (POWA) for counselling. We then went to Medico in Johannesburg for a medical examination and treatment. We didn't get help because there were neither nurses nor doctors on duty and they had no crime kits. They also said that it was not possible for a doctor who is based in Johannesburg to testify in a case originating in Krugersdorp.

They offered me a slice of bread and a painkiller. Muholi organised a car and we drove to Leratong hospital in Kagiso. There was no doctor on duty and no crime kits at the crisis centre. While waiting for a doctor, the police came by to drop the crime kit. They said they were rushing to Magaliesberg to attend to another urgent rape case.

The doctor came after three hours. I was examined and then he took the statement for the medical report. I told him that the guy raped me because I was a lesbian. As soon as he heard this he stopped writing and posed questions regarding my sexuality. He said: "Why are you a lesbian at this age? Do you know that it is against the constitution to make such a decision without the consent of a parent? You are wearing a cross of Christ, did you know that it is an abomination in the eyes of God to be lesbian?"

I asked him, "The guy raped me because he wanted to change me, are you saying that was a right thing to do?"

He didn't answer me, but instead he scratched off the report and wrote, "There is no sign of forceful penetration because the girl had already broken her virginity and the blood stains in the eyes are due to constant rubbing, and they might develop further if they are not treated." Without a medical report I had a weakened case.

The police arrived at nine o'clock that night. I opened a case and then went home, but could not stay long, as my safety was not guaranteed. I got a call around half past ten to inform me that the guy had been arrested and I'd be notified in advance about the case and court details.

I wanted to be away from Johannesburg, to ease my mind so I left for KwaZulu-Natal for a month. When I came back I heard that the guy had been released. I then called the sergeant who was handling the case. He told me the same thing: "They'll notify you in advance."

On the 28 August 2004 I saw my rapist; he approached me and threatened to kill me. I felt cold, betrayed, angry and very scared. I

93

called the sergeant again, but this time I couldn't get hold of him. I went to the station. They couldn't find the docket, and said it didn't exist. I was failed medically, and the justice system proved its non-existence. South Africa is celebrating twelve years of democracy, but with written policies that are not implemented. We are told to cooperate and not take the law into our own hands. Others harm us and get away with it; we have no way of getting justice.

Will South Africa ever change and accommodate everyone?

Closeted Love

Mavourneen Finalyson

Locking me out of your closet
feels sinful, birthing catholic
guilt, sexual confusion with
question upon tormented
attraction.

Words you utter soothing
attempts, hollow – without
commitment to your truth you deny
as you stroke my breast.
Would that I knew of authentic will
through tortured filter, homosexual
aloofness.

I fight shame which is not mine. But
I loved you whole.
Prevailing questions exhausting question.
Woman!
I crave you full.

ADDIE LINLEY chose to write her compelling story under a pseudonym. She is an academic, has two daughters from a heterosexual marriage and an adopted daughter with her current partner.

A LIFE IN-BETWEEN

ADDIE LINLEY[1]

I lived a heterosexual life until I was 45, so this cannot be an exclusively lesbian tale. I can't say for sure that I haven't always been one, but reached the point where all the past strands of inner dissonance I experienced when with boys and men, the too often reckless and dangerous heterosexual liaisons I had engaged in during my late 30s, and the horrible, debilitating lifetime of never feeling feminine, coalesced into an honest recognition of the reality of my sexual orientation only twelve years ago. I am now 57 and so there are many years of a confused and often fractured identity to account for if I am to say anything about who I am and the life I have led. Deciding where to begin was difficult, as was how I should organise the telling – by life phases, by "critical" events, by recurring motifs? In the end "life phases" seemed the most logical route to narrate my journey towards the fullness of my lesbian identity, not because the journey was linear, but because the past has created the present. And so it is with a remembering of childhood and adolescence that I begin this story.

CHILDHOOD AND ADOLESCENCE

As a young child, I was apparently very happy – my mother told me this when I was 40 – and if I think hard about it now, she was probably right. I was the proverbial tomboy. I can remember being four years old and at play school, and the only girl, together with three boys, to get a whack on the backside for climbing under the school fence to the house next door. I remember playing cricket and soccer with the boys who lived next door to us, and spending hours and hours with "Pup", my confidante, friend, protector and

---

"other mother" in her *khaya*[2] at the back of the property we lived on. Pup's proper name was Mrs Joyce Nkabinde. When I was about eight, we made balsam wood puppets at school and dressed them. I put mine in boy's clothes and was so proud of it, and Pup so admiring of it, that I gave it to her. Forever after that we addressed each other as "Pup" or "Puppety", right until the day she died, aged 65. I was the only white person at her funeral amidst hundreds of her community and family in the Catholic cathedral at Marianhill. Neither my parents nor siblings came, not even after 21 years of unbroken, loving and loyal service. Angry at first, I slowly realised that I was so grateful they were not there. Without them, I could hold the sacredness of the moment without interference.

But I digress.

I have a clear image of my mother shouting at me one Sunday morning when I was about nine years old, for "messing" my church dress even before we left the house. So angry, she smacked me hard and shut me in my room. My father must have taken my side, because church never happened that morning. Instead, my mother walked four kilometers to *her* mother's house and did not return until late that afternoon. Of what happened after that – that evening, the next day, the weeks that followed, how my parents reconciled (if they did) – I have no idea. Only the rage that I had "spoiled" my dress imprinted itself. She should have let me go in my T-shirt and shorts uniform and saved herself such despair and isolation.

I also remember stealing sweets from the local café – a conspiracy between two friends across the road, Willem and Delfie, his sister, to see how many we could take without being caught. Since I cannot remember ever being punished for this crime, I can only now assume we were such slick operators that no one ever noticed. And I used to rock-hop, alone, for miles down one of the cold Drakensberg streams that my father used to fish on our many trips to the mountains. My rule was that I should never put a foot in the water, which meant that often I took wild risks in leaping

---

2   Khaya: the commonly used word during the apartheid era to denote the living quarters of live-in black domestic workers (usually for white families).

from one boulder to another, dangerously beyond my stride. That my mother let me do this remains a mystery to me. Perhaps it was a relief to have me out of the way?

Though sent to Durban Girls' College, the "privilege" of a private school education escaped me. I was not a credit to the school or my parents. By the time I reached Grade 7 (the first time), I had visited the principal so many times that I had no fear of her whatsoever. I was one of a small "gang" who made the singing teacher cry, sharpened pencils into the bouffant hairdo of the Afrikaans teacher, and faked illness in order to be put into sick bay together. I never finished sewing any garment we began in Housecraft, but ate everything we cooked in those lessons. School, at that time, was a place of (mostly) fun. But some days were bad. Like the one on which my parents forbade me to have anything more to do with my best friend, Sandra. Out the blue, I was told she was a bad influence. In what way, they would not let on. The fact that she died in a motorbike accident, drunk and high at the age of twenty suggests they might have had cause for concern. All that lingers in my memory, however, is how hate-filled I was at the injunction, and that I ignored it entirely during school hours, and lied when I got home.

It wasn't until I was in high school that any liquid feelings of desire began to take hold. I remember being passionately devoted to our hockey coach, a short, tanned, strong young woman who "kicked ass" wherever she went. And I loved that I was considered a close friend of the two most popular and attractive girls in my class from Grades 8 – 12. They would hold overnight parties at one or other of their homes and invite the whole class. All the girls would drink wine quite openly, but I didn't touch a drop. Christian Scientists don't take alcohol. Instead, I played Florence Nightingale to anyone who overplayed their hand when drinking, holding drunken girls in my arms and mopping up their vomit for them.

But I also kissed Ronald when I was twelve. It wasn't much fun, but I knew I had to try it. And then I didn't kiss another boy until I was fifteen. By this time our family had moved cities and so we moved schools too, this time though, to a state school – unlike my brother who was sent to private schools until he completed his Matric. We now lived in an up-market suburb and, through a very obscure connection, got caught up in the private school clique that threw parties during school holidays. My sister and I were irregularly invited – when it was incumbent on the host to provide more girls. So we made up girl numbers and I learnt what it meant to be a wallflower. My sister has commanded the attention of men all her life, and back then it was no different. I can say with complete confidence, however, that I know all about wallflowering, and what an embarrassing and horrible job it actually is.

But I did get to go out with a few boys. Richard, for example, was a great guy who came as my partner to two school dances. We kissed and held hands and that felt good. But nothing more came of it.

And then there was Bill. Oh my god! He was the Adonis that every girl hankered after and somehow, somehow, he came to my Matric dance with me. I cannot now even remember how it all came to pass, but what I do recall (with enormous embarrassment at the time) was that, when we danced, I thought he must have a match box in his pocket. A hard thing kept rubbing my thighs, something I had never experienced before. Years later I heard that Bill had fallen on his head in a horse riding accident when he was twelve and had suffered some form of brain damage. If ever there was news to slubber the gloss of one particular triumph, that was it!

Weaving itself through all these years, however, was the Other Me. The girl who managed to get hold of "dirty" books from friends and read them under the bed covers, or at the bottom of the garden, alone. I had a ravaging thirst for the sexual details, the eroticism written into the pages of these books. The scenes I scanned provoked a delicious and irresistible response from my body and I never resisted it. It was as if I lived two lives: the one as dutiful, contributing, loving family member, the other as loner, inhabiting imaginary worlds of adult sexuality and difference. These books, though, reflected an entirely heterosexual framing of relationships. Much like the fact that I have never ever smoked weed or tried out any other form of mind-altering drug – simply because I have never been anywhere where I was offered it – so I did not know that there was a whole body of literature out there that focused on same-sex relationships. I just didn't know.

So powerful and all-pervasive was the "not knowing" of this life of mine, that not even the brutality and discrimination of the apartheid apparatus penetrated it. So closed, so wrapped up in middle class whiteness were we all, that I just never knew the reality of what went on. Not, that is, until I was very much older, a fact that still fills me with shock and remorse. But let me not dwell on that here. Let me move on.

FIRST LOVE AND MARRIAGE

Brian was the first man I ever truly loved. We married – I was 21 and he was 25 – and as I walked up the aisle (authentically virginal, too), in a beautiful, hand-tailored white wedding gown, I had no doubts whatever that we would grow old together. Of course, we have not done that and nor are we ever likely to. Such is the stuff of dreams. But, so great was our young compatibility that we were sure we would. We were so similar when we met in my first undergraduate year – shy, sexually inexperienced, used to being overlooked by the "opposite" sex, straight, both from solid, caring, but essentially constraining and conforming families. And so we both experienced our relationship as extraordinarily emancipating. Away from both sets of parents, we could do as we wanted.

At that time, men were allowed women visitors into their residence rooms (though the rule did not apply conversely), and so we spent hours and hours of intimate time together. But my sister had fallen pregnant "out of marriage", an event that so devastated my parents that Brian and I never went the whole way, contracting not to so that, a) we did not repeat my sister's deed, and b) because we were "good" kids and believed that "keeping ourselves for marriage" was the right thing to do. This too, I know now we were quite wrong about. Perhaps if we had learnt each other's levels of physical and sexual energies and needs *before* marrying, we'd have recognised their complete incompatibility and drifted apart. And perhaps if that had happened, I would have come to a greater understanding of myself much sooner.

Perhaps.

But I grew up, in the sixties and seventies, in a white, middle class, Christian Science home where *who* men and women *are*, that is, the essence of their Being, and the appropriate roles for each to perform, were very clearly defined. It was not that anyone in the family or our social circle contested these roles, or that we engaged in lively debate or imaginings of alternate gendered possibilities. It was not, in other words, because we had been challenged by them, or thought through them in considered (or even ill-considered) ways and had come to a conclusion about them. It was simply a given, a God-given reality that heterosexuality was the norm. And so there was never any need to discuss alternate sexualities, because in our world they did not exist. Not at that time. And not during the Second World War either it seems. This latter "fact" I learnt from my father. He has always insisted that there were no homosexual men in the South African armed forces when they fought the Desert War in North Africa, and later in Italy, in their defence of freedom against Nazism. He was there. He should know.

So, I grew up knowing only that there were *men* – some more "real" than others, and *women* – some more "attractive" than others (and therefore, more desirable to men). I also grew up knowing that I was not an "attractive" girl and that men ("real men" that is) seldom gave me a second glance. So when Brian suddenly came calling more often than anyone had ever done in my life before, and certainly since arriving at university, I look back and know that from the very start the odds were against him, and thus our marriage too. I came with too many suppressed feelings, dreams, fantasies, expectations for this one man at that time of my life (and his) to fathom and fulfil. These realisations came far too late to save the steadily unravelling connection between us, despite how harmoniously we parented together (and still do).

Becoming a mother, which I did for the first time six years after we married, was an experience filled with ambivalences and contradictions. I loved my two girls so much I could sometimes hardly breathe. They brought me a quality of love nothing could (or can still) match. They affirmed the essential "me" as whole, entirely good and sufficient. But, never instinctively having been driven to want to bear children, I also had dark moments of resentment and often a suffocating sense of entrapment. I resented the changes they imposed on our lives and Brian's complete and willing acceptance of these changes. Being a "good" mother, which I sincerely was and wanted to be, I was full of self-loathing and shame at how much I still wanted my "adult ideal" – of never ending selfishness, intimacy and the erotic. But I hid it all from everyone. Thus began the deeply complex matter of what it meant for me to be a mother.

LUST UNLEASHED

When my second daughter was eighteen months old, I went back to teaching. It was at this school that I met Dan. Ten years older than me, he turned my world upside down. Known to be a womanizer, a heavy drinker, and a bully when pushed, I'd been told to watch out for him. "If he comes on to you," my women colleagues said, "push him away". Well, he did, and I didn't. And instead of the womanizing, drinking, punitive wild card I'd been warned about, I found this seductive, experienced, gentle poet and literary man. We met in nearby forests and grassy hillsides, his leather jacket a blanket on the ground. I rode pillion on an 1100cc BMW touring motorbike for the first time in my life. For the very first time in my whole life I felt desired. For the first time, I felt woman. I was 34.

Over the next three years I lived the most profound lie, meeting Dan clandestinely and sustaining my relationship with him, whilst simultaneously going home each night to Brian. Dan watched how I grew in confidence because of him and slowly it dawned on both of us that "his creation" (his words) no longer belonged to him. Armed with what I then believed to be true femininity and womanliness at last, there was little he could do to hold me. And so, in a stream of insane consciousness, I ran wild, heady with the strength of my proven sexual prowess. I knew I was "good", and I learnt very quickly that men are staggeringly gullible when it comes to being sweet-talked. So I tested my abilities more times than once. When I tried to send my husband a guilt-infested warning by saying that I was "looking at other men" (too afraid at that point to admit to any real infidelity), he said only that reading a menu was not synonymous with eating everything on it. Loyal, naive, unaware, no suspicions crossed his mind. In the end of course, I told him, confessing however to only one affair, and though it took more than a year (with most of that time spent abroad as a family) the marriage did end – after seventeen years – with tears and great sadness on all sides.

Starting over was not easy. Though free to live honestly, free to follow my own desires, I now had full responsibility for two children. We found a new house and the three of us set up a new kind of home – one of women only. I found a temporary, part-time position at the local university and left school-based teaching behind for good. Though thoroughly untutored in the discourses of the Academy, and not altogether comfortable with this quite different world, the flexibility the job offered allowed me to parent singly in a way no other post would have made possible. Despite the "honesty" with which I could now live, I was wracked with guilt for breaking up what was really a profoundly harmonious *family* (as opposed to the marital relationship). Brian was an abiding and committed father and the girls ached for his former daily, but now absent, presence. Under the conditions of the divorce, alternate weekends with their father had to suffice.

And then I met Fred – fourteen years my senior, married, professorial, moneyed and living in a huge home on the right side of the tracks. We began an affair that lasted five years. Did his wife find out? Yes, eventually. Did his children? Yes. Did mine? No, and I am trusting they never will. He became my life. Three rings on the phone of an afternoon, an evening, a Saturday, a Sunday, just to signal he was thinking of me. I wallowed in the pool of desire that held us together, ignoring my part in the appalling betrayal of another woman, and his children. At least, I said to myself, I am not cheating on anyone. I am living an honest life. I did that. I truly convinced myself for the first four years that I was not at fault. I spent months and months in psychotherapy dealing with my "love" for Fred, not my part in the destruction of his home life – or myself.

We looked ahead to the time when we would be together. Again, I had no doubts that I loved this man. The wonder (as I construed it then) of my home effectively being on the *wrong* side of the tracks was that we could always meet there. The neighbourhood was not his and neither was it one he or his family would ever choose to live in. Nor would any of his associates. And so we were always "safe". He was careful too. He never wrote a single word to me in any medium, but he would give me things – an exquisite oak mirror he had made himself, expensive books, lunches out. I took up paddling in order to "legitimately" spend more time with him: a cover that I fooled myself no one saw through. A cover I think even Fred believed no one saw through, a cover I discovered so much later, that so many had always seen through.

It was only his wife we were waiting for. Noble, committed, state of the art family man, Fred said he could never leave his family. However, if ever his wife had an affair that would be it, he said. That would be when he would leave and we would be together. And of course she did have an affair. And of course he discovered he could not possibly leave her because, faced with a choice, he suddenly realised he needed her more than he needed me.

The Day The World Ended remains etched in a dark, fired memory of agonising emotional and physical pain. It was a Monday morning in February, and he phoned down to my office to say he had something to tell me. His face was taut and white when I walked in, his hands wringing each other over and over. I sat quite still. "She's having an affair," he finally said. I looked at him, my stomach rolling, flick-flacking with thrilled anticipation. My mind leapt ahead to the changes that would instantly be evoked in my life. The excitement, the certainty, the oh-so-badly awaited moment. His rebuttal, his pathetic, pitiful, pale-faced, yellow-bellied words that spoke his choice slammed into my ears, my face, my head, my legs. Unable to even speak, unable even to mouth one single word of hate-filled condemnation, I left the room.

Dazed, winded, wounded, I went straight to one of the handful of women friends who had paced me through the four years of madness. Uncharacteristically, I flung about, threw car keys, cried and cried. I felt violated, raped, torn apart. Then, with icy precision, I went home, packed my car full of all the gifts he had given me, including a canoe, and drove to his swanky home in its forest-like garden. No one was home. Carefully, I laid out everything I had brought with me on his lawn. The books, the mirror, the knick-knacks, everything. And left.

But that "event" that morning, that denial of everything I had believed to be my reality, was both an ending and a beginning. In the nightmare months that followed, I could not concentrate, I could not breathe; I did not go anywhere where there was a chance we would meet. Paralysing fear dominated my life. I could not tell my children that my world was in shreds. To them I had to be nothing but the mom they knew, but the front I put on for them and everyone else who had no knowledge of the affair wore me to an emotional standstill. I can't recall now exactly how or why or when that journey became easier but I do know it was a full year before I felt even remotely intact again. And in tandem with that "intactness" came the realisation, slowly, that I would never let a man penetrate me again. *In any way whatsoever.* The meaning behind all my years of trying to find a space for myself with men, all the images of myself playing out my "womanliness" through the sex act fell suddenly into place. I *had* been violated by Fred. Worse still, I had allowed myself to be violated, to be diminished by him. I saw for the first time the shocking truth that I was the cause of my own undoing, and that the literal and symbolic instrument of all my undoing, the instrument of violation, was the penis. I knew there and then that I would never want to "know" a man again, and that all my perceptions of maleness had undergone radical and irrevocable change.

In recalling all that I have here about my heterosexual lifespan, I am trying to capture how the "undertow" of relationships-as-sex dominated and determined their nature and shape. So much so that I, me, the woman I am, never emerged. Only the sex machine did. I've tried to track where it all came from. Certainly, my mother did not value beautiful women. She was threatened by them and trusted no one, especially men. She taught us not to trust anyone, but especially men, saying they only wanted one thing from you and that was "it". I can recall her saying that it was impossible for a woman to spend a night with a man without having sex. I know from my own experience that this is simply untrue, but I would never have told her I had done so because she would have said I lied. When my father went on business trips to Japan, there were vicious rows on his return. Whether he ever did actually have other women at home or away, I do not know, but he was party to her undoing through his own male stereotypical behaviour. Even at 89, he still speaks about a woman first in terms of her physicality – "nice boobs", "sexy body", or alternatively "very plain" or "nothing to look at" – and only then in terms of her social, emotional or intellectual attributes. So, while on the one hand our family did not talk relationships openly, on the other we children – well at least, in my recollected view – were only ever introduced to one construction of a relationship between men and women, namely that it revolved solely around the sex act. It is perhaps little wonder that my own sexuality was for so long in freefall.

THE BEGINNING OF NOW

Two years after the End-of-Fred, I went into psychotherapy with the express agenda of coming to know my sexuality. The period of recovery following Fred was characterised by regular and sustained introspection, a process which steadily generated more and more insights and revelations which I knew I needed help in understanding and responding to. In therapy I was able to delve into layers of my subconsciousness I had never accessed before. I recalled recurring dreams, old memories, my often-experienced desires for intimacy with women and my very real fear of and distaste for most men. Finally, I was able to embrace my lesbian identity with great joy, warm acceptance and huge relief. Though I had absolutely no intention of acting on what I now knew to be the truth about myself, I settled into a quality of inner peace I had seldom if ever enjoyed before. I could not imagine in my wildest dreams how living such an "alternate" reality could come about, and given my children's and my immediate family's lifetime of mainstream perceptions of who I was, I did not "go looking".

And then, only four months later, I met Alex. This very youthful, petite young woman moved into the office next door to me at work. The room was so large and she looked so small and lonely, that I felt I had to do the friendly thing and introduce myself as her colleague-in-the-next-door-office. Over the next week we chatted every day, then met for a drink, and finally, but within a very short time, we surrendered to the overwhelming chemistry flowing between us. We dreaded the periods when we could not be together, she driving kilometres to her flat out of town each evening and I returning to my children. As the weeks wore on, however, we both came to know, with a certainty that still astounds us, that whatever it was that we had, it was here to stay. Finding a way to "live" our love, however, troubled us both. From my Fred experience I knew that I would never again devalue myself in the self-interests of another. Conversely, I knew that I would never do this to anyone else. Since Alex was, and had always been secure in her lesbian identity, I knew that the only way I could invite her into my life was through an open door and into a space where we stood proudly and publicly side by side. The cataclysmic implications of what was happening, therefore, had to be confronted with complete honesty – and conveyed to my children – and soon. The fear of doing so completely undid me and when I eventually told my two girls, who by then were seventeen and twenty respectively, our world lay in tatters.

For the next two years, all four of us lived a tightrope existence. As a mother who had been the touchstone of her children's world, particularly since the divorce ten years previously, I stood accused of shocking betrayal and deep shaming – again. As a lesbian living honestly for the first time, I soared and swept through a magnificent discovery of the woman in me, finding her, for the first time, both within and outside the contexts of sexual intimacy and the erotic. As a partner, I stumbled from bold acknowledgements of my commitment to terrified uncertainty that I could ever sustain the courage and strength I needed to simply hold it all together. Caught in a maelstrom of antagonistic demands and needs, somehow my "partner" and "lesbian" subjectivities remained intact. My perceptions of my own integrity as a mother, however, were torn and scattered and I doubted that my children and I would ever be able to recover the depth of love and trust we had once known. That we did is a miracle, a testament to determination, maturity and love – on everyone's part.

And then came the next hurdle. Alex wanted a child of her own. She had told me of this desire on our first date, wanting it "out there" – to test my reactions, since her previous partner had been emotionally unable to manage fulfilling such a need. So in love, so completely and utterly swept up in this new life, so aware that I was already a mother that I could hardly deny her wanting the same, I glibly and smilingly said, "That's OK by me". And for the first two years of our relationship, the issue was not raised again. Of course we were all struggling to stay afloat during that time so I know now that it was only because of Alex's acute sensitivity and concern for our well being that she let the matter rest so long. But when she did eventually raise it there was no letting up or going back. For the first time, but by no means the last, Alex's single-mindedness became a force to be reckoned with.

Given my very precarious hold on motherhood, I did not cope well with, or ever fully understand, her driving need to have a baby. By this time, aged 50, my own two girls had finally gone off to London, relieving me of the stupefying worry that daily, nightly, round the clock responsibility brings. My most honest position was that I did not need or want any more children. Full of fear of "success", I construed her monthly absorption with her menstrual cycle as obsession, her determination to persist in trying as willful, selfish, ill-considered and child-like. However, after many artificial insemination procedures and in vitro fertilisation, we were finally told that she would never bear a child.

Relief flooded through me. Assuming she would accept her fate, I looked with thrilled anticipation towards a return to that place of "adults only" – my remembered and deeply ingrained ideal construct of the perfect relationship. But I should have known Alex better. Never one to give up on a journey begun, she moved immediately to talking of adoption. This sent me straight back over the edge of fear and resentment.

The months that followed were taxed with undercurrents of tension, undermining and superimposing themselves on what we both still knew was a profoundly bonded relationship, but now under threat. Slowly, I came to a point where I recognised the reality of the choices I had. I could either refuse to be part of an adoption process and thereby lose the relationship, or I could find a place in it, and keep my partner. Suddenly I was sailing in completely uncharted waters. I did not know how to be anything but a mother, yet I did not want this woman I loved to become one. My ignorance of "how women love women" angered and unsettled me. Used to being in charge, the "senior" member of the household, with an inherent sense of superiority (on account of my age and maturity!), I floundered hopelessly. Significantly, during all this it never once entered my mind that the child we were contemplating adopting would be anything but white. Such was the depth of my socialised subjectivity in relation to race.

It wasn't very long before it became perfectly apparent that there were no white children available – at least through state social welfare channels. Certain that it was now time for my construction of "our world" to hold sway, that is, one in which there were no more children, I said a silent prayer to the god of Older Women.

Being asked how I felt about a "child of colour" ripped into me with a terrifying intensity. Unable to stop myself, I said, "Absolutely not, not now, not ever." Shocked by my own reaction, I insisted it had nothing to do with colour. Everything, I said, was about the way in which goal posts in our relationship kept moving. Everything, I said, had to do with my partner's obsessive, compulsive demand to "have it all". Everything, I said, was about not wanting to be a mother again, and no one being willing to give me that. Everything, in the end, turned out to be about me.

I have always "gone off", sometimes literally, sometimes metaphysically, when hit by strangling degrees of dissonance. Though I could not, and would not, acknowledge to anyone but myself initially just how deep the level of self-doubt and recrimination my response to a black child had evoked in me, I knew I was on dangerous ground. Thinking "trans-historically", I began to try and access the multiple layers of my own conditioning. Having by now accepted an identity of "academic", I used theoretical tools at my disposal, ones that had already helped me see into the forces of social conditioning – class, gender, race, language and so on – that were central to my own teaching of post graduate students. Slowly I came to recognise that my racist *and* mothering "dispositions" were deeply rooted in my own upbringing, but were not necessarily "me" forever. By "objectifying" my own actions and responses through this intellectual engagement with them, I began to be able to calm the heat within me. Over the next month or so, as my intellectualised analysis of my reactions became more and more meaningful to me, I felt my defences begin to soften. I came to understand quite clearly, that all my earlier "whiteness", and my claims to being non-racist, were nevertheless entirely racist. I came to understand too, that splitting off my sexual self at the very young age I did, and sustaining this split throughout adulthood, *and* finding "being a mother" so very difficult, was not because I was flawed and perverted, but rather because the engendered ways of seeing, being and occupying space imprinted on me had pre-determined how I should construct this role.

Caela has been with us for seven years now – a beautiful, dark-eyed African child. She came to us at four months from the Princess Alice Home in Johannesburg. Abandoned in a park in the city two hours after birth, she has been the catalyst for the most remarkable change in all our lives. She has a birth mom and dad about whom we know nothing, two adoptive moms and two adoptive big sisters – my girls – who love her dearly. She has an extended family of aunts and uncles who love her, and whom she loves, beyond words, and she attends a multilingual, multicultural school nearby. The tongue of her middle class mothers is English, and so her language proficiency, values and beliefs reflect her context. Pensively, we note, however, her overt affinity towards our African friends and colleagues. She is immeasurably bright, with insights and observations beyond her years, but she can also be "simply 7" and a handful of nonsense and rebellion. Too much of this behaviour wears me out but reinforces my gratitude to Alex for having contracted to always step in when my age, and the fact that I have mothered two children to adulthood already, suggests she should. Being fourteen years younger than me, she has all the necessary energy and patience to keep us all on track in these moments!

Yes, Caela has enormous challenges to face – lesbian parents, no tangible "history" of her own, a first language English speaker in a brown skin in South Africa, to name the three most obvious. But there is so much of her. She has an impressive musical and singing talent, a great sense of humour, she thirsts after answers to curiosities and questions, and is physically strong and healthy. She can read, write, dance, swim, identify most wild life and common bird calls. When I hold her, dance with her, love her, I see only a child – and I am her mother, without fear. The legacies of my racial prejudice and relational expectations have dissolved into a dynamic and politicised home defined by five strong and vibrant women. The future for this lesbian, as woman, mother, partner and activist, looks good.

RANI SONI chose to write under a pseudonym. Brought up in a conservative Hindu Gujerati family, she has had numerous hurdles to overcome, but has succeeded in living a meaningful and spiritually fulfilling life as a lesbian.

LIVING A LIE: ISSUES OF IDENTITY

RANI SONI[1]

Why do I want to use a pseudonym for my story? I think there are a number of reasons. The other day I was talking to a friend of mine and she said at times she wondered if I was homophobic. I laughed my head off.

"Why do you say that?"

"Because you are very critical of gay and lesbian people who are very out there."

Actually, what offends me is anybody who is out there, in your face. It's nothing to do with the fact of being gay; anybody who is continually in your face with their views – political or other – really bothers me. And I think it's mainly a question of privacy that is the problem for me. I've always been a very private person. I come from a very conservative family, and one learns to respect that, as much as you make life choices, there is a sense that you don't impose them on your family, or anyone else.

Also, my family, who know about my homosexuality, don't really know what to do with it. My brother is quite cool about having a gay sister, and on the surface is quite open about it. But my sister-in-law, his wife, is the epitome of someone who says that she approves, but is totally against it, and there is a whole passive-aggressive behaviour around it. She has a strange attitude; there's a kind of falsehood about her response, like she is living a lie – not me who's living the lie, but her. I've tried to be quite up front and say from the beginning: This is who I am. Her response has been the whole emotional stuff of pretending it's fine when obviously it is not.

My father is still alive, and when I told him I was gay, he wanted me to go and see a therapist, and the doctor, and get medication for

---

1   Pseudonym

it. I sat there thinking, what pill is going to cure this? But when he had thought about it, he admitted it was a hard choice for me, and he would advise me to live in privacy, which is more his need rather than my mine. So, I vacillate, not so much being private about being gay, but private about my relationship. I openly admit that my colleagues probably know I'm gay, but I'm very careful about who I'm with, and who I talk to. I don't want it to be an issue, and I don't want to discuss it with anyone – I don't what to talk about my sex life with anyone. Even if I were heterosexual, I still wouldn't want to talk about it. At times I feel there is this bizarre curiosity, which makes me uncomfortable.

I've always questioned my sexuality, at least since I went to Varsity, although I had always been heterosexual. But I came to question my sexuality, because so often lesbian women would hit on me, or ask me out, and I began to think: What's going on here; what's wrong with me? And when I talked to my friends about it, and we had deep discussions, we all concluded that I was really heterosexual. Despite this, I remained single for a long time.

Then I met and fell in love with a woman – spiritually, because it never reached a sexual level at all. But I didn't make the connection that I was gay, because it was a soul connection that we had. In a sense I was living a lie in this relationship, and didn't know what was really going on. Throughout this fairly lengthy relationship this person would maintain that she was heterosexual, but she wanted to continue being with me. I really didn't know where I was, and kept thinking: It takes two to create something real. We lived together in a digs, at times with others and at times just the two of us. But never any sex. The fact that I was stoned and drunk for much of the time probably helped to keep me in there! I kept wondering whether I was sane or not, because nothing seemed to be real. In the end this rather weird relationship started messing me up, and I could see it was bad for me. So, eventually I disengaged from it.

I had begun to think that I was bisexual and, because I had been single for so long, I began to think maybe I'd been batting for the wrong side. I was tired of being lonely.

I met my partner while doing a theatre production and we immediately connected; I can't explain it any other way. She was a lot younger – there's a sixteen-year age difference. This was my first serious relationship. I had never done the dating thing. What with my conservative Gujerati background, I had not been allowed to go to a ten o'clock movie until I was 22. And all the *Guji* guys were scared of me, probably because I was too assertive, so I didn't get invited out. When I was 21 some of the community elders came to my father and said they were worried about me because I wasn't married yet. And my father said, "I think you need to have this conversation with Rani; I'll make the tea."

I've always been quite feminist. My brother believed that as a girl or boy you had to look a certain way and be a certain way, but I looked at all this *Guji* stuff and thought: I'm not going to get married; I want nothing to do with all this. For me, it was very much to do with rights; it was nothing to do with sexuality, but with gender rights. I thought: Why do *you* have the right to drive the car, and I can't do the same? And my brother could go to a nightclub till two or even five in the morning, but I was not allowed out.

And so, when I met my partner, I felt like I had waited my whole life for this. It was a very humbling experience for me and I had to work through a whole lot of my own issues about my body, and weight issues. When she first told me I was beautiful, I cried, because I thought, Oh, my god, are you sure? It's done so much for my confidence, and I just feel so settled. But at first I couldn't believe that anyone would want to spend her life with me, because of my own lack of self esteem.

So, it was only when I met my partner and suddenly we connected and we clicked, that I had this amazing sense of two human beings who had fallen in love. She was heterosexual before that and had had no hint that she was gay. I happened to meet someone and fall in love, and that person happened to be a woman. However, when she told her family that she was gay, although she didn't tell them about our relationship, there was a lot of conflict and abuse. Since then she has been able to make considerable peace with her family, and this journey is still in progress. Within my family, they are outwardly quite welcoming, and will say, "Come and see us," but then will do bizarre things, such as when my partner gave my sister-in-law a hug, she would say, "You don't have to touch me". There's an underlying kind of bitchiness, and she often makes it clear that she doesn't want to be touched by this "vile" person who might give her something.

So, we've got an agreement with each other that we don't ever have to spend much time with our respective families; if we feel the need to we do, but if we don't, then that's fine too. My dad has never been told who my partner is, but it's clear that he accepts it. My brother is in his own world, and doesn't give it much thought. I was, initially, very afraid of telling him about my relationship because, every time I thought about telling him, I kept hearing in my head the things he might say about it. I'm usually very defensive with him. But when I finally did tell him, it was such a shock because he just said, "Oh, that's cool!" – and a whole year of angst was just taken away. That has made a big difference to me; his accepting it has made it much more OK, somehow.

I wish that with my sister-in-law I could just sit her down one day and say, "Here's what I think", but I don't think she could hear it. I tried writing to her, but she said, "Don't even bother, I'll never accept it." And she has also said, "I don't want her in my house, as she is not welcome here." And then I apologise to her, because we're always so polite, but I think I'm actually fucked in the head for doing it. I say, "Sorry, I don't actually mean to impose on you," because, after all, it is her house. But my father lives there and we have to go to their house to see him. I've already lost my mom to cancer and I'm not prepared to lose the rest of my family because of her attitude to me being gay.

But, all the time she pretends that she had to help my brother come to accept us, and you listen to it, and you think who is daft here? I'm too polite to challenge her and, however angry I might feel, I know that things said in anger can never be taken back. She is totally cold, but she happens to be married to my brother, so we're stuck with her. In the end, reality is so relative, and as much as I want to say "this is my truth", she's never going to change and so I have to live with it. So, I'd rather invest my time and energy in the things I'd like to change, things that can be changed. I do know, however, that if she approached me directly, I would not back down from my position. But I don't think that day will ever happen.

I think that is why if I'm asked why I don't go public it's because I don't want to spend my time defending my life against hypocrites, people like this. It's her problem, but she'll never see it as that. I do have an uncle and aunt, who, when I talk about unconditional acceptance, *they* would be the example I'd use. Because they just, from the beginning, accepted us. It was hard for them, as I don't think they had ever met a gay person before in their lives, and suddenly here I was and here was this partner of mine. It took them about six months to be able to visit, but they did, and now we pop in and see them every week and we're very close. And that's what matters; that they can make that journey at their age. Of all the members of my family who I've told about this, my cousins from London have also been very accepting; they are, like, OK, when's the wedding? And there are my aunt's kids who don't care, because they see that I'm still the same person; I haven't suddenly got two heads.

Acceptance is so important. My brother and sister-in-law are very much into image, that's their currency, and my sister-in-law is forty-something, wanting to be twenty. She's going to grow old at some point, and she's going to have to deal with these things at some point. I don't believe my whole purpose in life is to share enlightenment with her; that's her journey, but I certainly don't have to live the lie with her. I think a large part of the problem is this continual politeness, so that any real engagement with issues is very rare. I don't even know if my brother's kids know, or how they deal with it in their family. When my father dies, maybe it will be different, but while he's still alive, I think he's too old to have to deal with the fact that his kids are fighting. After my mom died, I learnt that life is short.

My brother is the Alpha Male, the patriarch, but he doesn't have the ability to listen; say something ten times, and he'll come back and ask the same question. Whereas, my sister-in-law sees and hears everything. But is anything serious ever going to impact on her life? I have the strong feeling that her son of sixteen, my nephew, is gay, so both my partner and I watch with the radar out as this boy grows up, and that will be her karma at some point. Of course, whether he ever acts on it, or decides to do what, in my opinion, most of the *Guji* guys do – get married and live in the closet for the rest of his life – I don't know. But, at the moment his interests appear to lie elsewhere. So, maybe my karma is to exist in my sister-in-law's life, and her lessons will come in their own time.

For me, then, my sexuality is really a spiritual thing. I don't go around telling people about my religion, and what it means to me. It's a quiet acceptance of a spiritual presence, and I think this is how I've experienced being gay: it's just a quiet acceptance of who I actually am. It doesn't change the fact that I'm a good facilitator, or the fact that I'm a bad report writer. It doesn't change me, it just adds to who I am. I know who I am, and it helps to define who I am, but it's not the definition of who I am. I think another aspect of keeping one's life private, is that there are two people in a relationship. I could see myself saying: "Actually I don't give a toss about who knows; I've lived in this community for long enough for people to think it doesn't really matter." But there are two of us and, until we've both made that stand, until we're both ready to talk about the partnership, it can't happen.

When I was working for an Aids organisation, one of my team members came to me one day and said he had just found out that he was HIV positive. I asked whether he was going to tell the team. And he said, "Oh no, I would never admit something like that in this organisation." I thought that was living a lie because presumably you're working in Aids because of the people. The problem is that people expect you to respond according to a certain script, and when you can't respond within that script it's a very different world you live in. The level of pain you would have to go through is just too deep, because it's about your own identity. So, if I'm a coward, I'm at least a conscious coward. But it's a bizarre world we live in.

My activism is through theatre. All the plays I've done have had an aspect of gay relationships, and the difficulty of being gay in a relationship. These have expressed some of my more feminist views. But in terms of my own life, I just live it, and in living it and trying to be normal – in the sense that I believe I am normal – that should be the indication that I can do it. I've never been one to join a march, but I'd certainly write a poem or do a play about it. That's my way of getting through it. In the play I directed, which touched on issues of identity and relationships, for example,

I knew that I was questioning my own sexuality, and it seemed that a lot of others were doing the same. And I felt that to find an expression of that in a normal environment was very powerful. And there was no judgement, so that if some of the cast wanted to discuss relationships between women, and some wanted to discuss religion, that was fine.

However, what I do know is that it's so nice to be happy, and to feel I've reached a point in my life where I really am happy. I've never had anything that I could call "domestic bliss" and when you find it, it is wonderfully enlightening and comforting, although it's a very quiet relationship; very peaceful. There's something about falling in love that brings a new sense of clarity, like an awakening, and suddenly I see everything a lot clearer now. You have to learn to love yourself before you can truly love somebody else.

When you grow spiritually it's not usually like a lightning bolt, but like a quiet realisation and progression towards self. I believe you've got to actualise self before you can actualise God. For me Hinduism is an amazing religion, because it is quite open and free about God. Being a lesbian is part of actualising myself and my potential, and if I want to be authentic and true to myself I need to accept that, and to see what gifts I receive from that. Then I'm closer to God. I've always meditated, and if I meditate for an hour and get hand-cramp through the beads, and get my breathing so deep that I get high, then I somehow reach some form of enlightenment.

But this, being in love, challenges me to ask: Is this my karmic journey, is this my soul journey? I don't believe that God is a *sexual* being, but the Creator, the Divine Light. I don't believe God sees gender, and in a sense I don't believe love sees gender; so for me it is just that I happened to fall in love with a woman; I didn't look for a woman to fall in love with. I have connected with this person, this soul, on a soul-level, and the physical form is incidental, in a way. I'm still searching, and I'll keep seeking, and I like sitting and meditating and holding my beads. But God is here for me, and God is everywhere, in all creation.

ALLEYN DIESEL is an Honorary Research Fellow at the University of KwaZulu-Natal, specialising in the study of the place of women in Hinduism in South Africa, particularly their veneration of the Goddess. In 2007 she edited *Shakti: Stories of Indian Women in South Africa* (Wits University Press).

DOES YOUR MOTHER KNOW THAT YOU'RE OUT?

ALLEYN DIESEL

The Journey, then, involves exorcism of the internalised Godfather in his various manifestations (his name is legion). – Mary Daly

CHILDHOOD AND YOUTH

One of my earliest memories is of me and my paternal grandmother sitting on the floor arranging regimented rows of lead soldiers in bright European uniforms, as we imagined they might prepare for battle. Born in Pietermaritzburg in December 1942, near the end of the Second World War, I was not to meet my father until towards the end of 1945. He must have left with his regiment for the desert of North Africa sometime near the beginning of 1942, not to return home for two and a half years. So I spent my earliest years in a very loving all-woman family consisting of my mother and both my grandmothers. I seem to have clear memories of playing frequently with one or other of these wonderful, attentive grannies. My Grans were both in their own way strong women: my maternal grandmother was a trained nurse who had, as a girl, lived through the siege of Ladysmith, and my paternal grandmother came to South Africa from Glasgow and married a Free State farmer, helping to run the farm. An unspoken expectation assumed that women worked at some employment in one way or another, and were not merely submissive housewives and mothers.

I remember my mother playing the piano – the *Blue Danube*, one of my favourites, but most particularly *Keep the Home Fires Burning*, which, for some reason I did not understand, made her cry. She said she was crying for Daddy who was far away, fighting the enemy to keep us all safe. I was somewhat puzzled by this, as I couldn't imagine anyone else who might be needed in our idyllic little family group. However, I was taught to "Clap handies for Daddy", and to await his return with eager anticipation, which, for the most part, I forgot about.

When he eventually arrived, I was going on three years old. We went to the station to meet him, and soon after arriving home, he built me an exciting sandpit to play in, under a tree in our garden. But I soon discovered that he wasn't the wonderful, blue-eyed hero I'd been conditioned to expect. All too soon, in July 1946, I had a brother who took up all my father's attention and adoration, and I was pushed aside and ignored, or so it seemed to me. Everything my brother did was wonderful, and everything I did appeared to be wrong, stupid, irritating. I tried with everything I had to make myself acceptable. I became the assistant when he was fixing the car, I handed him the tools he needed when he was busy around the house and garden. There were moments when I really thought I was making it, and then I would do something that irritated him, and he would push me away. When my brother and I fought with each other I was frequently blamed for being in the wrong, and would often get beaten, and sent to my room.

I was very frightened of the dark, and often imagined that there were strange creatures in my room at night. Bookcases and shadows became dreaded monsters with large ears. I developed a terror of thunderstorms, and, like a frightened animal, was able to detect the first distant rumble of thunder long before anyone else heard it. At night I would cry out for my mother, and sometimes go through to their bedroom to climb into her bed for comfort. But if he became aware of this, my father would dismiss my fears and tell me to go back to my own bed. So my mother used to come to my bed to comfort me when I cried out in the night with fear at thunderstorms and nightmares.

As I grew older, mealtimes became particularly awful for the whole family, as again the criticism seemed endless, the meal frequently ending in a shouting match with me storming into my bedroom, slamming the door and refusing to come out. I was extremely fussy about my food, and was particularly thin, but that didn't worry me as I hated fat with a passion.

It was not all awful, of course, because I had my Grans, and my mother supported me, although she often had to be rather surreptitious about it. Because I was older than my brother, I sometimes got to go places with my father that my brother was either too young to do, or did not want to do. One of my happiest young memories is of him taking me to the motor races, first at the old Alexandra road circuit, and later to the Roy Hesketh track. What a thrill these days were, and I leant about cars and their capabilities, and loved the smell of Castrol racing fuel. Occasionally we went to a Western movie together at the old Bug House in Chapel Street. These dusty black and white movies filled me with a great sense of romanticism, giving vision to the Zane Grey cowboy novels which transported me to a different, exciting world on the wide cactus-strewn mesas of America. Occasionally, on a Sunday evening he would put records on the radiogram, his favourites being excerpts from Verdi's operas sung by Galli-Curci and Caruso. I have a clear, evocative memory of the limpid, aching quality of the emotions I detected. But these seemed to be little isolated pockets of happiness in my relationship with my father. I wished it could be different, and I seem to have spent a lot of energy trying to please him, and get his attention, but mostly my impression is that he ignored me, or criticised me.

I went to Scottsville primary school, just down the road from where we lived, and cried hysterically when my mother left me there on the first day. I felt totally panic-stricken, and somehow believed that my very existence depended on her, and that I would never survive in such alien circumstances. However, I seem to have settled in quite nicely, and muddled along in my own rather isolated way. But I had realised that in order to be acceptable to my father, something very important to me, I had to behave like a boy – especially to be tough and not to cry, or let people know when I was upset. This meant that throughout much of my primary school years I was teased and rejected by many of the girls, and when I managed to play with the boys, if I got into a fight and hit anyone, I was castigated as a very wicked and unsociable little girl. It was quite acceptable for the boys to slap and punch one another, but when I, a girl, did the same, it was completely unacceptable, sufficiently awful for my mother to be called to speak to the headmaster about my objectionable, tomboyish behaviour.

One Saturday morning I went off on my bicycle to the Scottsville hairdressers and got my hair cut short like a boy. My father didn't comment as far as I remember, but my mother said, "What a good-looking little boy you'd make" which made my year. A couple of Mother's stuffy friends said, "Girls can't have hair as short as that", and "Why don't you want to wear dresses and look pretty?" Yugh! How pathetically boring! This, of course, didn't help to raise my popularity stakes at school, but somehow it didn't worry me too much. I felt pleased that it was making a statement about who I really was. There were times when my life was made very miserable by various children who were obviously seriously offended by my gender bending, and I remember numerous occasions when I sat by myself at break feeling rejected and miserable. But I seem to have learnt to some extent to do my own thing, and take as little notice as possible of them.

Doing my own thing consisted of riding my bicycle long distances around Scottsville during the weekends, usually with a friend, and sometimes with my brother; all the way up to Oribi Village, and down to the Sewerage Farm, which was especially exciting when the river came down in flood. We also climbed trees, the tallest we could find, and explored streams, and houses under construction, often bringing all sorts of trophies home: stones, tiles, tadpoles. Some older neighbourhood boys built a bicycle race track on a vacant plot across from our house, and we spent most of the weekends tearing round this obstacle course, creating great mud puddles to splash through, and then fixing and cleaning our hammered bikes. I was fearless and reckless at this activity, and earned myself considerable admiration from these older boys, who I thought were really wonderful.

My mother, I must emphasise, was pretty unusual in that she did not share the conventional notions of sex-role stereotyping, and allowed me to wear shorts and shirts all weekend, and to enjoy these less than proper-little-girl activities. She was a primary school teacher, who had majored in English and Psychology at the University of Natal (where she met my father, who was doing a science degree), and her ideas on child raising and child development were, luckily for me, somewhat unusual and ahead of her time.

And so I muddled through to adolescence, and went to Pietermaritzburg Girls' High School. I remember loving school here, but I became increasingly naughty and uncooperative. Four of us formed a rebellious gang, where we had as our heroes James Dean (who had recently been killed driving a Porsche) and the sexy, sultry, sneering Elvis. Most of the other girls at school liked Pat Boon (whom we called Pat Baboon), and Johnny Ray, and thought that Elvis wasn't for nice girls. But then we had no aspiration to be nice girls. When I was in fourth form I got jaundice, and my mother was embarrassed that the doctor had to come, and I had about 40 pictures of Elvis stuck on the walls round my room. The gang bunked afternoon school to go to see Elvis's first movie *Love Me Tender* and our parents were called to the school by the headmistress, an elderly woman who was very shocked by the antics associated with Elvis the Pelvis. My mother was mortified because, as a teacher, she was particularly ashamed that her friends knew that she had such a rebellious daughter. We went to *Jailhouse Rock* and screamed and jived in the aisle. Mother despaired. Something about the potent alternative aura projected by Elvis seemed to release a wild, pent-up energy that was boiling away inside me, coupled with an unnamed longing and searching.

I became the dare devil of the class, and whenever the rest were bored or fed up with a lesson or teacher I would be dared to create a diversion, which I took great delight in doing. I climbed ladders which builders had left up against second storey windows, slid down banisters, wolf whistled at teachers, mocked the prefects, smoked in the lavs and at the bottom of the school grounds, rode my bike through the biggest puddles, smeared sideburns, like Elvis's down my cheeks, stuck on with Lifebuoy soap, and generally became the star turn.

At home things went from bad to worse because it was generally known that I was not doing well or behaving at school. I consistently came last in class, until it became a matter of honour to maintain that hard won position. One mortifying exam, I only came second to last, and was very fed up with myself. But my father had decided I really was up to no good and probably wasn't his kid, which he had, apparently, accused my mother of soon after he came home from the war and was something she told me about much later once, when I lay in bed with a bad fever. I, for my part, was quite sure that I had been adopted and didn't belong to them either. Meal times were still a battle ground, with my father complaining about something I had done, or the way I sat, or held my fork, or something, and I would yell insults, throw my food or fork across the table, and storm into my room, refusing to come out for the rest of the evening. I would then play my Elvis records instead of doing my homework.

Then in fourth form we got a new English teacher. I was not particularly interested in English, or any other school subject, so at first didn't register much. Quite soon I became aware that she was being nice to me and actually encouraging me. This was a novelty, as most teachers regarded me as a pest, to be tolerated with difficulty, or thrown out of the classroom. Gradually I began to enjoy English, and even tried to write some interesting essays, and I looked forward to English classes every day. Suddenly, I was passionate about *Far From the Madding Crowd*, *Silas Marner* and *A Tale of Two Cities*. A whole new world seemed to be opening up, filled with powerfully evocative situations and fascinating characters. Miss J became my hero. When I discovered that she ran a weekly SCA (Students' Christian Association) session during the lunch hour, two of us from the gang started going. To my great surprise, I found some of it interesting, and I began asking Miss J for books that I could read to find out more. Some fascinating films were shown about the amazing universe and how there must be some intelligent creator behind all this material world. I really got into theology. The wonderful irony then was that I purposely got myself thrown out of various classes so I could go to the library to read theology and philosophy. Of course, I then found out that Miss J went to the Baptist church and taught Bible class there, so I started going to that too. My mother was puzzled, but also much relieved as she could only perceive this as a change for the better. And so, inevitably, as an unhappy and mixed up teenager, I "got converted" and became a "committed" Christian, winning all the Sunday school prizes. But this certainly did not stop me from recklessly riding my bike and making a row to draw attention to myself. However, I did become somewhat more cooperative at school, and tried to work reasonably hard even at subjects I didn't like, which was most subjects.

But all these new interests couldn't disguise the fact that I was ANGRY, and had no rational idea of how to handle it – I just struck out in a confused and anguished fashion. My mother, who was loving and very principled and responsible, was in an extremely difficult position of trying to juggle her care for me, and how to deal with a husband who was also angry and immature. On the surface, I was rejecting her values, and learning those of my father with whom I had this love-hate relationship. So, my first real role model outside the family, Miss J, was very influential. Interestingly, rather surprisingly, she appeared to hold much the same values as my mother and, although I was unaware of it at the time, this helped me to begin to form a value system that I could consider my own and was, in fact, very close to many of the ideas I had unconsciously absorbed from my mother.

UNIVERSITY

When I went to Varsity in 1960, as my mother had always intended I should, and had saved the money to send me, I chose an Arts degree, not for my mother's sake, but because I had learnt to like English and Theology. Suddenly a whole new life opened up for me. I could choose subjects that I liked – English, Biblical Studies, Theology, later Art History – and for the first time in my life I was motivated to study and to work hard and with enthusiasm. For some time at high school my ambition had been to run away to the Wild West of the USA and become an energetic, rowdy cowboy. There I would dress as a boy and ride horses, and nobody would ever again know I was a girl. Girls were silly, frilly, and wimpish, couldn't run properly, or throw a ball, or ride bikes fast, and I wasn't having any of it. Now I found a whole realm of challenging new interests, and I did well, and enjoyed the image of myself as a student sitting at my desk reading, although I had many moments of anxiety that I wouldn't succeed – but I did, and no one was more surprised than myself.

On going into residence at Varsity I was surprised, and somewhat embarrassed, at how homesick I felt. I missed Ma tremendously, even though she was only up the hill at Hilton, and a phone call away. I went home every Saturday for the day, and wanted to share with her much of what we were studying in various classes. She was, of course, very interested, and began to read a number of the English set books, as well as some of the Biblical Studies and Theology works. I remember later, when I was doing Honours, she read a couple of the books on existentialism which I was finding fascinating. I didn't actually have any real discussions about the material with her, as there had always been this considerable reserve between us, and I didn't know how to conduct any sort of a personal dialogue with her. There was always a kind of embarrassment on my part, and I think at times on her side too, that anything too personal might arise, things too difficult to cope with. So there was a strange mixture of closeness and distance that I don't think was ever really bridged. But I needed to share much of my factual, as opposed to my emotional, interests and life with her.

One of the most exciting things about Varsity was being able to pursue my interest in religion, both in a personal faith way, and as an academic discipline. I did full courses in Biblical Studies and Theology, which was what was offered then, and later became one of the first two women in the department to go on to Honours and then Masters. My interest, even passion, in these subjects, grew steadily over the years, and branched out into Religious Studies, involving an exploration of other religious traditions. Some of us went together to churches of different denominations every Sunday evening to experience as much variety as we could.

This progression involved a long personal journey away from the Baptist church, back to Anglicanism (which was what I was nominally brought up in), leading later to a questioning of most of the cardinal doctrines of Christianity, and finally to a realisation that I was no longer able to fit myself into that box. I was never a fundamentalist, even in my five or so Baptist years, and being able to look at other denominations from a distance allowed me to appreciate the Anglican tradition anew. I found that I was strongly drawn to the ritual and colour, the richness of the complex liturgies (helped by TS Eliot), as well as the excruciatingly soaring and cascading music. My mother was extremely pleased when I accompanied her to church, and appeared to be safely established in a "respectable" fold. But still my old rebelliousness and questioning would not allow me to be a conventional or conservative anything!

From the early 1990s, with the encouragement of a colleague, I developed a consuming passion for studying Hinduism in Natal, particularly as it affects women. This research finally culminated in my PhD, which is something I had certainly never expected to do, but has proved to be very affirming.

At Varsity in the sixties I became passionately interested in the new Hippie and Beat Generation, and avidly read Jack Kerouac, Allen Ginsberg and others. Also the great anarchist Jean Genet, as well as Camus, Sartre and de Beauvoir. I enthusiastically espoused existentialism, doing a considerable amount of reading round the subject, and my motto became "Doubt everything". I could not for long manage to look or behave like a conventional Christian, which tended to upset many of my more conservative Christian friends. Whenever possible, I wore jeans, and went barefoot, experimented for a time with minimal bathing, and slept in my clothes. It was not considered respectable, then, to go to town, let alone to church, in trousers, and again my mother was somewhat puzzled and disappointed.

I also began to develop a political and social conscience through my association with other Christians in the SCA and Anglican Society. The early sixties were a time of considerable political protest at the increasingly restrictive laws being passed, and many political marches were held, starting on campus and proceeding to the City Hall. I benefited from the animated discussions taking place, both formally and informally, all round me. I was also an avid member of the Film Society where numerous challenging and disturbing foreign films were shown. It was a very stimulating time to be a student, and I loved practically every minute of my undergraduate years.

What about boys/men – the Other? Well, another great surprise about Varsity was that I suddenly had a number of young men coming to the residence to ask me out. Fine – well I liked boys, and was most interested in "male" subjects of conversation. I loved discussing and arguing and, fascinated as I was by the subjects I was studying, especially discussing theology with some of the young Anglican ordinands. But what a surprise when I discovered that this was not mainly what the boys were interested in. At school I had been a pretty asexual being, much too taken up with just surviving, and later with intellectual ideas. It was important to have close friends, and I had my few girl friends, but boys would do just as well. At Varsity I had to begin to come to terms with a whole new aspect of life: SEX.

My Christianity told me that sex before marriage was not acceptable, and I thought that was fine. But, more importantly, I sincerely believed that I did not want to "go the whole way" with someone whom I did not love. Many of my serious discussions with boys ended with groping, but I genuinely didn't find any of them physically attractive, and I knew how far I was prepared to go, which was not very far at all. I turned away a number of avid suitors, and it was not until I was in my first teaching post, at St Anne's Diocesan College, that I began to feel pretty strong stirrings of desire. But the groping just went a little further, and not nearly far enough for my partners. I think, too, that I was quite scared of the sexual thing, because our family has always been very reticent about physical expression of affection, and certainly never talked about sex. It was considered embarrassing to kiss and hug in public, and it hardly ever happened at home either. I have no memories of parents showing physical affection towards each other, and my father certainly never showed it towards me. Another thing that really terrified me was the possibility of becoming pregnant. That was about the worst thing I could imagine, and I was pretty certain that I would kill myself if it happened. I think I was terrified of my own anger, and knew that I would never cope with a yelling, demanding, smelly infant. I still find it difficult to handle small babies, although I find them fascinating creatures to watch from a distance – just as I do all creatures. A bit like game watching! But I find cats more interesting and cuddly.

"THE GREAT WORLD TOUR"

I went oversees for the first time in 1967 and again, looking back on my reactions to this experience, I realise how very closely, emotionally, I was bound to Mother. My travelling companion was a friend of an old neighbourhood friend who, at that time, I didn't know very well although I had been in the same English lectures as her at Varsity. We were away for five months, going up the east coast on the Lloyd-Triestino ship and through the Suez Canal, with a day trip to Cairo and the pyramids. I found life on board ship pretty claustrophobic, with not much of real interest except the excitement of going in at new ports. There was a disco every night, and I frequently found myself attempting to escape the unwanted attentions of various men, even being invited up to his cabin by the small Italian chief engineer. We left the ship at Brindisi and took a ferry to Athens, through the sheer, alarmingly close, grey cliffs of the Corinth Canal. Over the months we got on very well, and I learnt more about life and myself than ever before.

Greece was for me a profound experience in many ways that I have only much more recently been able to analyse. I felt, both geographically and psychologically, further away from home and my security than I ever had before. The whole atmosphere and life-style seemed incredibly "Eastern" and foreign, far from my familiar and secure surroundings. There were times when I experienced what seemed like a physical ache and fear at the strangeness of it all, as well as the intense excitement of new and amazing sights and experiences. But, little did I know then that I would find a whole web of spiritual connections here.

On our second or third morning in Athens, while we were standing looking at our map in Syntagma Square, traffic roaring and swirling past us, a small, bird-like elderly woman in a moth-eaten fur coat spoke to us. She had a strong French accent and, as a true Graecophile, had lived and worked as a teacher in the city for many years. Firstly she led us to better lodgings just off the square, talking all the while of her profound love for all things Classical. Many mornings as we set off on our sightseeing we just happened to bump into her, and she was always eager for a chat. She took us into the Hotel Grande Bretagne, far too splendid for us to have ventured into on our own. She swept us through the vast, luxurious lobby, greeting the liveried doormen in Greek like old friends, and up onto the roof where she pointed out to us the cardinal sites of the city. One of my truly unforgettable characters.

With growing excitement we explored the Acropolis, Agora and Plaka, marvelling at the antiquity and grandeur of what we were seeing, far older than anything we had ever encountered. The wonderful gloomy interiors of the numerous Orthodox churches with their rounded arches, all-pervading incense, numerous icons of the Virgin and other saints, candles, and smoky frescoes evoked a deep sense of reverence in me.

Several experiences in Greece revealed to me my, as yet unrealised, capacity to respond very powerfully to artistic and religious stimuli. I had, at high school, rejected all appreciation of classical music as wimpish and feeble. Rock music, it seemed to me then, was real and spoke to people in the modern world. So my mother's interest in Mozart, Beethoven and other composers was only for old fogies, and had no place in society any longer, although at Varsity I had begun to rediscover the joys of Classical music. In Athens we went to a production of Mozart's Don Giovanni at the opera house, sitting up in the "gods", seemingly teetering above the stage. I was blown over by the power of the music and the story, and wished Mother was there so I could share this with her, because I knew she would have loved it too. I found that I was continually thinking of Mother, and wishing that she could see many of the wonderful things with me. I wrote postcards home to her every third or fourth day, in an attempt to keep in touch with her and to share, in some way, this new, and at times alarming, experience with her.

Then there was the Athens archeological museum. Coming round a corner, and looking down the openings through the next few rooms, I was confronted with the huge bronze statue of Poseidon, ancient Lord of the Waters, throwing the trident. I was stopped rigid in my tracks by its overwhelming power that no picture or photo could ever capture or convey – and I found, rather to my horror and embarrassment, that tears were running down my cheeks at the sheer magnificence and energy of the figure. And a few days later in Delphi I had a similar, but even more powerful, experience with the charioteer. His hands still grasping the reins, his eyes glinted, moved, triggering a frisson which, on that late, cold spring evening in a silent, empty part of the gallery, hypnotised me, rooted me to the spot with his exquisite beauty and vitality. I had never seen anything so wondrous in my life, and again I had to wipe away tears that took me completely by surprise.

The next evening just before sunset we climbed up and up the steep, rough path to the stadium, that vast ancient sports arena, high above the archaic temple of Gaia, Earth Mother, Omphalos, Navel of the Earth. Silvery gnarled olive trees and pink almond blossom thrived in the arid earth at the side of the path. We stood, silent, right under the towering, almost menacing, grey cliffs of Mount Parnassus, with views down the deep, wild ravine to the Corinthian coast far below. The top of the mountain attracted light wisps of cloud, and far above the birds of prey, dark shapes, circled and circled in eerie silence. Despite the stillness, something barely perceptible seemed to pulsate in the air. As the light faded we reluctantly prepared to leave down the side path through the woods. I paused, looking back for one last attempt to absorb the atmosphere, and suddenly the massive grey rocks of the mountain seemed to be moving upwards and curling down over me like a tsunami – I began to feel crushed, my throat and chest so constricted I could barely breathe. My sense of panic in the presence of this terrifying power started me running, and I ran for my life down the rocky path through the darkening pine trees, stumbling over roots and rocks, gasping for breath, until I caught sight of the red, comforting roofs of the village below.

I experienced in a most direct and overwhelming way the reverence the ancient Greeks had felt in the presence of the mystical potency of nature, instinctively choosing sacred sites for their "numenosity" – so that we, thousands of years later, could still be enveloped by the mysterious intensity of these power-filled places. I could never explain this to Mother, but I went on writing the postcards.

In Rome, our next stopover, the art, architecture, and sense of historic power of the city was again a new and exciting experience. The Michelangelo Pietà in St Peter's was another of my heart-stopping pieces, but the Pietà in the Duomo in Florence was a complete surprise, as I had been unaware of its existence – totally astounding. I seemed to be doing a lot of uncharacteristic wiping away of tears. An abiding memory in Florence is of the horrifying evidence of the great flood of November 1966, just four months prior to our arrival: the high water mark in many narrow streets was clearly visible along the first floor level of the buildings, and the exquisite Santa Croce had gas heaters burning continually in an attempt to dry out the tiled floor. In Paris we stayed in a pretty basic pension near St Germain on the left bank, and my lasting memory is of walking along the Seine gazing in utter delight at the soaring flying buttresses of Notre Dame. Also, another opera: *La Boheme*, and the excitement of hearing it in Paris!

Arriving in England, where everyone was speaking English, seemed like coming home, and London was so amazing that I felt I had to keep stopping in the street to pinch myself and say, Hey, you're really in London! You're here in the city you've imagined and dreamt of so often, home to so much of the literature you find so haunting and evocative – there's Westminster Bridge with the great crowd streaming across it! I was aware of Mother's presence, too, every day, as they had been in London a few years earlier, and had loved every moment of it.

My father's maternal relatives were Scottish, and I stayed with his cousin Janet Macdonald and her husband Gordon McDonald, a doctor in Edinburgh. They were wonderful people – so friendly, accepting and interesting. We talked long over dinner every night. I had never met any relatives I liked so much and felt so close to, and kept contact with them until they died. My friend and I went on an organised tour of Scotland that included the Isle of Skye, because that is where my father's family originated – the Macdonalds of the Isles, reputedly associates of Bonnie Prince Charley. It was summer now and it stayed light until nearly 11 p.m., days long for exploring. At the village of Uig, on the coast of Skye, after dinner in the evening I wandered over the hills above the cliffs feeling the chill wind, watching the dark rain clouds lit up by the slanting rays of sun, and the gulls crying far out over the bay, and felt a deep harmony with the ancient wildness of the place. I loved it, and for the first time in my life was aware of feeling some deep connection with my beloved grandmother's family, my father's relatives.

Altogether, I was away for five months, and gained immeasurably from the experience, but when my fellow traveller said she wanted to look for a job in London, so that she could stay longer, I knew it was time for me to go home. I felt very strongly then that I could not settle down there and work – that my ties with home, especially to Mother, were too strong. If I were no longer taken up with the excitement of travel, I had to go back to my familiar, safe place, and take up life there again.

TEACHING

It was six months later, at the beginning of 1968, that I got the job at Natal Training College, settling into a fairly demanding and, for some years, most enjoyable period of my life, ostensibly teaching Biblical Studies, but slipping in as much Religious Studies as I reckoned I could get away with. I worked tremendously hard, with great enthusiasm, and in general felt that I got along with the students very well. I enjoyed them, and genuinely wished to challenge them to extend their horizons, so that a knowledge of how and why people of varying cultures and beliefs lived as they did might bring a sense of excitement, as well as tolerance for difference.

The rector who first employed me to teach Biblical Studies was adamant that he wanted me to convey a sense of the importance of the subject, that it was not just some filler that could be treated superficially, something that had to be added to a certificate as an unimportant extra requirement of Christian National Education. However, when, at the end of my first year, I failed a number of students who had imagined it was a pushover, he wasn't so happy. Calling me into his office, he tried to persuade me to raise the marks, and was angry when I refused. But essentially he was a rather silly, weak man, so he capitulated quite quickly, but he did not put me forward for promotion to lecturer during his term as head.

Later, one of the other heads was a particularly uptight "control freak" and soon reacted in a very threatened manner when he realised that I did not fit into the same mould as most of the other women staff members, who would do exactly as he required. Gradually over the years he made my life as difficult as he could, seemingly "spying" on me, trying to catch me out on small things like coming late for a lecture, which was very difficult as I am habitually particularly punctual. He watched out to see if I came on time in the morning, even if I didn't have an early lecture, and whether I left too early in the afternoon or snuck out during the day, which, in general was allowed. He would look for me on some pretext if he suspected I wasn't there. He even had the temerity to make veiled, critical comments on the way I dressed even though the dress code for teachers had been much relaxed by then. It became increasingly evident that he suspected that my single lifestyle wasn't entirely conventional, and he was obviously considerably threatened by it.

At some stage I had encountered homosexuality in my reading and thought quite a lot about it, coming to the conclusion that there was nothing wrong with it, as long as it was between consenting adults. I was, of course, madly in love with Miss J who was still a powerful influence in my life, but I was unable to recognise the exact nature of my feelings.

It was only when I was 27, and just before I moved to my teaching post at Training College that I met Jay. We talked intensely, and found we had many interests in common. Very soon we were kissing and making love in a most passionate and exciting way. My whole body and my head said, Yes, Yes, Yes, this is it; this is right and what I've been waiting for. But, although I had no real problem with accepting my sexuality myself, living in a society that generally condemned it was mostly agonisingly difficult, at times very scary and stressful.

The main reason that I designed and had my house built in 1973 was to create the privacy needed to conduct an "illicit" relationship. At work, too, I had to be extremely careful to hide the relationship from almost everyone. Working for the Natal Education Department, as I did at Training College, and teaching Biblical Studies, demanded absolute secrecy, as any knowledge of such depravity would have cost me my job.

The Rector suspected something that he didn't understand or like, and tried to get a hold on something that could be used to get rid of me. An exam paper where I set a critical question about the beliefs of Karl Marx, and the effects of his Christian upbringing on his ideas, was objected to by a parent, and there was a complaint. It was made out that I was promoting Communism in my lectures, and so corrupting the students. The rooigevaar! Reds under every bed! The Boss called me into his office and threatened me with a disciplinary enquiry, later saying he would withdraw it if I agreed to try for a post at the university, which, he maintained – probably correctly – would be more suitable for me. I refused, and fought for my life, and the vice-principal supported me, as did some other members of staff. Eventually it blew over, I suspect mainly because the rector came to realise that he was in danger of being drawn into the Nationalist Party ideology which he actually despised. But it was a very scary warning of the way the land lay.

Until the year before the Nationalist Government closed the college in 1987 in a kind of "scorched earth" policy as they detected the end of the regime, I was not promoted to lecturer, when all the other women who had joined the staff after me had either come in as lecturers or even senior lecturers. And I was more qualified than any of them. It seemed quite clear to me and my various friends on the staff that I was being punished for not toeing the party line, and for standing up to the Boss. He was a very threatened man, despite all his protestations about being innovative.

At the beginning of 1976, when my relationship with Jay broke up after six years, with much unhappiness, it was agony to try to hide that I was bleeding to death inside, and to pretend that I was just, inexplicably, feeling depressed. The grief of loss; a sense of no future. I had never felt so alone, and at times really wished I could die.

During my utter despair at my failing relationship, my lower back began to give me terrible trouble. It got worse and worse, until I was afraid that I might end up in a wheel chair, at the age of 33. I found it almost impossible to walk up straight, and continually got the most awful cramps down my legs – teaching, driving the car, and getting out of bed in the morning became an agonising exercise. I got to the stage of having to take a Beserol and smoke a Gauloises cigarette before the cramps would stop and allow me to get out of the bed. Also I found it very difficult to get out of the bath, as I couldn't sit up from lying on my back – nor could I bend over to make my bed. Mom suggested I go "home" to their place so she could help me bath. And so began a period of increasing physical dependence on Mother; she never complained and was constantly there to help and to try to comfort me. At least my back problem was a genuine physical ailment and could be openly talked about, one for which I got much-needed sympathy. Standing in front of a class was agony, and I often had to hold onto the blackboard behind me to try to keep myself upright. I did everything I could to disguise the pain as I didn't want the students to see how weak I was. Eventually, the physiotherapist suggested I see an orthopedic surgeon, who put me in a brace, like a Victorian corset, which helped to give stability to my back – I even slept in it. But then, just before we had to go out to the schools to start "critting" student lessons – which I hated, and was particularly dreading that year – the doctor decided to put me into hospital, in traction. What a relief! Just to be able to lie there, unable to put foot to the ground, and have the nurses do everything for me. Not to have to battle to get out of bed every morning, and drag myself through the day, trying to pretend that the pain was manageable. It was remarkable how quickly I overcame my profound fear of hospitals, and the smell associated with them. And there were some exceptionally attractive nurses.

Finally, an operation to remove a damaged disc and the pain was over, and I could try to start all over again, try to get my life together again. And gradually over many months I discovered I had the strength to be able to live and manage on my own, and do things that brought enjoyment.

And then, totally unexpectedly, I met Mary.

THE JOY OF LOVE

Mary is my third serious lover. There had been other women with whom I had made love, and I have never had guilt feelings about "one night stands", or brief affairs with women who I have not been in love with. The loving, of whatever sort, with a woman, always seemed to be some kind of genuine and honest expression of a feeling of deep affection. Since deciding that I am gay/lesbian, I had had one or two encounters with men where I did, more or less, "go all the way", but they were generally not particularly enjoyable, and certainly not in any way satisfying. They merely seemed to confirm my conviction that I do not find men sexually or emotionally fulfilling, and that I could not fall in love with one. Maybe many will think that I simply haven't met the right one, and they might be correct, but I'm not interested.

Mary. Well, we met in 1984 (Orwell's significant year), and certainly a great turning point in my life, and my perception of myself as a woman. It was so wonderful, for the first time, to live with someone, and to know that we could spend every night together, and enjoy lovely things together, every weekend, any time we felt like! It is Mary who has taught me what it means to be a feminist, to be proudly women-identified. And lesbians have the unique opportunity to be totally women-identified: not sleeping with the enemy! I had, before I met her, been becoming more and more interested in what I understood about feminism, but I didn't really have anyone with whom I could discuss and argue. She showed me that I didn't have to become a boy in order to have fun, be confident and independent, and live as I chose. What a relief it was to break those sexual stereotypes completely! To become a strong, loving, angry, rational, emotional, gentle woman. To feel, above all, that I could be angry; that there were some things one had a right to be angry about, and that this anger could become a powerful motivating factor in one's life. I began to feel that I was really able to take some kind of control of my life, and to quite like the person I had become.

My existentialism provided the tool to refuse the temptation to become a victim of circumstances: the whingeing attitude of "I can't help who I am". Even though some aspects of our lives are "givens" which we cannot change, we can avail ourselves of the freedom to choose what we make of what has been thrown our way, and take responsibility for who we are and what we wish to achieve in our lives.

With Mary I joined my first women-only organisation, the Black Sash, which provided an outlet for my anti-government, anti-apartheid feelings. Together with other like-minded and determined women we became involved in street protests with placards, writing letters to the paper on human rights issues. Several times we were arrested, either together or separately, and once a group of us was charged with an illegal gathering that led to a court case. Although it was quite scary, and had possible serious implications, the solidarity between the women, and our temerity to laugh at the snarling, boorish security policemen who took our fingerprints and mug shots, strengthened our resolve not to be

139

intimidated or distracted from our stand. The Enemy: Patriarchy in all its overwhelming, threatening ugliness. Disobeying the oppressive, illegitimate regime brought its own kind of thrill. Eventually the magistrate threw the case out of court, and castigated the Special Branch police for wasting the court's time. A small victory, but a great sense of belonging to a powerful movement with right on its side.

And we do almost everything together, and share how our day has been, and how we feel, and when we are happy, or unsure, or angry. We are best friends and lovers, and we share almost all our interests in common. We were delighted to discover when we first talked and talked that we are both avid Iris Murdoch fans, and couldn't wait for her next book to come out. We both felt we had lost a dear friend when we read of her death. Of course, we do some things separately, but not many. There is a theory that lesbian lovers tend to absorb each other, becoming too dependent on each other, and lose their separate identities. There is, possibly, some truth in this, but it need not be all negative. We certainly know that we have a closer and more supportive and trusting relationship than most of our straight friends, even our gay male friends. Mary was already "out" as a lesbian when I met her, and she terrified me by happily telling everyone she met about our new affair. I was still at Training College and needed to be very circumspect about my private life. Going to teach at Varsity in 1988, after I was made redundant by the closure of Training College, was the first time that I felt free, openly, to admit my sexual preference. It was amazingly liberating and affirming to find acceptance, and even positive support, there.

Largely because of Mary I began to realise that women are a respectable, even desirable, subject for academic research and writing. Teaching Religious Studies at Varsity for twelve years impressed upon me that religion is one of the last and most persistent bastions of male dominance. So my writing about Hindu women began in an attempt to make their lives more visible and appreciated; to help those who are unable to tell something of their own stories, and to do it in a supportive, honest, and non-judgemental context. My hope is that some traditional Indian women might, through my writing, gain the courage and the strength to claim some real independence from the patriarchal society in which they live. And, for my part, I love writing, get great satisfaction and a sense of achievement from it. It is in some way empowering for me too, as the writing of this account has been.

I have often wondered how men, the Other, see me. Well, it depends who they are, of course. The "average" sort of guy whom I encounter might well see me as unattractive (hairy legs!), somewhat unfriendly (doesn't under any circumstances flirt), lacking in a sense of humour (is offended by sexist and corny jokes), impatient (especially with macho posturing), too serious, and at times just plain rude. I think that some of the men I know quite well, and who know me fairly well, may see me as relatively capable, hardworking, reliable, honest, if somewhat intimidating, and at times quite amusing.

My mother has been, mostly without my realising it, or perhaps admitting it, a powerfully influential force in my life. She died, rather unexpectedly, in September 1997, on the third day of a tour to Italy Mary and I had embarked on. We were devastated, so far from home, but found some small comfort in lighting candles for her before the images of the Mother in countless richly adorned churches. Her death left me with a deep, aching grief. My father and I missed her terribly. This led me to try to work through the nature of my relationship with her, and what exactly she has meant to me. How emotionally close I was to her, even if there were many things we never talked about and I was unable to tell her. Like who I really am, who is most important in my life, although I suspect she did have possibly more than an inkling, but didn't feel she could talk about it either. How I needed her to be geographically close so I could see her frequently, even if that physical proximity seemed at times intrusive and irritating. But I always needed to be able to pop in and talk, even if I avoided saying the things that were really important.

What about my father? After Ma died he was pretty well wrecked without her, was very depressed, and his health deteriorated fast. He became quite pathetic and decrepit, and increasingly dependent on me for emotional support. What an irony! He definitely mellowed, and began to show, in various low-key ways, that he wanted some kind of forgiveness for his rejection of me, although he couldn't actually say so. But he hinted to Mary that he knew why I had been angry with him most of my life. I was not sure what forgiveness meant in this context. I certainly felt very sorry for him, and tried to help him in various ways, and talk to him on the phone every second day or so. But, in many ways, I knew that I still didn't like him very much, and I couldn't accept many of his right-wing values and some of the things he said about people. I was aware that I would miss him when he was gone, but then he had always been part of my life.

I certainly can't forgive the patriarchal system of which my father was my first and most devastating example. The ripple effects of war leave few people unscarred, and he and all our family were to some extent its victims. But the daily effects of patriarchy, which is largely responsible for creating wars, are far more insidious and pervasive. Because women suffer most from male domination, it is they who have to be conscientised to recognise its appalling effects, and so become motivated to do battle against the structural violence it perpetuates. I learnt that it is women who have most to gain by working for a new, more egalitarian, peaceful social order. My anger, our anger, and countless millions of other women's righteous anger will, hopefully, provide the motivation for bringing some sense of healing.

Dad died in June 1999, rather sooner than I had expected he would. He had been very unwell and frail since 28 May when he seemed to have a "mini stroke". He needed more and more done for him and I saw him every day and, in some way, got closer to him than I had ever been. In the last few months of his life he had shown more clearly that he wanted to be close to me, and to Mary, and said on many occasions how kind we were being to him, and how he appreciated it. He wanted to pay for all kinds of things for us, and loved being taken out to meals. Probably the last highlight of his life was my doctoral graduation ceremony, when we took him to the "VIP" cocktail party first, and then out to dinner afterwards. He was exhausted by the whole evening, but really enjoyed it and, of course, cried quite a lot because Mother was not able to be there. And I, too, missed her terribly, wishing so much that she could have known that somehow I had made it; achieved something really worthwhile.

Since his death I have missed him more than I could ever have imagined, which I'm quite pleased about, because I think this means that we had achieved some real closeness. I now know that I can somehow forgive him, because I realised from my own experience and what Ruth, their friend, says he told her, that he was so obviously tortured by how awful he believed he had been in the past. I feel, for the first time in my life, that I am able to appreciate some of the things that he was and did, and even to feel some sense of gratitude to him, as well as my strong feeling for Mom. And, as I grow older, I keep recognising them in things I do and say, something that is not altogether unpleasant – in fact, quite amusing and comforting.

And most amazingly, perhaps not surprisingly, shortly after mother died, I had a vivid and powerful dream of myself and Mary standing on board a ferry as it pulled away from the quayside, waving to my mother and father who were standing on the shore, in a characteristically Greek landscape with a backdrop of dark spreading Mediterranean pines and tall, thin, sad cypresses. The old deities retain their ancient all-pervading power, still manifesting themselves in the beauty and terror of the natural world, and all life.

MMAPASEKA "STEVE" LETSIKE At the time of writing this story, Mmapaseka "Steve" Letsike was project manager at OUT (LGBT) Well-Being, a non-profit organisation which promotes the rights of the LGBTI community, by providing physical and mental health services to this community. Currently she works for The Open Society Initiative for South Africa in Johannesburg, promoting their ideals of assisting people to understand their rights and responsibilities in an open and democratic society. She is passionate about human rights, and working for the implementation of the constitutional rights and the empowerment of those in the LGBTI community. She was honoured by being chosen as one of the 300 Young South Africans voted by the Mail & Guardian in June 2009.

THE "STEVE" IN ME HAS A RIGHT
MMAPASEKA "STEVE" LETSIKE

Twenty something years ago, a child was born. The child was named and recorded as a girl in the hospital files and based on what the doctors had seen. And, because children are only differentiated by the two sexes (male or female), and we are not even going to consider the third sex (intersex), which is ignored most of the time – so that most want to try to box the new born into the only two socially-constructed boxes – yes, it was confirmed: a girl I am. I am not intersex, and I worry about those young ones who are born, with or without their parent's expectation of whether they would like to have a girl or a boy.

As a girl, I guess I had no choice but to be given my grandmother's name, saying it's a family tradition to get an elder's name, but still we had no choice. But I won't say the name …, never mind, it's not a train smash, life goes on. This particular girl had two siblings: a brother Stephen, named after the grandfather, and a sister Peggy, named after the aunt. And later, after a couple of years, she had another sibling, the younger brother Peter, named after the uncle. What did we do to deserve this? But I guess it has been a family practice where, when a child is born, the child will be named after an elderly person in the family.

I think it's a Catch 22 situation. When I grew up my parents had a lot of expectations, and they brought me dolls and all that, and I was expected to only have girl friends. It was easy, I did the opposite; I would climb trees and play with brick stones, reflections of my ideal cars. Nevertheless, I continued to play with boys a lot … And importantly I used to identify as a boy. By then I had boy friends and we would do things together: play, ride bicycles, take the train to town, and it used to be fun, then, as we were young with no worries.

I had to fight for my childhood. MINE: not the childhood that I was expected to display based on socially-constructed norms. But, did my family care? They all wanted the girl in me, and at some point I gave in, particularly because of the confused definitions of culture that we have adopted. I believed in humanity, while my family and community believed in systems; but those systems are made and could be changed. But it's hard to change systems, and they also depend on multiple layers. So you can imagine when you start setting levels of systems that we believe in, and that we all want to be correct – such as the likes of religion, tradition, what we were taught, what our leaders say, expectations, experience, needs and what benefits us … the list is endless – it complicates things.

So, you can imagine the child in those days, pre- and post-apartheid. Some days, together with my struggle, I displayed the boy in me, or rather the tomboy in me, because that was the identity expected of the girl child. But still I identified as a boy.

I have this wonderful complicated family, very close, although there is much which keeps us separate based on what we don't agree about. But it is a lovely family. The family that kept me on my toes, when they would refuse most of what I wanted to do. They instilled good discipline and morals for their children's development.

I guess I was the lucky one to keep my childhood; but it wasn't an easy journey, when a family keeps on pushing the fact that one should rely on religious, traditional, cultural morals, as it is good for people. I didn't think they were not good. I thought at times all an individual needs is a good life experience as all elderly people have experienced theirs. Our families have many expectations and would do anything for their expectations to be met – and they all say this is good for you. Well, sometimes it's not. I see it with a lot of friends, and also when I travel and see all the young women and men displaying their families' world-views and needs. In this century we are still confronted with people who are unable to start living their own lives; they separate, but exude their needs, and all they live to do is feed the expectations of their family members. Expectations which could be based on many ideas, such as the economy, or social, religious or cultural issues, or fear of our parents disowning us. But at the end of the day we live in a world that is full of opportunities and a world that is waiting for us to grab and fulfil those opportunities.

I did almost everything that I thought was expected of me, but I also thought my life was as important as theirs, and after school I would have to live on my own. This is what I remember of my life now. When I was six, I was attending Sub A (now known as Grade 1) at Makgwaraneng Primary School. I was always regarded as a strong young one by my late mother, Johanna, and my grandfather, Stephen. I would run and do what was expected of me, because it is good to listen to your elders and do as they say, but, hey, I used to make it difficult for people. I remember my mother used to tell my sister and me that when we walked to school we must hold each other's hand and walk together. One morning I decided to walk without holding my sister's hand, and she got angry because we needed to get to school on time, and I *would* walk on my own: "Don't touch me!" She walked a little faster and I was left behind. I did not know how to cross the road, which was a main road. I had learned looking left and right, and only to cross when it was safe. I tried, and I managed to cross half way, but when I got to the other side of the road all I remember is being hit by the mini bus. I was under that mini bus, and I could only cry and call for my mother. And that is what we did before we went to the hospital: they took me home to get my mother. It was one of the things that was said about me: I was trying to be taller in everything I did.

I never got to spend much time with my mother and father, as I lost both of them in the same year, when I was only seven years old. My brother Trompie was thirteen years old, my sister Lesego (Peggy) was nine years old, and my younger brother was only five months old. I only had my two grandmothers and one grandfather who I was very close to, and fond of as well. He used to be my sunshine – he understood me, and never in his living days made me feel less of a person or less of a child. My grandfather and I loved each other very much. I remember most of the things we used to do together. When I came back from crèche or school I used to find him in the lounge drinking his beer, and he would pour me only one cup of beer, just to sit with him and not go outside. I still remember my uncle had a Spaza shop (mini supermarket) that had games like Pacman, Street Fighter, a gambling machine and more. I used to be the lucky one, as he would give me R1 to play the machine and I would come back having won R30, more or less, but

I would always give it to him. I think one of the things was that we were always there for each other, including when he got paid every month and he would give me money to go spoil myself as well.

Ag! most memories I still cherish, and will share with my daughter and maybe with my grandchildren one day, if I have any. You know, losing my grandfather in 1998, and two years later one of my grandmothers, I thought I would never get anywhere. But I had been taught that culture, tradition and religion are important, so I was able to believe that the ancestors are always around, which I still believe. And I remained with my living ancestors, my grandmother who is 77 years old (mother's mother), and my great grandmother who is 106 years old now (my grandfather's mother).

I am spiritually connected to God Almighty, even though I don't usually go to church to praise him; I do it in my own comfort zone. I used to go to church when I was young. For my grannies, I attended both the Lutheran Church and St John Apostolic church. I was baptized and confirmed in both the churches. After my confirmation in church, I had said to Reverend Khoza at the Lutheran Church that they would never see me again. Truly, that did happen. The reason was that all girls after confirmation are not allowed to wear pants any more, but are required to wear skirts. The same went for St John Apostolic church. If one is uncomfortable about dressing according to the rules and regulations, people should just let you be. I have always said that one does not bring fashion or clothing to school, church, or even the work-place; you bring your mind, heart, skills, and so on. If I go to church, I am there to praise God, if I am in school I am there to learn and build my knowledge, if I am at work I am there to work. All of these have nothing to do with my attire, how I dress.

One day I went to the Lutheran Church after not setting foot in it for thirteen years, and to my surprise when I got there they still had the same system of women on the one side and men on the other side. I went there in my pants, my jacket and shirt, and because I am a woman I went to sit as expected in the women's section. And everyone was shocked and was wondering "Why is this man sitting with the women?" After the church service, I went to several elders, including those I still remembered. When I got to them I greeted them with all due respect like we always do, and

I said, "Do you remember who I am? I am Mmapaseka, the late Squeza's granddaughter."

And they all remembered, saying, "Aoo, Mmapaseka, is that really you? We haven't seen you in ages, look how old you have grown." And one of them asked me, "Why don't you come to church any more?"

I said to them, "You have realised what people have been saying about the man in the women's section." He said, "Yes" and I said that was the reason why I wasn't coming to church. "But I am here now, and I am only paying a visit to see how you guys are doing."

It felt good to be remembered and recognised, and all I wanted was to be. But none of them wanted me to live my life as I wanted; they all wanted me to live according to their expectations.

When we were young we used to play house and you would find four or five children playing house. I liked being the father, and if I was not the father I would want to be the young boy, somebody's brother. And I loved it. During my days at Mboweni Higher Primary School, I would do everything: be in the school choir, the debating group for the school competitions, sports (netball and soccer), as well as being part of the drama group. I refused to play the girl – I wanted so badly to be a boy – and I managed to get the part after speaking to the director (Bethuel) of the group. I was then named "Ike" in the drama group. By then I had realised there was another girl like me in the same school whose name was Mahlaole (Sorrow). She was a girl, but also wanted to be a boy. So we then became friends and we would do everything together. We would borrow each other's clothes. I would steal my brother's trousers to be comfortable and act with my brother's clothes to represent the Ike in me. I had grown to love being me, and when I say me, I mean a boy in those days. I met a couple of lesbian girls in the same school and remember that I hated them, because I kept on asking myself, "Why do these girls pretend to be boys but still identify as girls?" It really caused me confusion. I did not want to be around them, not understanding why, but because I saw myself and identified as a boy. And, growing up in a heterosexual environment, you are either a boy or a girl. There

MMAPASEKA "STEVE" LETSIKE

would surely be no girl who would dress up like a boy and pretend to be a boy, but still identify as a girl.

My life as a young boy was great and challenging. I played boy's soccer, and I used to be a star. And that is how I got my name "Steve". A family friend said I played like Steve Mokone (the first black South African to play soccer in Europe), and started calling me Steve. All my friends started calling me by the name Steve, and I loved it, identifying myself as *"I am Steve"*. Most people recognised my dislike of a binary gender expression. Although I was legally named Mmapaseka, I was given multiple male names throughout my young days that represented my boyhood. My mathematics teacher – who was also my soccer coach in school – used to call me Rrapaseka, which was the male equivalent of my real name.

A challenge came when I couldn't play for the boy's team any more and had to make a transformation to play for a team called City Sharks Ladies Football Club. The reason given was that I couldn't play with boys as the rules and regulations stipulate that girls must play with girls, and boys with boys – rules which I thought could have been amended. It really made me feel so bad and upset, but for the love of the game I had no choice. I had to go back to the same people who I had shown dislike for and apologise for my reactions. Later I took these moments as a learning curve.

These experiences taught me a lot; I had given myself an opportunity to be open-minded and open-hearted about myself. It displayed my growth, and the achievements and goals that I had to reach. I furthered my studies and was enrolled at Hofmeyr High School. My other granny used to teach in the same school. Most teachers knew who I was and expected quite a lot from me. It was great, as I also expected to be treated the same as any learner in the school. I would go back to my high school days if I could, as it was great being a child and being me at the same time. I remember when a group of teachers called me and asked me to come with my friend whose name then was Brian (the goal keeper). We were then asked, "Why you do like girls?" Another question was, "When you look at yourself in the mirror what do you see?" Brian was older than me, and she replied, "I see a boy". They all expressed amusement about what she said.

One teacher said to me, "You know what, Mmapaseka (calling me by my real name), if Squeza (my granny's nickname) was still here you not would be doing all this; poor Squeza must be turning in her graveyard because of you living this nonsense lifestyle."

I then said, "Mem, you know what, at least Squeza let me be, she never made me feel bad about myself. I am a child and I all I want is to be me." All the teachers did was to make us feel bad, and consider getting boyfriends, rather than being tomboys. And the other one said, "Being a tomboy does not mean you should like girls, so you'd better pull up and get your acts together." By then I thought, That is it, I can't take being in that school any more, but I had to because I didn't like the other schools around my township.

That school followed the rules and guidelines, like the code of conduct which stipulated the uniform and how learners should dress. Girls wore skirts and school socks, and the boys long grey trousers, shirts and ties. As a girl I was required to dress in a skirt, but because I refused, my granny was called several times to my school, and told she had to buy skirts for me. In protest I burnt all the skirts that were bought for me with an iron, and I used to tell my teachers that I wouldn't be able to dress up in a burnt skirt. It took years of practice of doing that and playing that game with them, so that I dressed in long grey trousers full time. I became the first lesbian woman to dress in boy's clothing on a regular basis. I learnt to pull even more strings when I became part of the Learner Representative Committee/Student Representative Committee, and also played a role on the School Governing Body. It was a great adventure for me, as well as developing some of the sporting activities, such as ladies' soccer and taking our school to the top in the Gauteng North District.

Amazingly enough, in those days you had to be someone to be allowed to say something, because of issues of power and its limitation. But for me, I always say the personal is political, and the most important thing is how you put it into practice. At that time I never thought about things in a feminist way, I always thought about being able to be me. Even if it came with all the challenges and hiccups in life, I still enjoyed it. I had never stopped being involved in community work, as I had a passion for change, seeing that there is a lot to change in my community, especially attitudes and the mindset. I had fought and challenged my school, my fellow learners and teachers about a lot of things, and I was able to stand up for myself and the voiceless. There were quite a lot of protests in school during those days: over free education when Kader Asmal was in office as Minister of Education, over abusive teachers and in support of those who were still learning mathematics in Afrikaans. We even protested for Matric dances – even if the majority of the learners failed – because it was their last year in school and they wanted to enjoy their last year of schooling together. Gone are those days, and if I were to choose, I would still return to my high school days; it was hectic, scary, challenging, fun and crazy. But one thing that I wouldn't want is to go back to my experiences of being abused sexually.

As one grows up and creates one's own path, at some points I was unfortunate and at some I was fortunate. But I was able to pull through life and its challenges. I managed to complete my Matric even if people thought I wouldn't pull through. It was tough back then, and I remember how I wanted so badly to continue my studies, even applying for financial aid or a student loan, because my granny couldn't afford it and that might cause her trouble in the long run. My only sibling who had the opportunity to be taken to a higher education level was my brother. We also thought that he would be able to get a job and be able to assist us in obtaining higher education, but it turned out that we were hoping for nothing, as the most important thing for him was his own career and needs.

I remember a friend of mine, Ponstho, who had spent the whole year without doing anything: no school, no work, nothing at all. Pontsho was a year ahead of me in our schooling. On 3 January 2005 I had dragged Pontsho to come with me to search for a university or technical college that would accept us to study through a loan or financial assistance. I only had R60 to transport us to and from town and the surroundings of Pretoria. We didn't have any food, so we had each bought snacks costing us R1. I was finally accepted by Tshwane University of Technology and Pontsho was accepted by Rosebank College, but one striking thing about this attempt to become academic students was that it required money, which we didn't have. Then we decided to go back home to consider plan B for our future development for building our careers.

While I was at home I volunteered to some organisations, including OUT LGBT Well-Being (Lesbian/Gay/Bisexual/ Transsexual), and served on the ANC Youth league. I also did karate and joined several community drama groups. I was employed at a Spaza shop to be able to live. It was difficult, but I managed to put up with all the challenges that I faced – and some were extremely painful, nearly making me lose faith in life – but I eventually made it. I had to catch a wakeup call one day when I had an opportunity to go to work for the Department of Social Development, where I had applied for a job. All the interviewers were expecting a girl, a girl dressed in a skirt with high heels, long hair and the Naomi Campbell walk. Unfortunately for them, I came in dressed in my long-sleeved shirt, long fine-ironed pants, and black square-toed shoes, not to forget my tie … ooh, and my hair shaved. You should have seen all of them when I entered the room; most of their mouths were wide open, and their eyes shocked, as if someone was glued up against the wall. For a minute they were all quiet, and I thought to myself, There goes a job opportunity!

One of them asked me, "Are you Mmapaseka? Are you the applicant that applied for this job? Are you really a woman?"

I replied, "Yes I am a woman, shall we start with the interview."

After the interview, I thought that was the last of it, I would never hear from them again. To my amazement I was wrong. They contacted me the same afternoon, and I was requested to report for duty the following day. That is how my real life started.

Heading the Youth Programme, together with my other colleague, was fantastic, as I had an opportunity to develop career-wise and individually. I met with the intellectuals, the academics, the movers and shakers of life, including a very close friend of mine, Dr Johann Broodryk (the first white person to obtain the doctorate in Ubuntu Philosophy in South Africa). I enrolled at the University of South Africa to start furthering my studies and it felt good to pay my own fees, even though I would have loved it if my parents had been alive and able to pay for me, rather than having to struggle to get a head start in life.

153

Dr Broodryk taught me many things in life, especially about humour, which we call Ubuntu. He even dragged me along to the book launches of many authors, and I didn't miss his own launch, where I would actually be his master of ceremonies for the event. I guess that was one of the things that I have learnt and the beginning of my journey of putting Human Rights issues at the heart. I always knew that I was a Human Rights Defender, and I knew that I wanted to pursue that, as for me the personal is political and my focus always has to do with how one puts it into practice. I then started my adventure of learning about the struggle of people, not only blacks or same-sex individuals, but people living with HIV and Aids, women and foreigners. My focus had to do with the rights of every marginalised person and the most discriminated-against groups.

I had a calling as well as a need to leave the Department of Social Development, determined by the politics of personhood. As a feminist, an activist, an advocate and defender of human rights, I had to answer my calling. Finally, in 2005 I moved to OUT LGBT Well-Being, formally and permanently. It was a heated situation when I arrived at OUT, the period when the Civil Union Bill (same-sex marriage) was under discussion. I had colleagues, mentors and friends such as Melanie Judge, Fikile Vilakazi, Wendy Isaack, Carrie Shelver, Kerry Williams, just to name a few. We had to travel around the country that year when Parliament, the Home Affairs Portfolio Committee, had public hearings. It was hectic due to the fact that we had to be there, and always defend the LGBTI (Lesbian/Gay/Bisexual/Transsexual/Intersex) community.

There was a point when one of the Portfolio Committee members (in fact the chairperson) said to us, "I have seen you from other provinces and all that, but what I would appreciate is for the people in this province to speak for themselves."

We need to look at the facts here, as we were in Mpumalanga and I would regard Mpumalanga as a very conservative province. But we were able to respond and said: "Chairperson, with all due respect, we are quite sure that you are tired of our faces, but you should know by now that the LGBTI group is a minority community, and we are here representing the voiceless and marginalised groups, so you will have to put up with us till the public hearings are complete."

During that time I was flabbergasted when in the very same province, Mpumalanga, there was this old man in his mid-eighties who stood up and commented by saying, "You know, during our time, we were refused to express our feelings, we were forced to even marry the partners that we didn't choose ourselves. I think it's important to allow the following generation space and rights to choose who they love and who they want to marry. It would be unfair to repeat the same mistakes that were done by our parents and the government then, and I would not like to live my life seeing that mistake being repeated again." I think it was sweet and honest of him to stand up for his community like that in public; you don't find people like him often.

We eventually had a victory in 2006 when the Deputy President Phumzile Mlambo-Ngcuka (acting as the President on that occasion) signed the Civil Union Bill into law on the 30 November 2006, just a day before same-sex marriage would have been legalised by the court order from the Constitutional Court. It was a great victory for each and every individual who had contributed to the work of same-sex marriage in South Africa.

On the other hand, while we were busy with marriage, there were other issues: the Sexual Offences Act, Domestic Violence Act, and more. While we acknowledge the fact that one's choice of sexual orientation is recognised in South Africa, it's in the hands of government to try to educate communities about diversity. But it seems we thought wrong – not in this day and age. In 2006 in Cape Town Zwelisa was stoned to death, in 2007 we were faced with the tragic and brutal murders of Salome and Sizakele and the N1 incident that involved a shooting of a lesbian on the highway, in 2008 Eudy Simelane was murdered and Donna was tortured and murdered. These are just a few of the better-known incidents which are a nightmare for us in the LGBTI community. We knew this was happening, but in 2007 we really saw the rise of this brutal homophobic violence. It was very hard that we had to deal with the political part of it, to seek justice, while this was so close to our hearts, our personhood. South Africa does not have hate crime legislation, so LGBTI people's cases are not prioritised and addressed in a manner that highlights the motive for these incidents; it makes our lives a living hell as we all know that these kinds of cases and incidents are based on hatred, and lack of knowledge of what diversity and Ubuntu mean. Part of my work, together with other stakeholders, is to fight these perpetrators and to seek justice for the voiceless.

We have an obligation to create awareness, to celebrate our struggle and embrace our pride in who we are. South Africa has seen the excessive and radical moments, and those are what we remember in the annual Gay Pride celebrations, from 1990 to date. We have seen the growth of Pride celebrations which are now held in almost every province (whereas originally only Gauteng held one). And we are currently seeing a different purpose in the Pride celebrations. For instance, if you look at the politics of the main Pride and Soweto Pride, that in Soweto is more political because the issues are not only race and sexual orientation, but beyond that include culture, religion, education, gender and more. Also, in a township your neighbour knows what you are up to, with whom and when, whereas in town everybody minds their own business. So the visibility creates vulnerability. But at the end of the day transformation has taken place: we used to see only white people in the Jo'burg Pride march, but now we have a more multi-racial approach, including not only black, but also Indian and coloured people, as well as people from different age-groups and different backgrounds. The overall goal is to celebrate our lives and create visibility in a collective manner.

I enjoy my job to the fullest; in fact my life is my job and my job is my life – an everyday thing. I had always seen myself as confident and with high self-esteem – all the time with a beaming smile and a firm handshake. Being the Advocacy and Mainstreaming Manager at OUT has groomed me a lot. I have learnt to work in a comprehensive and holistic manner, and my role is to ensure that our rights are also protected.

Former President of South Africa Nelson Mandela once said to Walter Sisulu: "We walked side by side through the valley of death, nursing each other's bruises, holding each other up when our steps faltered."

156

These words speak of the struggle of black people then, but for me currently they speak about the struggle of being a homosexual in South Africa. We are all protected by the Constitution, but the implementation of the laws is not yet extended to everybody.

As we have seen, there has been an increase in homophobic attacks, stigmatisation and discrimination against LGBTI people. The situation is not unique to South Africa. We are seeing Uganda and Rwanda tabling Anti-Homosexuality Bills that involve some form of imprisonment, and possibly even the death penalty. This while we have policies, declarations, treaties and principles – such as the World Conference on Women held in Beijing, the Yogyakarta Principles and Japan–US treaties – that are supposed to be followed, rather than having selfish leaderships pushing their own personal agendas, in the process putting their own people's lives at stake. After witnessing the horrific trauma of homophobic attack, torture, arrests, brutal murder, rape and more, African leaders in post-independence states should strive to govern in a manner that ensures that all Africans are afforded the highest form of respect in their roles as agents of their own future.

But external power is limited. It has no impact on a person's willingness to please and appease others. When someone is popular, that person has been made popular by other people. This means that someone who is perceived to be powerful does not necessarily own that power – it belongs to the group. The power I am talking about is not only political power, but male power, religious power, cultural power, imperial and military power. We see that abuse of power with President Jacob Zuma and his rape trial. We see it with most of our politicians. In the past decade South Africa has made incredible progress against immense odds with regard to LGBTI people and our struggles. But we have to continue to work on these issues with undivided attention, so that we are able to eradicate and reduce some critical issues that are faced by our communities.

I stand firmly on my rights and the rights of my people. I will fight the struggle to a point where rights become a lived reality for everyone. As we all know, discipline is the most powerful weapon to achieve liberation; an organisation can only carry out its mandate if there is discipline, and where there is no discipline there can be no real progress. And to that I dedicate my duties as a human rights defender: my involvement with other campaigns, including the birth of the 777 Campaign (anti-hate crime campaign), the One-in-Nine Campaign (in solidarity with Women Who Speak Out – only one in nine rape cases are reported), serving in the office of the Women's Sector of the South African National AIDS Council (SANAC), led by the Deputy President Kgalema Motlanthe, and on a personal level, my participation in a variety of community work, including at my previous primary school Makwaraneng, where I have served as deputy chairperson in the past and currently serve as treasurer on the school governing body.

I am, according to the law, a community member not because of what I am doing, but because of what I stand for, because of what I think and because of my conscience. I will stand and fight with my people and share the hazards of war with them. I'm an ordinary person, and have made serious mistakes. I have serious weaknesses. I am learning. I am what I am, both as a result of people who respected me and helped me, and because of those who did not respect me and treated me badly. I will not divert my attention from my task, which is to unite the world. I regard myself, in the first place, as an African patriot.

Midrand, South Africa

Pathways

Mavourneen Finlayson

cover me aching
to inhale you,
fill my breasts
stinging hard nipples
with lustful skin

seductive heat
glistening humid bodies,
your sultry shoulder
divine to taste

take my hand,
uncover the pathway
leading into you
where passion penetrates
every magnetic inch

take my head beyond reason
enter me sensually,
intoxicate perceptions
with quivering depth

SHIFRA JACOBSON "I am deeply interested in authenticity. I studied Movement Therapy in Special Needs Education at the Laban Centre in Goldsmiths, South London. I am an Adult and Popular Educator with an Advanced Diploma in Adult Education and a Post Graduate Diploma in Women & Gender Studies from University of the Western Cape. I am an alignment and massage practitioner, and bodywork specialist. For the last twenty years I have been a trainer/facilitator, focusing on diversity, gender and anti-bias training. Six of my poems have been published in a book *RAINFIRE – Women in leadership in South Africa*, August 2005. I have played a part in actively promoting social change in this country for the past 22 years. I am a multi-skilled educator and have contributed to many publications and training manuals, including *Agenda* (empowering women for gender equity) and *Investigating My Life*, a grade seven educators' guide. I work part-time for Jewish Care Cape, an umbrella organisation for the seven welfare organisations in the Western Cape."

THEN AND NOW
SHIFRA JACOBSON

My story and how to write succinctly about 56 years of a very varied life? Nevertheless I will try.

The Gamsu family, my paternal Grandmother's side of the family, are descended from the scholar Nocham Ish Gamzu who lived in the first century of the common era in the town of Gimzo which still exists in Palestine/Israel today. His grave has recently been found in the ancient Galilean stronghold of Jewish learning, Safed/Zefat, and the street in which it is located has now been named after him. The oral history of the family locates it, later, in Spain prior to the Inquisition where a well-known General Gamsu, a favourite of Isabella, the 15th century Queen of Castile, refused to convert to Christianity. He left his Spanish estate and went to Holland. Later the family moved to Russia.

I was born into a culturally rich and diverse Jewish family, but we were everything but financially rich. My dad was gregarious, socially adept and embraced diversity. My father's side were Bundists, Socialist Jewish workers. Many of the Jewish immigrants who came to South Africa had been inculcated with humanitarian and egalitarian ideals. In some cases these were rooted in traditional Jewish teachings; in others, Socialist and Marxist ideas widespread in Eastern Europe were the basis for these ideals. Some of the immigrants espoused those values that in 1897 had resulted in the General Union of Jewish Workers in Lithuania, Poland and Russia, better known as the Bund. Radical activism was a way of life that some Jews brought to the tip of Africa. My paternal grandfather, Solly Jacobson, was one of the founder members of the South African Communist party. My grandmother, Fanny (Gamsu), was a founder member of the Garment Workers Union. My father grew up in Chapel Street, District Six, from 1918 to 1926. So, yes, I was born into activism at a very young age. My mother's side of the family brought a mix of Austrian and Polish Jewish ancestry.

What does that mean for me today? Shifra is a Hebrew name derived from the Tanakh, the Scriptures: Shiphrah and Puah were Moses' midwives in the house of the king of Egypt and it is rumoured that they lay together as lovers and lesbians. I am proud to incorporate this ancestral heritage into my daily life. I understand that we all originate somewhere, and find ourselves somewhere else, therefore ancestry and origin (although constructed) have always fascinated me because I am a mixture, and these cells of mine are infused and dripping with remembrances of ancient times of Mesopotamia, and being in Pharaoh's court. So, yes, I am an ancient Jewish South African Lesbian, and mother of two black girls – young women, ancestrally Xhosa, English-speaking – my adopted daughters.

My sexuality is my own now, and of course I will always be a lesbian because I prefer women in so many ways over men. That is not to say that I don't like some men, but generally as a group they do not spark my interest or desire.

My maternal grandfather committed suicide in Namibia in 1929. From there my Gran and her three children went to Upington as they had some family there. Later they came to Cape Town. As a destitute single-parent family they became one of the first families to live at the then Jewish orphanage, and my Polish granny worked at Ackerman's shop as a seamstress for forty-odd years.

I grew up heterosexual in that I was completely surrounded by the notion and structure that girls like boys and boys like girls, and that is how it is. Less from my family and more from the mainstream Jewish community, was the notion that because of anti-Semitism and the Holocaust, we girls and women must marry in order to procreate and keep our race/nation proliferating. Honestly, from an early age I never felt that I was the marrying type; however, somewhere in my consciousness I thought that that was what I was expected to do. My parents sent me to the Jewish day school, Herzlia, in Cape Town, although they could never afford the fees and so, for my entire schooling, I was supported as a beneficiary of Jewish welfare. This was embarrassing and shameful in many instances, and early on I realised that there was nothing glamorous about being poor.

I came out as a lesbian in 1978, in London. It was the time of the radical women's movement taking hold. We stormed the Houses of Parliament when the bill on abortion was being discussed. I had my arms jack-knifed by the police, but this did not stop me taking action on property and buildings, especially on billboards that represented women in derogatory ways.

I had been sexually involved with men for many years, in fact since the age of thirteen (I was very physically developed), until the age of twenty-one with the same guy. I was popular with the boys, but at some point in my early twenties I was beginning to feel very frustrated with men at an emotional and sexual level. Like many women at that time, I thought there was something wrong with me because I just did not feel satisfied in any of my relationships or sexual encounters with men. I had always felt equal, even superior, to men and I couldn't for the life of me understand why men treated women as subordinates. Anyhow, I couldn't accept this and thought there must be something different and better out there. Slowly I began to realise that everything in our society promoted the normative ideal of white, heterosexual, able-bodied males. I certainly did not conform to that, and realised that the brainwashing, socialisation, and socially-constructed notion of men being better than women had really started to bug me. I mean, as a child, teenager and young adult I was exposed to men who were termed *moffies*, and they were usually coloured and my mom's hairdresser. Lesbians were a no-no. I think their invisibility as "real women" kept me from encountering very many.

I do remember, when I was about seventeen, I was a member of the first contemporary dance company in South Africa which was very progressive because there were people of colour in our group. We also performed at the Space and Little Theatre where the government allowed a quota of black people to attend the shows. Well, it was during this time that I met an older woman who said she was a lesbian and was very interested in me. I ran a mile (raw homophobia) and told my mom about this woman who didn't look like a man and who was very feminine, etc. I could not understand what was happening because in my mind, from what I had been fed, lesbians looked and acted like men; the propaganda was so intense. My mom disrupted this stereotype for me and explained that all kinds of diverse people and genders can be gay and that you don't have to look a certain way in order to be one.

About twelve years later, when I was comfortable with my identity as a lesbian, I phoned my mom from London and straight out (or "queer out") I told her I was a lesbian. I asked her how she felt. She first asked me if I thought it was a phase I was going through, and when I said no, it was for real, she asked me if I was happy. I said yes, and she said, well that was all that was important for her: that if I was happy, then she was happy. Now, ain't that amazing? My mom proved to be an ardent supporter of gay rights, so that when my former partner and I had a commitment ceremony in 1994, with 200 family friends and colleagues present, she was so proud of us. When we adopted our first child two years later she was in her element. Now my dad's reaction was completely different. He would not speak to me for the two years after I came out and went out of his way to disapprove of my lifestyle. Once I was back in South Africa in 1988, very active in the Defiance Campaign and in a loving partnership, he really changed and accepted my former partner as his daughter-in-law and would introduce her to his friends as such. Both parents accepted and loved my adopted daughters, their adopted grandchildren, so blessedly.

I had left South Africa in 1975 after attending my first ever political protest on the steps of St George's cathedral. It was back then, on Academic Freedom Day, and Helen Joseph (bless her soul) was the speaker. We were all sitting on the steps and were warned by the police, who had batons and dogs, to move back. We defied them and resisted, and the next thing I knew I was being *klapped* over the head by a young, steely, blue-eyed boy of about eighteen, and then I was bitten by his police dog. I had six stitches and left the country within two weeks.

I was 22 and, as I was Jewish, I simply flew to Israel without a hitch. This was because "The Law of Return" accepted Jewish people as if it was a given right to return to the "homeland", even though in that "homeland" Palestinian people, as well as Jews, had lived there forever, but they did not have the same right of return. Wrong, very wrong. After being in Israel for a short while, I became aware of the fact that racism and discrimination flourished. The darker your skin, the more you were marked as Jewish or Arab from Africa, Asia and the Middle East and not as Eastern or Western European, and the more you were discriminated against. This seemed so similar to apartheid, and the way that Arab and Palestinian people were treated made my blood curdle. However, the contradictions for me were mixed in with a great love that I felt for the terrain and its people, so I endeavoured to live there for a couple more years, although my soul and spirit were still searching for something different.

That is when I took myself off to London in 1978. As I said before, these were great times! Because I had a South African passport I had to keep leaving England every few months for Paris in order to have my visa renewed. Eventually I had to choose: it was deportation back to South Africa or a marriage of convenience. I chose the latter and although that was risky in terms of the British Home Office and immigration laws, there was no way that I wanted to come back to apartheid South Africa. My British husband and I never lived together, and within two years I had my British passport. Soon after that we quietly divorced. During this time, I had become active in coalition politics and was very involved in the British anti-apartheid movement, the ANC, the women's liberation movement, gay and lesbian rights, and the anti-fascist movement, as there was a surge of National Front fascism at the time.

I returned to Israel/Palestine in 1981. I lived in Jerusalem and was involved romantically, spiritually, sexually and emotionally for the next six years with a wonderful Sephardi/Mizrachi Israeli woman (Sephardi Jews were descended from the Iberian Peninsula and were expelled in 1492, and Mizrachi Jews are from Arab and North African lands). We eventually separated by mutual agreement and have retained a strong friendship until today. Jerusalem is a most beautiful city – with the highest density of light in the world – albeit deeply divided religiously and politically, undeniably, because of Islamophobia. While I was living in Jewish Jerusalem I contributed strongly to the formation of a women and lesbians' community. We were out and proud, despite the severe homophobia from the Jewish fundamentalist religious right through to the ordinary members of a very macho society. During the day I worked in the "Katamonim" neighbourhood – originally built to house new immigrants – with third-generation Jewish immigrants from Africa, Asia and the Middle East. I was also involved in solidarity work with Palestinian women living under occupation in the West Bank.

It was time, though, for me to leave Israel. It had become claustrophobic and the militarism and some of the policies of the Israeli government wore me down. As I now had the option of being able to travel freely to England, I returned there in 1986. Back in London now, too complicated for detail, I met and befriended Lamont, a young gay black American man who had been discharged from Nato in Germany. Lamont had contracted HIV/Aids and needed access to health care where he was living in Germany. He did not have permanent residency there and therefore was not eligible for state healthcare. As I now had an EEC passport, I married Lamont, which meant that as my husband he could then access health care. We married in London at the Brixton registry office, and needless to say our retinue of friends and family were formidably and mainly gay and lesbian folk. Sadly, those were the severely ignorant and treacherous days of the HIV/Aids virus: There were no anti-retrovirals and people with HIV/Aids were treated badly through ignorance, prejudice and fear. Lamont, my dear soul brother, died in 1993 at the age of 32.

There are gaps and there are losses; leaving and staying, and coming and going, are not for the faint-hearted.

In 1988 I came home at the start or continuation of the Defiance Campaign. I had studied movement therapy, adult and popular education, so I was ready to work for social change. I was also ready for a life partner. It all happened in 1994. The legal end of apartheid, and a lesbian commitment ceremony "like never before": like nothing that Cape Town had seen. We wrote the vows, my late mom did the catering, well-known activists (returned exiles), lent us their magical garden and home. There were approximately 200 friends, family and colleagues present. It was a gathering of note and we declared our love publicly. Everything seemed possible, and it was. With our new Constitution we were able to imagine anything and we knew that we had won our legal and social rights as lesbians, as women loving women.

And so, the idea of family, new kinds of family, crept into our consciousness. It became possible to envisage a life inclusive of children as well. A year of artificial insemination and then discovering that I was infertile was followed by reproductive technology of fertility treatment: the morass of pain and expense while trying to become pregnant was harrowing. The sperm donor and I had to pretend to be married, as there was a law prohibiting lesbians and single women's right to human tissue. So we had to pretend we were married and not gay or lesbian. This was the only way that we could have access through medical aid to fertility treatment that had been, and was still, the exclusive right of heterosexual couples. After a long, draining and emotionally traumatic time of not being able to become pregnant, and a protracted battle to gain access to invasive fertility treatment, I discovered that I was infertile due to scarred fallopian tubes.

After two years of trying, the natural conclusion was to adopt a child, because ultimately that is what we wanted: a child. Then started the process of adoption. At first, at the open adoption meeting, the staff were taken aback as we were openly gay and they immediately told us that they had no white babies. We said we hadn't come for a *white* baby, we just wanted a baby! They said, well we probably will have an African baby for you. We said we would be delighted and honoured! After the checks on our home, our histories, our salaries, and the attendance at a monthly adoption group, and after nine months and one day, a little five-week young baby dropped into our arms, our hearts and our lives. In the interim our predominately gay friends and family had organised a baby shower of at least 30 people at a well known gay restaurant of that time. Because the agency was not used to gay people adopting, and because the law had changed in our favour again, we were very clear about our rights. During our interviews with the social workers, initially we were asked ignorant questions loaded with bias, such as "who is the man and who is the woman?" and "what about sex in relation to the child?". We were horrified at such stereotypical and prejudiced attitudes. However, we realised this was not wilful ignorance and so we went out of our way to educate the social workers about the real meaning of gay and lesbian lifestyles. Three years later we had our second child, only eleven days old, and for her we waited seven months. She was tiny and adorable.

The rest is history, to use an old cliché. The girls are now thirteen and ten. I am now divorced, and a single mom. How could I have known that that relationship would not last forever? How could I have known that at 56 I would have two young children and be on my own? Would I have it any other way? No, this is now my everyday lived-reality. The girls are great company and gorgeous children, and I and the other parent have joint care. It works!

Who am I, then, in the present? I am still a lesbian, and have a transgendered lover far away. The girls are with me every second week, and I have a wonderful circle of diverse friends. I am finally happy. The severe trauma of divorce and loss has taken some years to heal. But I am content, happy on my own for now; this is the current reality of my life. I have learnt over the years that sexuality is fluid, and that my multiple identities grow and change. Who knows what the future might hold …? That is the wonder of life.

One thing is for sure, though: I will always be an out and proud lesbian member of the global LGBTI community.

Love Letter

Mavourneen Finlayson

I remember
in candlelight,
bronzed memories,
facets of your fullness.

I come to face
my love for you:
we entwined, eager,
hungry with desire.

Strong lustful urges
sucking air
cooling damp lips,
rooting the dizziness
searching anchoring ground.

Driven intensely to consume
moving with rhythmic heat –
sensuality raw and wild,
fingers extend forever
melting into cosmic bliss.
With you, I dance.

"PONIE" NOZIPHO NGCOBO is a Project Officer at the Gay and Lesbian Network in Pietermaritzburg.

DISCOVERING MY IDENTITY
"PONIE" NOZIPHO NGCOBO

I come originally from the rural area of Elanskop in KwaZulu-Natal, where I grew up in a family of seven: my Mom, my granny and my siblings. Our family was strongly religious and I went to the Roman Catholic Church every Sunday. Because we were such a strict family we were often not allowed to go outdoors to play, so I used to spend most of my time indoors. I went to a Roman Catholic primary school, and then for high school I was sent to a boarding school in Pinetown, the St Francis College at Marianhill, which was for girls and boys, although we were sort of separated in class.

At school the girls used to play "Moms and Babies", a game where you formed a relationship with someone who asked you to be their baby and then you would play this role with them. When I was in Standard 9 I asked some girl to be my baby and we used to kiss and touch each other, and I realised then that I had strong feelings for her. But because of that incident I was chased from St Francis, expelled. So then my mother sent me to Montebello Girls' High School which was a girls-only boarding school in Dalton. There were quite a lot of tomboys there who dressed like boys and played soccer, and there were some others who I think were truly lesbian as they had close relationships with other girls, although I had never heard the term "lesbian" then. And I also had my first relationship with a girl there. It made me feel very happy, especially when I kissed her. I liked that.

This led me to try to understand myself, so I used to spend most of my time in the library, or asking some girls who were older than me, but there weren't really any books about homosexuality or lesbianism. So in the holidays I used to spend much time in the town library searching for books and that's how I began to find out what lesbianism means. I still wasn't sure whether I was part of it, or whether I was still going to be like my friends, who talked all the time about boyfriends. But I didn't have those feelings at all.

I did my Matric in 1996, and went to M L Sultan Technicon (now called Durban University of Technology) to study for public management. Here there were a lot of different people from different races and backgrounds. I continued to do my research on homosexuality: reading books, going onto the Internet, and talking to others who had more experience about doing research. I also now saw some other girls who I thought: *Oh, she's like me, yes, she is like me.* And so I began to be able to talk to them, and they introduced me to the Compass group for homosexuals on campus. I joined the group, but wasn't active because I didn't know clearly what was happening to me. Although I was still a kind of tomboy, wearing whatever I liked, I was accepted, and at home people just thought that was the way they dressed at the Technicon.

After three years, when I finished my course and went back home, I told my girl cousin about myself. It was raining and my mother was at school where she was a teacher.

My cousin said, "I knew a long time ago; didn't you ever notice?"

So I said, "Oh, OK, now who's going to tell my mother?"

She said she would tell her at the weekend as she was going to be with us. When my cousin told my mother, she was so upset that for two to three weeks she didn't go to school, and she cried non-stop and wouldn't talk to me. I decided to visit my aunt about this, and my aunt spoke to my mother, who then said that maybe she would accept what I said as I was probably just in a phase. She also said that, because I had spent so long in the boarding school, maybe I hadn't met that somebody special – a boy. I hope that one day she's going to change. But she was worried about what she was going to say at church, because she's from a religious family and goes to church, and at that time I was an altar server. Surprisingly, when she went to tell the priest, he said, "Hadn't you noticed? This is the reality". When she came back from there she told me to go and talk to the priest. He said I had to feel free and that my mother was accepting it so far, and I must decide whether I was sure about it.

In my community I was qualified but unemployed, and I now started dating many girls; I was dating and dating, and nobody gave me a problem and they treated me like everybody else. Even the families of the girls I was dating were quite cool.

In 2003 I was invited by Radio Maritzburg to be on a talk show about homosexuality, and that's where I met Anthony Waldhausen, who was also part of the group being interviewed, and he told me that he wanted to set up an LGBT organisation. He asked me to keep in touch so I could be part of various functions, and I could volunteer to help. There were a lot of social events, like parties and pageants, which is where I met many new people. So, when they set up the Gay and Lesbian Network in Pietermaritzburg in 2006, and we got funding, I enjoyed so much being part of this organisation. As I got more involved I began counselling – mostly African people, like those who are still in the closet, still having issues with their families, or who need support or information.

In 2006, in September, I met this girl at a party. Although I had other girl friends at the time, we started dating. She was straight so she couldn't really understand why I said I loved her, and all those things. But we went on dating, because I was feeling that, as I was getting older, I needed a stable relationship and she went along with it. In 2007 we decided to get married, although she still didn't think she was lesbian, but she said she loved me and she wanted to live with me. So in August we went to Home Affairs to get married. We had booked an appointment, but when we got there, we were told to wait, and there was much delay and nothing happened, and then they said we must wait for someone else to come before they could do it. And then it turned out they couldn't do it that day, so we had to go away. There is a number there if you have problems, so I ended up calling that number, and told the women who answered the phone that I had a problem. She said we must go to Home Affairs again, and when we went for the second time everything was fast and quick. Afterwards we had a party and had a "white wedding" where my partner wore a white gown and I wore a suit, like a traditional wedding. For me it was the best day of my life, and I felt really loved by her and by the other people, because there were so many there, and she said it was great too.

Unfortunately we soon started having problems. I think it was because she wasn't really lesbian, and she still had feelings for boys and began cheating on me. And then she started doing abusive things to me, emotionally and physically. She shouted at me in front of my friends and was very aggressive.

I am a "butch" lesbian – I like dressing in "men's clothes" and hate wearing skirts. Even in church I used to wear my brother's things. I feel most comfortable like this, and it gives me more freedom. I also look like my father. But I am a soft, soft person, and I was expecting love and happiness, and the joy of a lifetime, but instead I got the opposite. I think I was the victim of abuse. It was so sad for me. I didn't think that women would do things like that to other women.

We lived in a flat in central town, and we both did the cooking although she only did what she felt like. But I used to do most of the cleaning during the weekends as she was often out doing other things. And so eventually, after about three years, it broke up and she moved out, and we are now in the process of a divorce and I have to let it go. But I think I allow myself to be exploited as I'm frightened of losing the person I love, so I allow things to happen.

I have recently met someone new, but I'm scared to love again, and so I'm trying to take it easy and slow. She comes to visit often and spends most of the time with me, and she is sweet, gentle and kind; also very loving. So far this is just what I need, but I hope it's not going to change.

At the Network, I was firstly a volunteer, which means you only get paid for expenses. In 2006 the Network got some funding and so I was formally employed with a salary. We've grown a lot and now there are six altogether on the staff. I love working here. There are other opportunities for me elsewhere, but I feel at home here. I'm with my people and I can really help other people and I love that. There is so much support here, and I meet so many people, and there is so much to do, especially to sensitise the community about LGBT issues and to help create tolerance. We are planning to go out more and more to the communities to conduct workshops to deal with these issues.

There is still a lot of homophobia out there: for example at taxi ranks if you are seen holding hands with your partner, you are often called names. When I was still married we sometimes went to a social club, where some of her old boyfriends were, and they would sometimes say, "Come here and we'll show you what a woman should do."

Once, when we went to the clinic because my partner was sick and I accompanied her, when we came away from there some boys, including one she knew, came and wanted to talk to her. When she said she didn't want to talk, they started grabbing us and calling us "stabane" (homosexual; literally hermaphrodite). They were pulling us and saying, "We'll show you what a woman is." We went to a police station to open a case of assault and because we had some bruises the police were kind to us and assisted us to lay a charge. At first the police kept contact with us, but I think after about two months we never heard any more from them and I didn't do any follow-up. I think that maybe my partner told them to drop it because she knew the one boy, but I don't really know, because she was often very on and off.

In 2007, when we did our Gay Pride street parade past the City Hall, there were lots of protestors, especially religious people and priests with Bibles, who denounced us.

It's going to take a long time to get things to change, but I think people who have attended our workshops are getting to be more accepting.

ALTHEA LAINE chose to write under a pseudonym for this collection. She was in four unsatisfactory marriages to men before she discovered her "authentic" self and has married her current partner under the Civil Union Act.

LOOKING FOR MISTER – OR IS IT MS? – RIGHT: ON BEING CLASSIFIED LESBIAN

ALTHEA LAINE[1]

Getting married is something I know a lot about. I have organised or helped organise at least six weddings. Five of these have been my own. By now I have enough wedding dresses to open a bridal hire shop. It's a joke amongst my friends and I tell my daughter that she needn't shop for a gown, she can just choose from mine. One of my favourite stories comes from when I became engaged to Richard, my last ex. At the party, one of my nieces asked if they were coming to the wedding, which was to be a grand Medieval–Celtic affair. I explained that the costs were too high for children to attend, so unfortunately no. My niece exclaimed in a very loud voice, right next to my future mother-in-law, "Ah no Aunty Althea, we *love* your weddings!"

I also know a lot about divorce by now and am reminded of Mae West's laconic comment, "A woman scorned quickly learns her way around a courtroom." Don't let anyone kid you; divorce doesn't get easier each time, it just gets more expensive. I don't really know why I got married so much, it just seemed important to make a commitment each time, and I guess I kept hoping that each partner was The One. One friend merely refers to me as a "serial marrier" and leaves it at that.

When I met Diana, fell in love and moved in with her, most people I knew sat back and said, "So, *that's* her problem!" It was as if everyone else knew I was "gay" except me. I hasten to add that I do not mean to fight the label or to hurt anyone who has fought hard to have it, keep it and be proud of it. Diana herself has spent over twenty years battling for recognition and feeling isolated.

---

1   Pseudonym

When she was at school she believed she and Martina Navratilova were the only gay people in the world! Forgive me that I don't want this label, but I actually don't want *any* label. Why do I have to fall into a category?

If I listed all the jobs I have done in my life, all the types of people to whom I've been attracted and have married, and all the roles I have played, I would appear to be worse than Sybil with her seven personalities. The thing is, I believe that's true of most of us. We women are mothers, sisters, wives, girlfriends, workers, nieces, aunts, grandma's, care-givers ... what does it matter who we choose as a life partner? Should it matter? During all my marriages to men I was never referred to as heterosexual. My labels came from just trying so much, not because of who they were.

Diana and I have been together now for seven years, better than my batting average over all the last 25 years and last year we got married, once the Civil Union Act allowed for it. This time I know it's the last time, because she is The One. We are very different as people but we blend together like breathing in and out. Our world values and views are the same; our likes and dislikes are the same; our appreciation of all things beautiful is the same, and we love each other to death. For the first time in my life I have a real partner and it's not because she is a woman, it's because she's Diana and she and I work well together. We have deep mutual respect and we properly support each other in all we do. I don't know of another couple that can work together 24/7/365 the way we do and not get sick of each other. We choose to spend all our free time together and can't bear to be apart.

This marriage doesn't compare with any other I've had, gender notwithstanding. Each one has had its pitfalls and highlights, though I must say at least one nearly cost me my life. My daughter was born from my first marriage when I was only 22 years old. Her father was and is a complete shite, having rejected her from his life when she was only nine, because I chose to send her to a multi-racial school; then not at all the norm. I am eternally thankful for Sarah now; she gives me perspective I wouldn't have had if I weren't a mother. She is also very supportive of this relationship and we have become very close in this last year.

My second marriage was when my daughter was four and I reconnected with an old university flame living in exile and we moved overseas to join him. It had all the ingredients for a heady, romantic, exotic story, but fell apart because, when the chips were down, he couldn't accept Sarah and becoming an instant father. The irony was that he later came to have two children of his own, one of them autistic, and is now a single dad. My third marriage occurred many years later when my daughter was thirteen. "Third time lucky" I hoped and she walked me down the aisle. My father toasted the marriage as a "Cleopatra meets her Anthony" at the wedding and all agreed he was gentle and sweet and sensitive. There was a substantial age gap, but who was counting?

Four months later he went home to his mum because it was too much hard work and responsibility. We hadn't even received the wedding photos back! In addition, he had the temerity to try and sue me for maintenance! He cost me my self-worth and I tried to take my life, as all I saw was the bleakness of failure and lasting love being out of reach. I felt discarded and ugly. I couldn't see the wood for trees – or even the branches. My counsellor went to great lengths to try and show me that each situation had its lessons. It took me many years to see why that particular situation was good for me. It was only really last year that I understood that having my life on a knife-edge was an important step in finding out that my self-worth came from *me*, and no one else.

Husband number four was a big surprise in a way, if such a thing is possible. I was certain I wouldn't marry again and he pestered me. Then a life-threatening situation I found myself in in one of the other African countries made me change my mind. I thought what the heck … we don't know if we have five minutes or five years left. If it works it does and if it doesn't, well it doesn't. Not exactly a good basis for a marriage.

So here I am, after four marriages to men. It's a lot, I know, to anyone actually! There isn't really a pattern. There has been a doctor, a journalist, an architect and an engineer. To say nothing of all the other men I dated and/or lived with, including an IT specialist, a company executive and a photographer. The only pattern has been the constant craving for a real partner, an equal who would love me as I had loved them; someone who would genuinely be there for me, come hell or high water. Someone I could respect and rely on. Someone I could love and not tire of – and vice versa.

I didn't set out to find a good woman. One of my friends who is gay used to tell me the only thing I lacked was "a good woman". Maybe she was right and maybe not. I am not drawn to other women. I don't see them in a sexual light. I don't see anyone romantically, other than my Diana. I love her deeply because of who she is. If I were asked to find one word to describe her it would be "kind". She is the epitome of kindness. She is caring and gentle. She wouldn't hurt a fly – no kidding. When we sold the house we bought together last year, she got me to do the Polyfilla thing where ants were in the way because she couldn't bear to hurt them.

I met Diana when Richard and I were falling apart, right at the end of our marriage. It was at a crowded crew table in a restaurant belonging to a friend. We were put together because our host believed we would "get on like a house on fire". And we did! We became best friends instantly. She was attracted to me, something I didn't realise for months. I just loved her company and spent lots of time in it. When Richard and I got to the point of no return it was Diana who comforted me and helped me through it. As time went on and I realised I was falling in love with her, I had an all-fall-down breakdown. It was probably due to all the stress that had accompanied me in that last year and the culmination of things breaking down with Richard, added to which was the realisation that I was in love with a woman!

My family were deeply religious and my daughter very bound to a particular church at that time. I believed any relationship with Diana would have cost me all of that. It was a terribly difficult place to be. Did I just go for it and see what happened? Could I afford to? There were no guarantees – as there aren't in *any* kind of relationship. It's just that, when you are in the same field as everyone else, being measured in the same way, it seemed such a risk to "cross the fence". Would anyone on the "other side" ever accept me back again if the relationship didn't work? It all felt terribly drastic then, very black or white.

I chose to try. I chose to possibly bring down my family's wrath. I chose not to hide our relationship and to risk it all. I suppose I chose that in the same way I chose to marry each time that I did. None of them was guaranteed and none of them lasted but it didn't stop me trying to find my own path and my happiness. I guess that's what it's about for me. It's not about being gay or "straight" (how I *hate* that term! It implies all else is bent). It's about being happy, compatible and together. In the last seven years I've gone through some sort of "conscientising" experience with Diana. I've seen prejudice and felt it. I've also reacted in anger to so-called Gay Pride marches and events, as if those represent all gay people. What gives a bunch of people who want to cross-dress and act wildly the right to speak for all gay people?

From where I sit, and based on the friends we have from all persuasions in life, most gay people appear to be perfectly normal people, just trying to be happy. Many have kids, either of their own or adopted. All just enjoy going out to eat, watching movies, picnicking with family, playing games, sharing birthdays and all the regular things people do. *None* of them is kinky or weird or obviously dysfunctional. One of my ex-husbands turned out to be a sex addict, for goodness sake, and put me at huge risk of illness. Another is serially unfaithful to his partners and another is violent and abusive.

I don't really get the hoo-hah around me about having to choose what category of humanity I am supposed to belong in. I am a loving, loyal person, passionate about life and love. I have found the love of my life and she's a she. There shouldn't be any hoo-hah. It should just be wonderful that we've found each other and so much love at this stage of our lives. It should be fantastic that we have a relationship to be envied because it is so equal and so healthy. That should be it. I am not so naive to think people will leave it at that and I am increasingly undisturbed by what people think. Our relationship will stand the test of time and that's all that counts.

A last word: I recently watched an Oprah show with a Pastor Ted Haggert in the United States. He seemed to be protesting at the gay label and it caused an outcry. It made me think I should end this story differently to what I had intended: I don't fight the gay label because I am ashamed about gayness. I don't fight the label to pretend anything. I just don't understand why we need labels at all. I fully accept the gay community's fight for recognition and

I support it. I find it abhorrent that people judge others based on their choice of partners. I find it outrageous that people cannot be left alone to find love and acceptance, as long as it is between consenting adults. I just don't want my life explained away, especially as it relates to having had so many marriages, etc., on the basis of "Well she was always gay and that's why". Life is not so black and white. This choice of mine is about the individual in my life, Diana.

> *My darling, our anniversary is coming up. I want to say again that I can't believe how amazingly lucky I am to have found you. Thank you for your love and for how happy you make me. I hope I can continue to make you happy too and just thank the Universe for us. If I ever lost you I would not be able, nor would I attempt, to replace this with anything else at all. — Yours always.*

Come to me

Mavourneen Finlayson

Obscurities and obstacles
hold no faith
as dawn to come
with sugar-coated dreams.

Delight expanding inside,
with sweetness and desire
to lie with you beside an erotic fire.

Come to me –
let me feel your skin,
we can make it Holy.

ZANELE MUHOLI is currently working on a long-term visual project that interrogates the state of hate crimes in South African townships.

2002:	co-founded the Forum for the Empowerment of Women (FEW), a black lesbian organisation based in Gauteng
2003:	completed an Advanced Photography course at Market Photo Workshop in Newtown, Johannesburg
2005:	recipient of the Tollman Award for Visual Arts
2006:	recipient of the first BHP Billiton/Wits University Visual Arts Fellowship
2007-2009	studied MFA: Documentary Media at Ryerson University, Toronto, Canada
2009:	Ida Ely Rubin Artist-in-Residence at the Massachusetts Institute of Technology; awarded a Fanny Ann Eddy accolade by IRN-Africa for her contributions to the study of sexuality in Africa; won the Casa Africa prize for the best woman photographer and a Fondation Blachère prize at Bamako biennale of African photography.
2010:	co-directed *Difficult Love*, a documentary commission by the SABC on her work

Publications:
Only half the Picture (2006)
Faces and Phases, Prestel (2010)

Exhibitions:
Group shows include *Life Less Ordinary* at Djanogly Gallery, Nottingham, UK; Undercover: *Performing and transforming black female identities* at Spelman College Museum, Atlanta, USA; and Rebelle: *Art and feminism* 1969-2009 at the Museum voor Moderne Kunst Arnhem, the Netherlands.

Muholi's work was included on the 29th São Paulo Biennale (2010)

Recent solo shows have taken place at the Gladstone Hotel in Toronto and at Fred, London

Currently showing on group exhibition at Arnhem Museum of Modern Art with Dineo Bopape and Marlene Dumas.

Websites:	www.zanelemuholi.com
	www.michaelstevenson.com/contemporary/artists/muholi.htm

THINKING THROUGH LESBIAN RAPE

ZANELE MUHOLI

BEING INSIDE/OUTSIDE

While South Africa celebrates ten years of freedom and political democracy, there are those within our borders who are still outsiders, who have yet to find substantial meaning in this celebration. Despite formal constitutional protections against discrimination based on a person's gender and sexual orientation[1] – one of the liberation struggle's most impressive achievements – black lesbian women are still refused entry into the nation's most public spaces and are punished for their same-sex desires and relationships. The lived realities and experiences of lesbian-identified women, such as those living in and around urban townships, are still overwhelmingly dominated by a set of intersecting raced, classed and heterogendered politics that blur the lines between our apartheid past and our new constitutional democracy. As lesbians, educational discrimination and unemployment continue to shape our collective experience of poverty.[2] Our blackness still excludes

---

1   In 1996, South Africa's Constitution was amended to include the Bill of Rights, which legally guarantees that everyone's right to their inherent dignity is respected and protected. Chapter 9 states that "The state may not unfairly discriminate directly or indirectly against anyone on one or more grounds, including race, gender, sex, pregnancy, marital status, ethnic or social origin, colour, sexual orientation, age, disability, religion, conscience, belief, culture, language and birth." It was the first constitution in the world to offer such protections to lesbian, transsexual/transgender, bisexual, and gay peoples.

2   Due to structurally unequal gender relations of power, some girls and women are not afforded the opportunities to complete even basic education. Even now, young lesbians who do not finish Matric report being forced out of school for not conforming to gender-specific dress codes or for being "out" at school. This violates constitutional rights to gender and

us from the mainstream, mainly white, gay and lesbian voice. Physical assaults and sexual violence against our sexual/gender queer bodies encourages our invisibility. Post-assault victimisation by state institutions and representatives carefully shapes how, and to whom, we will choose to speak about our lives.

In what follows, I will highlight the issue of hate crimes against lesbians living in townships, in order to raise awareness about the realities of lesbian lives amongst women, feminists and gender rights activists in South Africa. Yet I need to push beyond simple exposition, and begin to unpack why our black sexual agency and autonomy is so threatening to how this new nation imagines itself. As black lesbians, we need to initiate the process of theorising hate crimes against us so that we may become the agents articulating our sexualities and genders through our own diverse voices.

I write as a proud daughter, Zulu, and lesbian living and working in urban Gauteng. I am a community worker and organiser. I spend most of my time with the women who live their lives as lesbians, as lesbian men, as femme and butch mothers, as women loving women who push against the boundaries of who is, and what is, an "African" woman. We have taught each other about our experiences. My community is those women who are too poor and "uneducated", too African to some and too un-African to others to be entrusted with any meaningful participation as citizens of this country. I locate myself as both an insider and outsider of this community. I am an insider as it is here where I find my past, where I find some of my own life experiences reflected back to me, where I find legitimisation for loving women. But I am also an outsider as I am currently employed and tertiary educated, both of which afford me a degree of (unfair) access to social, economic and cultural resources not available to the vast majority of my sisters.

It is partially this fluid position as insider/outsider that has moved me to claim this privileged space within the pages of a feminist journal that my community will most likely never have the chance to read. But claiming this space does not come without a price to myself. I have had to learn to speak a language that is

---

sexual equality. This information has been collected by the author from interviews with 47 black lesbians between December 2002 and April 2004.

foreign to me, to present my knowledge in a manner that is more familiar to the colonisers than the colonised. It is at this moment between performance, articulation and agency where both the continuities and the breaks with our colonial past are made clear to me. I am left searching for how to negotiate the path ahead, and I conclude tentatively that it may only be through this process of reciprocal dialogue, which we as reader and author can create, that will move us into a new space where a politics of decolonisation is possible. But mostly, I just need to talk things through and be heard.

HATE CRIMES

For the past two years I have listened to, and recorded, the stories of hate crimes against 47 lesbian women and lesbian men from different Gauteng townships (Soweto, East Rand, West Rand, Alexandra, Katorus, Vereeniging, Orange Farm). I have also interviewed one perpetrator of lesbophobic hate crime. I have taken these journeys into my community in order to let these women speak and represent themselves in their own languages and their own words.[3] While relatively few resources are spent on studying the nature and dynamic of violence against women, even fewer are spent on the particular form of homophobic violence that non-heterosexual people such as lesbian, gay, bisexual, transgendered and transsexual people face. This, in itself, is a barrier to the meaningful realisation of legal protections in people's everyday lives. The women range in age from 16 to 43, though the majority are under the age of 25.

According to Donna Smith, CEO for the Forum for the Empowerment of Women, hate crimes take many forms, ranging from verbal assault, physical and sexual violence including gang rape, harassment, intimidation, homelessness, stalking, abduction and murder. A hate crime is an unjustifiable act committed with the specific intent of depriving a person of some right or benefit

---

3   These journeys have been taken with the support of Behind the Mask and the Forum for the Empowerment of Women (FEW), the only black lesbian organisation operating openly in South Africa.

because s/he belongs to a particular group. It is motivated by hatred of the group to which s/he belongs. It often takes the form of a violent crime such as rape, but includes verbal abuse, psychological abuse and various forms of intimidation and fear. A hate crime can be state-sponsored and many communities endorse hate crimes, as the testimonies of "curative rapes" against lesbians prove. Although anti-hate crime legislation has not yet been coded into South African law, lesbian, gay, bisexual, transgender/transsexual (LGBT) activists are currently working on this.[4]

Of the 47 women I have interviewed so far, 20 were raped explicitly because of their sexual and gender non-conformity, 4 experienced attempted rape, 17 were physically assaulted (3 with a weapon), 8 were verbally abused, and 2 were abducted. Twenty-nine women knew their attackers and only 16 survivors reported these hate crimes to the police. Many of these women experienced these hate crimes more than once. The silence in my community over the issue of hate crime has meant that it has, at times, been difficult to access women who experience lesbophobia. In many cases, the women could not relate to the terms "lesbophobia" or "hate crime." However, when asked in their own languages if they had ever experienced discomfort or assault due to their lesbian identity, they were eager to share their stories with someone who understood, someone who was like them.

I have learned that women choose their silence for a multitude of reasons. For instance, some butch lesbians spoke to me about their silence in terms of the emotional trauma they feel when speaking about their rape, an admission that cuts into their gendered and sexualised selves in very different ways than it does for heterosexual or femme women. For many butch lesbians, their masculine identities are structured through the power they possess not to be touched intimately during sexual encounters. Consequently, revealing intimate violation to anyone is painful, and can be delegitimising and disempowering. Thirty-one women

---

4   The definition of hate crime and its key features has been formulated by Donna Smith, CEO for the Forum for the Empowerment of Women, Braamfontein, Johannesburg. Author's private communication with Smith.

interviewed define themselves as butch lesbians or lesbian men. This exposes the reality that sexuality is always constructed within, and mediated through, gender identity and that any analysis of lesbophobic hate crimes must incorporate also the interplay between sexual and gendered relations of power.

Women also spoke of their silence in terms of the fear of exposure that comes with telling their stories, since many black LGBTs are not yet "out" to their families and communities. But mostly, women spoke about the shame and humiliation that comes along with the systematic revictimisation by the very people who are constitutionally obliged to protect their rights as women, as lesbians, as rape survivors. The women spoke of the police who do not take lesbian rape seriously; assault crisis and shelter workers who are not sensitised to the specific emotional traumas and needs that come with a homophobic assault and rape; and health care workers who are either uncomfortable with or hostile to women who claim their lesbian identity when reporting assault or rape.

The reality of being black and lesbian in South Africa is that we become "outsiders" inside our townships or rural communities because there are those who have defined homosexuality in racial and ethnic terms as "un-African". Some make the argument that those who identify as LGBT are mimicking western or "white" culture. "Black lesbianism" is acknowledged and constructed through a heteronormative lens and is recognised as situational, as "a fashion" or a phase "because her friends are doing it" or as a response to frustration with a boyfriend.[5] What is conveniently forgotten is that African cultures have historically accommodated same-sex desires and relationships. More recently, lesbian sangomas are claiming their lesbian identities and their sexualities publicly to highlight the fact that their culture and their spirituality has not always been based on heterosexism and that their traditions have

---

5   Defining homosexuality in racial and ethnic terms is a phenomenon among both white and black South Africans. Some gay white South Africans believe that "there is no such thing as a black gay – gay is a white thing". See Gevisser in Drucker (2000). For a more historical and in-depth analysis of African homophobia which situates homosexuality within a context of western imperialism, see Epprecht (2001).

not always been restricted to the homosexual/heterosexual binary (Morgan, 2003).

TWO VOICES FROM MY JOURNEYS
VOICE ONE

The most recent rape motivated by lesbophobia that has come to my attention was committed against a teenage lesbian who was raped repeatedly in Kagiso on 7 March 2004, by a "friend" who was aware of, and pretended to be comfortable with, her sexual orientation. I was with "Kid" (pseudonym) the following day, which allows me to insert myself as both narrator and subject of Kid's post-rape experience. The incident happened at night after the man and Kid spent the afternoon sharing food and drinks at a local eatery. She did not suspect that he would become violent towards her since he had requested to meet other gays and lesbians, and both their families were aware of their friendship. The extent to which violence against lesbians is rooted in a deep fear of female erotic autonomy from patriarchal familial, social, and community structures is sadly made clear by the fact that the majority of lesbians are victimised by someone familiar to them or to their families.

The following account of Kid's ordeal is in her own words, though I have translated them from the original Zulu interview.

> On Sunday afternoon I went to make a call at a phone around the corner where I met with this guy. We started chatting as usual and he asked me to accompany him to buy food and drinks. We then went there, bought some few items and we stayed there till late. I noticed that it was really late and was worried about my safety. I told him that I wanted to go home since I had the house keys with me. He said to me, "Do not worry, I will accompany you." A few minutes later we left the place, but he told me that he needed to go to his room first because it was chilly that night and I had on warm clothes and could see

that he did not. On our way I noticed that he was drunk but I could think of nothing else except being accompanied home. Then we arrived and entered the outside room attached to the side of the house. He started asking me funny questions. He demanded to know what I do in Johannesburg so frequently, and I told him that I go there to visit my friends and check my girlfriend. He said I was lying and accused me of being involved with foreign guys who in return for whatever favours I give them, give me money. As I was trying to process this, [his words were] followed by a slap and heavy blows with fists. He took a screwdriver and threatened to stab me with it. I attempted to fight back, but the man was stronger than me. He forced me to take off my clothes and told me that he wanted to prove to me that I was a woman, that he always wanted to have a child with me and added that he was going to rape me and give me AIDS as well. I cried but that did not stop him from raping me. He started at 22h30 for about an hour, slept for a while and woke up and did it for a second time at about 2am. I was in so much pain. As he raped me, he kept on asking me if I loved him, and I was crying. He then went back to his sleep.

Kid managed to escape afterwards. She did not tell anyone about the rape and cried until morning. She phoned me, a woman she barely knew, and took the train to Johannesburg so we could meet. I could only think of one place to take her and that was People Opposing Women Abuse (POWA) in Berea where she was able to receive a debriefing and post-rape counselling. We were then referred to Medico at Hillbrow Clinic. And this is where the revictimisation began. The nurse at the clinic informed us of two problems. First, we could not be attended to because the police had not brought a crime kit which is part of standard procedure when attending to rape survivors. Second, the doctor at the clinic would have difficulty finding the time to testify in court as many other court testimonies were already a burden on her time. The nurse then referred us to Leratong Hospital in Krugersdorp.

What must be appreciated in all of this is that Kid is poor, unemployed, and living with her aunt who is not only disabled but also the sole breadwinner in the household. Taking the train into

Johannesburg from Kagiso is expensive, not to mention dangerous. But this was her only mode of transportation as Johannesburg was in the midst of a general taxi strike. Trying to navigate Johannesburg without a car is a hectic experience on most days. But imagine for a moment the emotional and physical pain of it after your body has been violated and raped, when it feels like your body is an exhibit for everyone, and when it feels like everyone knows you have been "marked." In a socio-cultural context where rape is still a fairly taboo subject, these feelings are overwhelming. And yet this young woman chose not to hide.

Since there were no taxis available and police transport was available only between the hours of 16h00 and 16h30, I organised private transport to Leratong Hospital. Kid and I arrived there at 16h35 and were attended to by a trauma unit counsellor who called the doctor and the police station nearby. Again, there was no crime kit immediately available and another wait ensued for the police to arrive. But when the police officer finally arrived, he did not feel the need to take a statement right away, claiming he had another case to attend to. The doctor was not available either. We felt a sense of complete helplessness just waiting for someone to take us seriously, to care that a woman had been terrorised and raped. That a woman was waiting to hear if her rapist impregnated her, or worse, infected her with HIV. We waited for three hours before an on-duty doctor could see us. During this wait, a female doctor came by, but stated she would not see us as she was off-duty. Would she attend if this was a life or death situation, I wondered?

When an on-duty doctor – male – finally did arrive, he appeared sleepy and resentful at having been called at all. He examined Kid and handed over the file to the trauma unit counsellor who informed her that she was neither pregnant nor thankfully, HIV positive. However, by that time Kid had already experienced further humiliation and victimisation by the doctor who very crudely remarked that he could not see any signs of forceful penetration, and that she was not a virgin. His insensitive commentary suggested to us that he questioned why we even bothered to come to the hospital at all. Additionally, upon being informed by us that this crime committed against Kid was a lesbophobic sexual attack, the doctor interrogated Kid's integrity and identity by asking why she was a lesbian while still claiming to be a Christian. Kid felt defenceless against this onslaught. All she could do was cry more.

The attending doctor was Nigerian, hailing from a country in which homosexuality is still legally punishable by the state. It is difficult to come to terms with how homophobia is constructed by individuals and how I should understand this man's reaction. Is homophobia and lesbophobia national? Cultural? Unfortunately, homophobia expresses itself in all nations and cultures. Our constitution has yet to change attitudes in a society that is still fundamentally structured around heterosexuality.

After the doctor's examination, we were finally seen by the same police officer who was too busy earlier. He took Kid's statement and issued a case number. I silently sat by, wondering why hours earlier I had to argue with him not to prolong the agony for Kid by making her tell and retell her traumatic experience of the night before. By the time we left the hospital it was 22h30 – 6 hours after we arrived at the hospital, and 12 hours after Kid arrived in Johannesburg looking for help, support and comfort. Sadly, I knew that despite the long wait of the day, there was a longer wait still to come for justice and for healing. For us lesbians, who are raped and bashed on a daily basis, accessing services and service providers who will treat us with dignity and integrity is still a struggle in the new South Africa. It makes the promises and protections of the Constitution meaningless for women who are too poor to afford the safety of private transport and safe living spaces, too poor to afford private health care, too poor for private rape insurance.

VOICE TWO

Last year, I also had the opportunity to interview a perpetrator of lesbophobic hate crime, a rapist. He gave me much sought-after insight into what motivated his, and perhaps any rapist's, hate crime. This rare exchange between a black lesbian (and one time potential target of his rage) and a man who made the conscious decision to control lesbian women through rape was not lost on either of us, despite the unplanned and spontaneous nature of our exchange. The following is what "Xolani" (pseudonym) confessed

195

to me. I use the word confessed here because I neither requested the interview with him, nor prompted him to explain his actions. He simply asked if he could speak to me because he had something on his mind.

> It happened in 1996 when me and three of my gangsters raped a lesbian friend of ours... We all knew that she was a virgin, but we wanted to prove her wrong – that she was not a man... One day she came to us after school, to hang out like always... We had already planned what we wanted to do... We took turns raping her and told her that if she reported us to the police we were going to kill her family. She did not go to the police as she was scared for her life. I repent for what we did and wish I could apologise to her for what we did. It was just ignorance that led to that brutality[6]

As he continued to speak I turned the tape recorder on and listened. What could I say? What I needed to do was process.

UNPACKING HATE CRIME

As I have listened to the life journeys of the women of my community in their struggle to claim and live their identities, I am filled with a deep sense of sadness and respect for them. For a long while now, I have had the need to unpack the very specific acts of sexual violence against the bodies of black lesbian women. I have begun this process with my friend, colleague and writing mentor for the Writing Program, Sabine Neidhardt. Despite coming from very different social backgrounds and experiences, we have each been able to use our unique experiences and knowledge to move beyond simply telling the story of black lesbian rape. I am a Zulu lesbian from the "global South" – Umlazi township outside of Durban to be exact. My political education dates back to watching my mother get up in the early morning hours in the service of

---

6   The interview between the author and "Xolani" took place in a township outside of Johannesburg. The interview was conducted in Zulu, translated by the author herself.

caring for someone else's children and home. I am an activist, photographer of women, and a reporter within the Gauteng LGBT community. Sabine is a lesbian "whitey" from the "global North". She became a closet feminist at the age of 8 after she told her father to stop beating her mother, though now, at the age of 30, she works openly as a feminist in the academic hierarchy. This need we both feel for getting beyond telling the stories, has been motivated by our dissatisfaction at the lack of attention paid to the realities of many black lesbian lives. I feel this dissatisfaction with the LGBT and the women's movement; Sabine feels it within academia. We increasingly recognise that ongoing conversations about differently positioned women's experiences of violence need to take place inside and outside South Africa between grassroots organisers and intellectuals, between anti-racist, gender rights and queer rights activists. Moreover, we recognise that transnational feminist solidarities are a necessity in order that a politics of decolonisation within women's and feminist organising, globally and locally, can take place to push us beyond conceptions of rape as violence against the generic category of women. Amina Mama (in Alexander et al, 1997) argues:

> ... prevailing gender ideologies have much bearing on the types of violence that are manifested in a given context.

As such, we believe that as we share the stories of black lesbian realities, we need collectively to begin to interrogate how gender is structured through race and sexuality, and class. Why do we witness black butches contracting HIV from heterosexual men who rape them? Why, in the postcolonial gender trajectory of South African township life, does heterosexual black masculinity appear to be invested in raping black lesbian women? These are important questions we need to ask ourselves.

According to many anti-colonial feminists, all patriarchies, whether operating in colonialist or neoliberal capitalist periods, function on "sameness" and on the persistence of fixed identity – heterosexual/homosexual, women/men, femininity/masculinity, black/white, coloured/Indian. They argue that patriarchies must function in this way in order to consolidate masculine dominance within colonial and capitalist processes. Sabine and I would like to position the lesbophobic rape of black South African women into such a framing of patriarchies, and suggest that it is the disruption of this sameness and the challenge posed by black lesbian women to the fixity of what is an "African woman" (in itself an identity imposed by a colonialist order), that makes non-heterosexual women's gender, sexual, and erotic autonomy so disturbing. It appears to us that it is this constructed and artificially fixed identity of "African woman" that Xolani and Kid's rapist need to police and to enforce as they rape lesbians. The rape of black lesbians reconsolidates and reinforces African women's identity as heterosexuals, as mothers, and as women.[7]

Amina Mama's work theorises contemporary violence against women in Africa by linking this violence to the continent's history of imperialism and colonialism. If we accept, as anti-colonial, anti-racist feminists, that colonialism itself was out of necessity a violent and gendered process, we must subsequently trace the current expressions of violence against African women – and black lesbians – back to precisely that period which saw a marked decrease in African and non-white women's social and political status, and a marked increase in violence, particularly sexual violence, against black female bodies (in Alexander et al, 1997). Consequently, we believe we must look at how western colonialist and imperialist conceptions of heterosexuality and gender, both historically and in the various current postcolonial contexts, have been and are still employed to stabilise racialised and gendered hierarchies. These hierarchies consistently position white heterosexual men at the top of the hierarchy while feminising (which in a heteropatriarchal social order means subordinating) all other identities: non-white men, queers, straight women, butches and so on. To ignore this trajectory is to come dangerously close to treating race, gender,

---

7   I wish to thank Sabine Neidhardt for her intellectual contributions to this
     point. My own entry into theorising lesbophobic hate crimes has been
     informed by the ongoing conversations with Sabine, who is presently re-
     searching and writing her dissertation on the politics of (re)heterosexu-
     alisation, structural violence and race in post-colonial South Africa. She
     has also shared with me many of the black feminist and post-colonial texts
     that have influenced her own thinking.

class and sexuality as mutually exclusive categories of experience and analysis that have no historical context to them. We must begin, in other words, to systematically address the intersecting categories and multiple embodied experiences of women. And that will only happen when we speak and listen to differently positioned women, whether heterosexual, lesbian, coloured, transsexual, white or poor.

My location as an activist and community worker within the lesbian community of Gauteng allows me to testify to the constant revictimisation that lesbians face after experiencing the trauma of rape. I see first-hand how these women's sexualities and their genders are questioned and interrogated by police, doctors and the media. I hear my wider African community deny these women the right to live their sexual and gender identities. I know that the rape of black lesbians is a weapon used to discipline our erotic and sexual autonomy. I also can appreciate that the silence within the township lesbian community about lesbophobic rape is partially responsible for the disconnection between these women and those gender rights and feminist activists who work to stop violence against women. However, I wish to extend an invitation to those who work against gender-based violence to come into dialogue with black lesbian women so that we can collectively create the kind of world in which we all feel safe.

REFERENCES

Epprecht M (2001) 'What an Abomination, a Rottenness of Culture: Reflections upon the Gay Rights Movement in Southern Africa', in *Canadian Journal of Development Studies* (XXII), 1091-1107.

Gevisser M (2000) 'Mandela's stepchildren: homosexual identity in post-apartheid South Africa', in P Drucker (ed) *Different Rainbows*, London: Gay Men's Press.

Mama A (1997) 'Sheroes and Villains: Conceptualising Colonial and Contemporary Violence Against Women in Africa', in MJ Alexander and CT Mohanty (eds) *Feminist Genealogies, Colonial Legacies, Democratic Futures*, New York: Routledge.

Morgan R (2003) 'So It is African Although they were Hiding it: Same-sex Sangomas and the Indigenous Oral Archive', in *Comma*, 1, 75-82.

This article was originally published in Agenda, *Vol. 61, 2004*

ADDITIONAL READING

Gevisser M & Cameron E (eds). *Defiant Desire: Gay and Lesbian Lives in South Africa*. Braamfontein: Ravan Press, 1994.

Govinden D. *Sister Outsiders: The Representation of Identity and Difference in Selected Writings by South African Indian Women*. Pretoria: University of SA Press, 2008.

Malan R & Johaardien A (compilers). *Yes, I Am! Writing by South African gay men*. Cape Town: Junkets, 2010.

Morgan R, Marais C & Wellbeloved J (eds). *Trans: Transgender Life Stories From South Africa*. Fanele, imprint of Jacana, 2009.

Morgan R & Wieringa S. *Tommy Boys, Lesbian Men and Ancestral Wives*. Johannesburg: Jacana Media, 2005.

Stobie C. *Somewhere in the Double Rainbow: Representations of Bisexuality in Post-Apartheid Novels*. Pietermaritzburg: UKZN Press, 2007.

Van Wyk E. *Miriam Dancing: Outing the stories of women who love women*. Cape Town: Aqua, 2009.

Van Zyl M & Steyn M (eds). *Performing Queer: Shaping Sexualities 1994-2004*. Vol. One. Roggebaai: Kwela Books, 2005.

OTHER MODJAJI TITLES

Go Tell the Sun
Wame Molefhe

Invisible Earthquake
A Women's Journal Through Stillbirth
Malika Ndlovu

Hester se Brood
Hester van der Walt

This Place I Call Home
Meg Vandermerwe

The Thin Line
Arja Salafranca

Undisciplined Heart
Jane Katjavivi

Whiplash
Tracey Farren

http://modjaji.book.co.za